"We've got company."

Andrea found herself facing the barrel of Neil's automatic handgun. She understood his intent right away. He thought he could protect her from an Aiding and Abetting charge.

"Save the theatrics," she hissed. She'd never been so angry in her life. Men could be so blindingly stupid, and Caufield was king of the mountain. Neither one of them had to be sacrificed.

The cops banged on the door and bellowed another warning. "This is the state police, Dr. Vogel. Open up, now!"

Andrea defied them, scooping up papers with no intention of opening the door until Nick was safely concealed.

Neil followed her and grabbed her by the arm. "These aren't theatrics, Vogel. Consider yourself my hostage."

ABOUT THE AUTHOR

Carly Bishop has been an avid reader all her life, and she takes special pride in creating characters who risk it all for the emotional brass ring. *Falling Stars* is a story that came naturally from her interest in anthropology, medicine and forensics, as well as her job as a hematologist. Carly lives in Denver with her husband and fifteen-year-old daughter, Sarah.

Books by Carly Bishop

HARLEQUIN INTRIGUE
170—FUGITIVE HEART

HARLEQUIN DREAMSCAPE
PRINCE OF DREAMS

Falling Stars

Carly Bishop

Harlequin Books

TORONTO • NEW YORK • LONDON
AMSTERDAM • PARIS • SYDNEY • HAMBURG
STOCKHOLM • ATHENS • TOKYO • MILAN
MADRID • WARSAW • BUDAPEST • AUCKLAND

To Steve

Harlequin Intrigue edition published June 1993

ISBN 0-373-22232-7

FALLING STARS

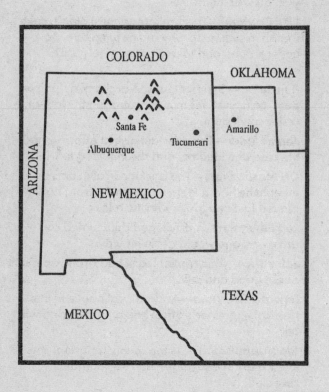

CAST OF CHARACTERS

Dr. Andrea Vogel—A spectacular murder trial made this forensic pathologist a star, but all she wanted was the truth.

Neil Caufield—This brilliant scientist didn't make foolish mistakes, so why did he jump bail, go underground and take on a vengeful justice system?

Ben Solter—Syndicated, self-acclaimed "poison pen" columnist, his murder outraged the law-and-order contingent.

Janine Tyler—The assistant district attorney had the case of a lifetime, and she intended to win.

Dr. Mason Piers—The chief medical examiner thought he had a team player in Andrea, but he played fast and loose with the rules.

Leif Elbertson—A privileged child turned con artist—no one would get in his way.

John Brice—This criminologist had strong opinions about good and evil.

Edward Gresham—Andrea's colleague in the medical examiner's office had an ax to grind with her.

Ida Happelsmith—As the county historian, she knew a great deal more than her journals revealed.

Vicki Thornbloom—A bed-and-breakfast proprietor who knew when to take a warning seriously.

Chapter One

The witness box dwarfed her. Made her seem younger, like a little girl playing deadly grown-up games.

Her onyx-black hair was parted in the middle and drawn into a classic, heavy forties-style roll that suited her heart-shaped face and exceptional green eyes. Her unwittingly sultry Louisiana-belle voice required a microphone to be heard in this imposing New Mexico courtroom.

Or *was* the sultriness unwitting?

On trial for murder in the first degree, Neil Caulfield sat in the chair of the accused near the end of the third day, and he couldn't take his eyes off her.

The lady was neither a little girl nor a Southern debutante. Andrea Vogel—*Doctor* Andrea K. Vogel, deputy medical examiner—sat poised to destroy everything Neil had spent the last twenty years of his life recouping.

The prosecuting attorney made sure the facts about the good Dr. Vogel were perfectly clear. She was thirty-two. She'd graduated from medical school—Tulane University, New Orleans—with honors.

The attorney continued feeding Andrea Vogel's credentials into the record. Neil shifted in his chair. His throat was dry and his guts were in a knot. He felt cold. The last time he'd been in a courtroom like this, he'd been fifteen, defiant and scared out of his mind.

Thirty-five now, he was clean-shaven and clean living in a 44 Long suit and striped tie. Twenty years had done nothing to mitigate the feelings, the fear, the ceaseless foreboding. Janine Tyler's voice cut through his thoughts. He knew just what direction this prosecuting attorney was headed. He wished she were defending rather than prosecuting him.

"You have also established an expert reputation on the identification of murder/homicide victims—"

"Objection!" Dale Fetcher, Neil's attorney, interrupted. "No one is contesting the identity of the deceased here!"

"I'll withdraw the question. But, in fact, you *are* considered the star—the premier player—of late, in the M.E.'s office, isn't that so, Dr. Vogel?"

"Your Honor!" Fetcher rose again to complain. Neil had the sinking sensation that his counsel's constant objections had already alienated the Honorable Julio Medina. "Is there anyone left in the state of New Mexico unfamiliar with the reputation of this witness?" The newspapers had been touting Andrea Vogel's rising star status from the start of the trial. But then, the murder victim, Ben Solter, had been one of their own, a nationally syndicated columnist writing out of Santa Fe, New Mexico.

The prosecutor began her protest. "I'm merely trying to—"

"I don't care what you're trying to do, counselor. I will allow the witness to answer," the judge warned. "Then I will expect you to cut to the chase. Am I clear? Good. Dr. Vogel?"

Neil sensed that she was uncomfortable with the limelight. He could see distaste in the way her delicate eyebrows pinched inward. But her uneasiness wouldn't stop her from nailing him to the proverbial wall.

"There are no premier players in the medical examiner's office, Ms. Tyler. I do my job, and I do it well."

Tyler smiled her satisfaction and picked a piece of lint from her pinstripes. "Now then, Dr. Vogel. What was your ruling as to the cause of death of Ben Solter?"

"The victim died of cardiac arrest brought on by a lethal injection of Zolgen B."

Tyler stopped in front of the jurors and leaned against the jury-box railing. Closing her hands into loose fists, she began to beat them together, imitating the sound and rhythm of a living heart. *Thud...thud...thud...* "In other words, his heart—" abruptly Tyler's hands opened and spread wide "—just stopped?"

The jurors hung on the assistant district attorney's every word and gesture. Neil had to hand it to her. The theatrics made his skin crawl, made the jury members shift uncomfortably in their chairs, but she was doing her job.

Vogel was unmoved. She simply answered the question. "Yes."

"Tell us now, Doctor. What is Zolgen?"

"Zolgen is an experimental medication developed by Neil Caulfield as an antidote to narcotics addiction. As of this time, the medication is pending a final FDA approval for the marketplace."

The crowded courtroom buzzed at her statement. Neil swallowed hard and let his glance at Andrea Vogel develop into a cold, hard stare.

She looked away.

Despite her show of cool expertise, the lady couldn't handle his stare, and Neil felt perversely gratified. Zolgen was his baby, and he was damned proud of it—had every right to be proud—and Vogel knew it, as well. It stopped dependency cold. And if even he didn't know why it had proven most effective in adolescents, that hardly seemed a drawback.

"And is Zolgen being tested only by Neil Caulfield?" Tyler asked.

"No," Vogel answered. She risked another look at Neil, then continued. "Trial studies are always conducted across the nation by qualified physicians. Zolgen has proved an unquestioned success in every study I have seen."

But Assistant District Attorney Janine Tyler couldn't have cared less, Neil thought. To her, Zolgen was merely the cause of death in the most important case of her career. "Zolgen has been tested all over the country, Doctor?"

"Yes."

"But you said Zolgen B was the fatal compound administered to Ben Solter."

"Again, yes." Vogel hesitated for a moment, looked down first at her hands, and then directly at Neil. "Zolgen B is a chemical variant which was abandoned early in Caulfield's research."

"And the coroner's investigators discovered dozens of vials of Zolgen B under refrigeration in Caulfield's laboratory?"

"Yes."

"A compound with no viable medical application?"

"No *known* medical application," Vogel corrected the assistant district attorney. "No responsible research lab arbitrarily disposes of rejects which might prove valuable in other applications."

Tyler waved aside Vogel's statement in irritation. "Please confine yourself to the question, Dr. Vogel."

"Your *Honor*," Fetcher said, rising, "the prosecution is attempting to stifle its own witness!"

"Dr. Vogel, keep your testimony to the point."

"All right," Tyler continued, not bothering to disguise her smug pleasure in the judge's directive. "Let's move on to the nature of Zolgen. The substance has created quite a public furor, hasn't it?"

Again, Andrea Vogel glanced down at her hands. "Unfortunately...yes."

Her soft Southern drawl was more pronounced in that one word, *unfortunately,* than in all her prior testimony. Neil's pulse hammered in his head. He didn't need her professional pity. He needed the truth, and the M.E.'s office should have come up with it. *She* should have come up with it.

"Unfortunately, Dr. Vogel? Why so?" Tyler asked.

Her chin rose, just as it had when she'd been asked to call herself the M.E.'s star player. "Because our society will benefit from Caulfield's work immeasurably. The medical uses of Zolgen will approach a complete cure to drug addiction."

"But the victim, Ben Solter, didn't see it that way, did he?"

"No."

"Please remind the jury, Dr. Vogel, what Solter's quite vehement objections to Zolgen therapy were?"

Vogel straightened in her chair. "Mr. Solter was on record as being of the opinion that Zolgen represented a stopgap measure that would return dangerous criminals to the streets. He believed utilizing any drug to cure substance abuse is absurd, and that dependency is best cured by total abstinence."

"And, in fact, Ben Solter's rhetoric whipped up quite a backlash against Zolgen, which provided the defendant with motive enough to murder Solter, didn't it?"

"Objection!" Fetcher shouted.

Tyler held up a hand. "Withdrawn, Your Honor. Tell us, Dr. Vogel, is there support for Ben Solter's theory against the use of drugs to treat addiction in the medical community?"

"Some," Vogel acknowledged. "But the argument, in my opinion, is medieval."

"*Medieval,* Doctor?" Tyler mocked. "In what sense?"

"Taken to the extreme, Solter's argument makes the treatment of *any* medical condition with drugs unacceptable."

"So let's be perfectly clear here," Tyler continued. "Prior testimony by the arresting police officers tells us that the defendant was discovered over the body of the deceased."

Vogel said nothing.

"Please answer, Dr. Vogel."

"That was the testimony of the officers, yes."

"The defendant is a biochemist?"

"Yes."

"He formulated Zolgen and all its variants?"

"Yes."

"And Zolgen B was the substance identified in the syringe used to inject the decedent?"

"In the syringe supplied to my investigators, yes."

"And, finally, the defendant knew that Zolgen B had no useful or current medical application?"

"I have no knowledge of what Mr. Caulfield knew—"

"All the same, Dr. Vogel, Neil Caulfield—" Tyler swung around and stared pointedly at Neil "—knew the Zolgen B injection would kill his victim!"

Pandemonium broke out in the courtroom. Neil supposed Vogel's testimony was at an end, because she sank back into her chair. But the pounding of the pulse in his head was so loud he didn't hear her answer. He only saw her nod, and her vermilion lips shape themselves around a *yes*.

He felt the accusing stare of each and every juror. Andrea Vogel hadn't done him any favors with her determined remarks about his work changing society. Or saving kids.

Ben Solter, nationally syndicated, self-proclaimed law-and-order poison pen, was dead. Zolgen B had killed him.

For the second time in his life, Neil had run afoul of the criminal justice system. The first time he'd been confined in juvenile detention and then prison. He'd fought his way back, all the way to the highest honors ever conferred on a scientist. To respectability.

That wouldn't happen this time. Even if the truth came out, his reputation was destroyed. He wasn't going to be sticking around to have the jury foreman read him the writing on the wall.

How do you find in the matter of the People vs. Caulfield?

Guilty, Your Honor.

He imagined the court clerk entering the verdict into the records. They could take his reputation and stuff it. They wouldn't take his freedom.

Not again.

ON THE MONDAY MORNING following her Friday court appearance, Andrea entered the medical examiner's offices with a sense of foreboding. She had never before chafed at testifying in court as to her professional findings in the cause of a death. She believed in fair play and justice. Neil Caulfield's case still disturbed her, for a number of good reasons.

While her position in the medical examiner's office suited her, Assistant District Attorney Janine Tyler's case didn't, and Andrea had gotten precious little sleep in the last forty-eight hours. She worried that her answers could be misconstrued. She worried because the sum of her answers was so at odds with what she believed possible.

She admired Neil Caulfield's work, she'd detested the politics of Ben Solter, and though it wasn't her job to make such judgments, she couldn't believe a man of Caulfield's caliber and compassion had chosen to murder another human being.

She put down her briefcase next to the file cabinet of current cases, locked her purse in the bottom desk drawer and washed her hands at the small white sink common to every staff pathologist's office.

Not everything in her small domain was strictly functional. On the shelves beside her desk, alongside medicolegal and forensic investigation texts, was a collection of plants. On one wall she'd tacked a poster of Einstein, with a quotation touting imagination over knowledge.

Knowledge. She couldn't help feeling the awful, stinging irony. What good had it done the state of New Mexico, or Neil Caulfield, or her, to have her knowledge point up conclusions she doubted, construed in a way that would probably send an innocent man to prison? And what of Caulfield's knowledge, going to waste in the state penitentiary?

She pulled a paper towel from the dispenser to dry her hands. Reviewing her caseload in the morgue labs, she changed quickly into her surgical garb and checked the schedule. She had no court appearances and no requests of outside investigations—so far—which left her with a few spare moments to see her boss, Mason Piers, the chief medical examiner.

A fellow staff pathologist, Edward Gresham, stopped her near the stairwell door, just short of the construction area where a new voice-activated security system was being installed. "Well, Andrea, how is our very own little 'rising star'?"

Andrea frowned. Gresham galled her on a variety of levels. Of everyone in the M.E.'s office, Gresham most resented her newfound celebrity. Forty-seven and well into his middle-age paunch, Gresham counted himself heir apparent to the medical examiner's office. He didn't care for women in pathology, particularly forensic pathology, particularly a Southern woman. He wanted no competition from her, and he made no secret of it.

"Tyler wants Caulfield's conviction, Ed, and she'd make a 'rising star' out of the Cookie Monster if it helped her case. The attention will fade as fast as it came up." Though he merely grunted in response, the pinched look around

Gresham's eyes remained. "For that matter, please feel free to trade cases with me if some spectacular murder comes along that you want to handle."

"Talk is cheap, Vogel," he said, scowling. "Just let's remember that, shall we?"

Before Andrea could respond, Gresham marched off in the direction of the morgue. Ed would do anything to have the last word. She watched his measured retreat with distaste, then pushed open the stairwell door.

She stepped from the linoleum-covered hall floor to the carpeted beige environs of the M.E.'s office and greeted his secretary. Linda McMurphy sat talking on the telephone, holding her glasses. She twitched the bifocals to indicate that Andrea should go on into Piers's office.

Andrea knocked twice, then opened the door. Piers was adding cream to his coffee. She assumed his guilty expression meant that he'd been warned off cream by his personal physician but was ignoring the advice.

Piers held up the empty plastic creamer, confirming her guess. "Caught me, didn't you? Well, a single shortcoming in this vice-ridden world has to be congratulated and not scolded, don't you think?"

"We're not counting your pipe-smoking today?"

Piers glowered. Andrea smiled. She'd had her disagreements with Mason Piers, and she expected another unpleasant discussion this morning, but he could be charming. He was unremarkable in his features, with a silvery head of hair and not an ounce to spare on his gaunt frame. His wife, Cindy, was a strong feminist, and Andrea's staunchest supporter.

Andrea seated herself in the chair across Piers's desk, and folded her hands. "Mason, I have to say again that I can't buy Tyler's case against Caulfield."

"I'm not open to discussion on this one, Andrea. The case is ironclad. Caulfield was caught red-handed—"

"With a syringe in hand. I know. But of all the fatal injections a biochemist like Caulfield could concoct, why on earth would he use Zolgen? And not only Zolgen, but a variant only he possessed?"

Piers shrugged. "Murderers are not rational folks, Vogel. They use guns they've licensed themselves, custom-made knives, their own prescription drugs—all manner of self-incriminating methods. A clever defense attorney can always make the case that the suspect was handily framed in just that manner."

"But Caulfield's attorney hasn't even hinted at the possibility!"

"Case closed," Piers said gesturing in finality. "If his lawyer isn't attempting to throw doubt on that issue, why should it concern you?"

Andrea turned the gold bangle at her wrist. "For one thing, I don't believe a man like Neil Caulfield, who was nominated by the Nobel Prize committees for awards in biochemistry, would murder—"

"Andrea," Piers interrupted wearily, "I hesitate to point out the obvious here, but you cannot play doctor and juror at the same time. What you can or cannot believe is entirely irrelevant."

She straightened in her chair. Piers had admonished her before, but there was something in his attitude that made her feel uneasy, something intractable in his reaction to what she considered legitimate queries. But she wasn't a woman to back off because of her superior's ruffled feathers.

The truth was, finally, all that mattered.

"The point, Mason, is that this office is charged with discovery. Motive isn't my only concern. Other things bother me, as you well know. Things which have to do with our investigation of this case."

Piers gave one of his long-suffering sighs and scrubbed the knuckle of his thumb over his right eyebrow, always a dead giveaway to mounting frustration. "Remind me."

"I always believed the inquest was cut short. The investigators were called off almost immediately. We don't know—because there was no exhaustive field collection of evidence—who else might have been in that house—"

"Or who else may have actually committed the murder?"

"Exactly."

"Caulfield actually committed the murder," Piers snapped. "Like it or not, I am the chief medical examiner, and the responsibility for calling off our part of the investigation was all mine. I did so in tandem with the police—and with ample justification." He pulled a pipe from his middle desk drawer, filled it, tamped down the tobacco and lit it.

"You have very little respect for the funding constraints of this office," he went on. "To devote time and resources and personnel to the collection of irrelevant and unnecessary evidence in an open-and-shut case is...irresponsible."

Dollars and cents ruled Piers's decisions. Andrea had heard him spout off from this soapbox many times before. "What is truly irresponsible, Mason, is to settle for whatever presents itself as the truth for the sake of simplicity."

Piers clamped the pipe in his mouth and drew hard on the heavy-scented tobacco. He took the pipe from his mouth, planted both elbows atop his desk and pointed the stem at her. "Dr. Vogel," he said sternly, "as deputy medical examiner, you may either support the rulings of this office or get the hell out."

"My country, right or wrong?" Andrea fired back. "I'm sorry, Mason, but I refuse to act out of blind loyalty. I won't compromise my work—"

His complexion reddened in anger. "Who's asking? I admire your persistence, and I would never presume to interfere with your work, but I will not tolerate your second-guessing my determinations. This is not the first time we've had occasion to disagree in this manner, but it is becoming more and more irritating.''

''The Bartlett baby,'' Andrea stated flatly, recalling the last occasion she'd gone to the mat with Piers. Seven-month-old Melissa Bartlett had died of circulatory collapse after ingesting furosemide, a potent diuretic used by the Bartlett nanny.

Andrea had been strongly inclined to rule the baby's death an intentional overdose, but Rodman Bartlett was very wealthy, politically active and not without the power to sway public opinion—or that of his medical colleagues, either.

No one could prove that the Bartlett nanny had given the baby her own diuretic, the extremely bereaved father had said. His daughter might well have found pills spilled on the nursery carpet and put them into her own mouth. Without proof, without any believable motivation for the nanny to have committed such a terrible crime, surely the M.E. would find the baby's tragic death accidental.

Andrea had not only thought the father's bereavement bogus as a three-dollar bill, she couldn't believe that in his five-million-dollar home such potentially fatal medications could be found lying around the nursery floor.

Bartlett, however, had prevailed, and Mason Piers had ruled the baby's death an accidental overdose.

''Yes, the Bartlett child,'' Piers acknowledged. ''And now, to all appearances, we're having the same discussion. Your job, Dr. Vogel, is to arrive at the cause of death. Anything else is pure speculation you are not entitled to discuss.''

''I'm charged with discerning the truth. I'm able to offer informed conjecture in a court of law. If I weren't, I'd be of no use to this office, Mason. Perhaps,'' she concluded softly, ''my insistence upon the truth is a nuisance to you, and I should resign.''

Piers stared at her in disbelief. "Are you threatening me, Dr. Vogel?" He didn't wait for an answer. "I object to your tactics, and I resent your using that cultured, superior Louisiana drawl with me."

"And I resent your treating me like some naughty child, Mason." Andrea's chin lifted a bit. Her heart knocked hard, because she sensed what was coming. "I admire your work, as well, but I won't confine myself to whatever answers prove most convenient for this office. I can't believe that you would insist upon it, either, but if that's what you want, I'll resign."

Piers sank into his high-backed, oxblood leather chair, drawing hard on his pipe tobacco. He refused to meet her eyes. His jaw jutted out, then his teeth clenched together over his pipe stem. It was a standing joke in the M.E.'s office that in death, Mason Piers would be identifiable by the exact fit of that meerschaum pipe to the worn places on his teeth.

Maybe, she reflected uneasily, such gallows humor came to mind now so she could avoid admitting that her principles were about to march her out of these offices forever. As a deputy medical examiner, she was a sworn officer of the court. Sworn, on her honor, to act in the interests of justice.

Piers finally cracked under the pressure of her refusal to take back the offer to resign. He jerked the pipe from between his teeth, banged it upside down into a crystal ashtray, then sent it clattering across his desk top. "What would it take to get you to reconsider?"

A ray of hope flickered for Andrea. "Stop Caulfield's trial. It's well within your jurisdiction as the medical examiner to require the investigation be reopened."

"With what justification?" he demanded, sitting straight and tall in his chair. "'I'm sorry, Your Honor, but my deputy just can't believe Caulfield committed that murder.'"

"Truthfully, Mason," she responded softly to counteract his blustering, "I don't know if Caulfield murdered Ben Solter or not. But Janine Tyler's prosecution is too pat, and the investigation was cut short. Either we conduct another investigation, or I will resign my position."

Again Piers seemed to retreat into himself, as if doubts and uncertainties plagued him. "If you leave, Andrea," he stormed at her, "you are sworn to absolute silence as to the affairs of this—"

"Dr. Piers..." His warning was cut off by the voice of his secretary over the office intercom. "The district attorney's office on line five, sir. Tyler sounds fit to be tied, or I wouldn't have interrupted you."

Looking more relieved than annoyed at the interruption, Piers reached for his receiver and punched the button. "Piers here."

Andrea sank back into her chair. She had anticipated an argument, but she couldn't fathom his rigid stance against reopening the Solter murder investigation. Mason Piers had become the sort of bureaucrat the office of the medical examiner demanded, but until the Bartlett nanny case, he'd supported her findings to a fare-thee-well. From the start of this investigation, however, he had seemed overanxious that the case proceed to trial without delay.

He had been her mentor as well as her boss, but something had changed. He had changed. She knew why she was prepared to walk out on her career, but she had no idea why Mason sat there clinging to the wrong decision.

Now, answering the assistant district attorney's call, Mason's face had gone as bloodless as a dead man's. His eyes widened, and he stood up. "You're certain? Yes. I'll tell her. What will happen now?"

Tyler's answer was short. Piers recradled the receiver a few seconds later.

"Caulfield has skipped bail," he announced. "They've checked his residence, his labs, his office, everywhere."

Andrea checked her watch. "It's only nine-fifteen. Can they be so sure yet? If he got caught in traffic—"

"He's AWOL, Vogel," Piers snapped, all traces of uncertainty vanished. "The minute he missed showing up to trial, he's guilty of criminal flight. How does that jibe with your theory that the case should be reopened?"

She returned his uncompromising stare. Piers's question presumed that jumping bail proved Caulfield's guilt. Andrea had always mistrusted the way things looked at first glance.

Piers offered her one last conciliatory gesture. Smiling benignly, he began, "Andrea, my dear, if it walks like a duck and quacks like a duck..." He shrugged eloquently, as if the answer were a foregone conclusion.

It's a duck.

"Or maybe," she returned in her most cultured, respectful Louisiana drawl, knowing that she would close the door on the last few years of her life in the next few hours, "it's only a very clever mynah bird."

AT THE CLOSE OF BUSINESS each afternoon, Clerk of the Court Jay Frost produced a final transcript for the day... then made an unauthorized copy. This copy was fed into a self-service fax machine at the nearest shopping mall, and sent to a number Frost had been provided with weeks before.

At the receiving end of that unauthorized copy, Leif Elbertson abandoned his telescope—he was an admirer of the heavens—poured filtered and deionized water from a pewter decanter, tossed in equally purified ice cubes and settled himself down to read the ill-gotten fax transmission.

He laughed when he read the part about the district attorney thumping her fists together, miming the victim's heartbeat, and then the ominous silence. Signifying death.

"Ah, Janine," Leif murmured into the quiet after his laughter evaporated. "How do I love thy prosecutorial theatrics? Let me count the ways."

His question was rhetorical. Facetious. He had no intention of counting anything. The woman had a job to do. A responsibility, not to be taken lightly, to put Neil Caulfield behind bars, if not into the executioner's hands.

Leif sipped at a glass of his iced, purified water and stared out into the gathering twilight at the silhouettes of his power-generating windmills. His home was a fortress. No one could approach without triggering the sophisticated alarm system he had installed.

He was dependent upon no one, and his self-sufficiency gave him comfort. He had drilled a well, without a care as to how deep the rig had to penetrate. The windmills provided energy for his home. His vehicle, all-terrain, four-wheel drive, ran on ethanol. He purchased fresh meat and produce in town when he drove the twenty miles to pick up his mail, but his basement was both an arsenal of weapons and ammunition and a pantry stocked with dried and canned food that would last a decade.

He had foreseen the day when the scum of the earth would rise up and overwhelm men of reason such as himself. Scum like Neil Caulfield.

Leif had prepared himself. He had little else but time and money to burn, and it wasn't often that one could indulge in a moment's appreciation of life's cosmic jokes.

Like Caulfield getting his just deserts.

Leif brought the tumbler of iced water to his lips and tossed back a hefty swallow to wash away the bitter taste evoked by Caulfield's name. A Nobel-nominated biochemist, indeed. More like a bleeding-heart liberal who preyed upon the weak and spouted platitudes of hope with his precious Zolgen.

Comfortable now, his thirst slaked and his taste buds cleansed, Leif read on. He had nearly completed the testimony of Deputy Medical Examiner Andrea Vogel when the telephone rang. Leif slipped the page he had just completed to the end of the sheaf, rose from his chair and went to answer the summons. The telephone was to be used by his compatriots only under the most pressing conditions.

He answered. Listened. Crumpled pages of the report and then hurled the wad to the floor.

Caulfield was gone. Disappeared. No one knew where or how or even when.

Only Caulfield's death would serve the Cause now. In jumping bail, he had sealed his own fate. If justice were to survive in this day and age, *Neil Caulfield must die.*

Along with any man, woman or child who gave Caulfield so much as a moment's succor.

Chapter Two

In the wake of her "rising star" notoriety and her resignation, half a dozen job offers came from pathology groups around the country.

Andrea gave serious consideration to only two of them. One, a surgical pathology fellowship at Sloan-Kettering in New York, tempted her more than another position offered in forensics in the San Diego area.

In the end, she rejected both offers. She wasn't ready to leave Santa Fe, and the offer of a position as a full-time pathology consultant to the New Mexico Antiquities Foundation intrigued her. She accepted it. If Andrea missed the challenges and the pressure of a medical examiner's life, she appreciated the lack of politics and infighting.

The position in New York had tempted her most because her college roommate and dearest friend lived in Manhattan, working as a producer on many choice PBS programs. Seven months after Andrea's decision to stay in Santa Fe, she had her first chance ever to work with Miriam Silverman.

Sitting in her lab amid the chaos Miri had introduced with her production team, Andrea skimmed the introduction to the "Medical Detectives" segment due to be videotaped on a PBS grant for the "Science Observer" program. The intro touted her forensics background.

Dr. Andrea Vogel is uniquely qualified to show us how artifacts, the clues, relics and microscopic evidence from the ancients, are evaluated for disease states. A former medical examiner for Santa Fe County, Dr. Vogel brings the unique perspective of a forensic pathologist to bear on the diseases suffered by our ancestors....

She hesitated to object, but the foundation had asked that her previous ties to the medicolegal establishment in the state be downplayed.

"I'm afraid this script isn't going to fly, Miri." Andrea surveyed the small crowd gathered in her high-tech museum lab and frowned. "In fact, I—I'm not sure this is going to work at all."

Miriam groaned. "Take five, guys," she instructed her crew. "Andrea, this is going to work. It *has* to, you know. The production grant specifies the medical investigations of the New Mexico Antiquities Foundation, and you're the star."

It was Andrea's turn to groan. "A fallen star, maybe." She reached for her can of ginger ale and shrugged. "The foundation would rather its name not be connected in any way to forensics. That's not what we're about." Sipping at the cold soda, she wished there didn't have to be so many people around for one small PBS production. "Besides, I left my surgical scrubs behind for several good reasons, Miri, which haven't changed in the past seven months."

Miriam slid her clipboard across the low-gloss gray countertop of Andrea's worktable and prepared to hold her ground. "Time flies. Look, I know you didn't leave the M.E.'s office on the best of terms, but—"

Andrea laughed, and tucked stray wisps of her hair back into place. "A masterpiece of understatement, Miri. My fellow doctors resented my being there, and they resented it more when I left."

Miriam's startling blue eyes, deeply set in her plain-featured face, hardened. She plunked down on a tall stool next to Andrea's comparison microscope and offered her usual explanation. "They felt threatened, Boo. Everyone does."

Boo.

Within their first week as freshmen at Tulane, Miriam had begun calling Andrea *Boo* because the depth and understanding of little Andrea Vogel's answers, aloud or written, had scared off even her university professors. Not to mention the boys. Her boyfriends were always the ones clever enough to court the girl with all the answers.

A few had claimed to appreciate her petite stature, her peaches-and-cream complexion, her optimistic nature, but even those suitors faded fast when they discovered they weren't dealing with a pretty little girl, but a smart woman with a mind of her own.

"You deserved better than that," Miriam offered quietly.

Better than what? Andrea wondered. Colleagues who mistrusted her? Or boyfriends who only cared about getting the answers right? She gave herself a mental scolding and Miriam a warning glance. "I'm not going to change my mind, Miri. Can we just get on with this?"

She bent to pull a pile of notes from the cabinet below. Miriam, bless her, finally conceded, and turned to her text supervisor to come up with an intro sans any mention of Andrea's forensics background.

There were half a dozen other conversations going on around Miriam and her text supervisor, but a lone man making himself at home at her desk snagged Andrea's attention.

Casually dressed in faded, nondescript blue jeans, he wore a soft brown polo shirt, his forearms and biceps exposed. And he appeared deeply engrossed in one of her reference books. He looked as though he belonged here—which she knew he didn't. She couldn't help wondering if he deliberately cultivated that appearance, and if so, why.

Her quick, professional assessments kicked in. Six-four in height, give or take an inch; weight near two hundred and thirty pounds. He had a mesomorphic body shape—tall, athletic build—but his forearms and shoulders were broader and more powerful than his frame suggested. He was bearded, with arrogantly rugged, almost Gallic, features and a dark complexion. His thick, slightly long brown hair defied categorization, with shades ranging from gold to mahogany under the fluorescent lab lights.

When he looked up from the reference book, his eyes went straight to Andrea's, and none of her quick judgments explained the sudden alarm that clawed at her throat.

At the edges of her attention, she heard Miriam instructing her crew as they began again to tape an introduction to the New Mexico Antiquities Foundation and its pathology research consultant, Dr. Andrea Vogel. The intro gave her the excuse to break off eye contact with the man so comfortably ensconced at her desk.

Nevertheless, her body remained poised at the edge of a fight-or-flight response. Her arms were covered in gooseflesh, and her heart thudded too fast. Even as she acknowledged her own physiological response, she scolded herself for fearing he could hear the pounding of her heart.

"Dr. Vogel, would you explain the mission of the New Mexico Antiquities Foundation?" the interviewer asked, leading into the program text.

She knew him.

She dragged her attention off her own uneasy, threatened responses and focused herself on the question at hand.

"New Mexico transcends the ordinary in every sense," she responded. "The state is home to more historical and cultural variants than we see anywhere else on the North American continent. The foundation is committed to preserving the antiquities, of course. But more than that, we study them, classify and authenticate them."

"And by authenticate, you mean—?"

"That we've built our reputation on what is real—everything from dating and identifying skeletal remains to anthropologic measurements to disease states."

In spite of her concentration, Andrea felt the keen, too-intense attention of the stranger at her desk—like a sparrow vividly aware of an owl's threatening presence. But that was crazy. He had done nothing overt to trigger her alarm. Sometimes an ancient relic didn't jibe, either, as if a melody she knew well had been subtly altered and the notes weren't the ones she expected. Something about this man struck the same false chord.

"We look for the cause of death in the remains of our ancestors, in the hope of understanding their world a little better. Simply put," she concluded, "historical accuracy—the truth of our ancestors—is our goal."

"Something like 'provenance' in the art world?" her interviewer asked.

"Yes."

"Or, in modern-day criminal investigations, the chain of evidence?"

Andrea hesitated. The regard of the man at her desk took a quantum leap in intensity. She—or her answer to that particular query—had every facet of his attention. The question itself violated the spirit of her agreement with Miriam not to mention her past occupation. On the other hand, it didn't seem worth the effort to object.

"That's fair to say, yes," she agreed. "In the end, all scientific investigation aims at revealing and protecting the truth."

She felt the stranger's scorn leveled straight at her, and she glanced again in the direction of her desk. He was gone. The book remained on her desk, closed but not replaced between her bookends. And there remained in her chair the impression of his body, of his weight.

"Cut," Miriam called. "That'll do it."

Andrea relaxed, letting the tension in her upper body diffuse as she leaned into the counter. Those few minutes of narrative had taken more out of her than the rare days she spent in excavation of human remains under the unforgiving New Mexico sun.

She didn't know whether that had more to do with the videotaping or the now absent man who seemed so... familiar. But Miriam was outlining the schedule for the balance of the day, and Andrea had no time to examine the alternatives.

"You look a little green around the gills, Boo."

"I'm no good at this, Miri—"

"That was perfect," her friend contradicted. "Derek can replay it right now for you. Would that make you feel any better?"

"No." What might make her feel better was to know what business that man had in her lab. And if he had any business here, why was he gone now? She almost asked Miriam who he was, what he did on the video crew, but her friend was already talking again.

"So. Will you trust me to know my job?"

Andrea smiled. Shrugging, she tilted her head. "Do I have a choice?"

"None," Miriam returned. "Now, at this point we'll cut to narrative and edit in the reconstructions. We'll need your voice-over descriptions, then we'll go to the computerized versions to compare. Okay so far?"

Andrea spent the rest of the afternoon narrating and displaying one investigative technique after another, in no apparent order. The fragmented hours left her feeling confused and out of her element. Miri's crew finished up and called a halt around five o'clock. It took them another hour to collect themselves and disband.

When the last small group had gone in search of fajitas and tequila before their flight, Andrea put her lab back in order. At last she grabbed the watering can above the sink where Miriam stood washing her hands.

"Miri, who was the guy sitting at my desk when we started this afternoon?" The memory, the image of the man occupying her territory, lingered still.

Shaking her wet hands, Miriam reached for a paper towel. "None of my people were sitting at your desk, Boo. They have all had the fear of God instilled in them about touching anything in places like this."

"Well, it's not like anything on my desk could really be harmed. Do you remember seeing him? He was buried in that reference over there." She gestured with a nod of her head. "He had on a brown polo shirt—"

"With shoulders out to—" Miriam measured off a width twice her own with her hands in the air " —here?"

Andrea nodded. "That's the one. He isn't one of yours?"

"I thought he was one of yours," Miriam answered. "He looked vaguely familiar, now that you mention it."

Andrea shivered, though the sun still blistered outside and the climate-controlled lab never varied in temperature more than a single degree. "If he isn't one of yours, and he isn't one of mine, who was he?"

"Beats me. A groupie, maybe? We get them all the time. You'd be surprised how many people think they want to make programs for PBS.... He didn't stick around very long, though. I don't remember him being here after we got started. What do you think?"

Andrea shook her head and turned off the faucet. "I've seen him. I know I have, and it bothers me that I can't recall where or when."

"It'll come to you sooner or later," Miriam answered, plunking herself onto the closest stool. "Anyway, Boo, we did it. Ten straight hours."

Andrea topped off the watering can and laughed. "For one segment's worth of a 'Science Observer' special."

Miriam cracked a tired grin. "I know. Ten hours reduced to fifteen minutes. I resent it bitterly, but that's the way it works. The weird part," she groused, gesturing to the begonias and bleeding hearts Andrea was so busy watering, "is that the piece is going to look like we trumped up a greenhouse set for the Antiquities lab."

Pinching a withered leaf from a lush white begonia plant, Andrea scolded back. "Climate control is vital in a lab like this, you know. These babies kick out oxygen like crazy."

Miriam eyed her knowingly. "That's what I like best about you, Boo. Your endlessly creative excuses. Remember the honors lit class, when you told old man Miller you really couldn't read *Moby Dick* again because your Greenpeace consciousness wouldn't allow it?"

"Well, that was true—"

"Phooey. Why don't you just admit you'd rather be babying begonias than piles of old bones?"

"I wouldn't!"

"You would," Miriam needled—the way only an old friend dared. "You missed your true calling. When you left the M.E.'s office, you should have opened a real greenhouse."

"Or a vineyard? I'm sitting on prime New Mexico mountainside, you know."

"Exactly."

Her commentary, Andrea knew, was just Miriam's contrary way of expressing her opinion that Andrea should never have left the medical examiner's office in the first place. Or that she should have taken the pathologist position at Sloan-Kettering so they could be roommates again.

"Consulting here in pathology for the Antiquities research projects is very important, Miri."

"But the Bartlett nanny did it, Boo."

She shouldn't have been surprised. Miri had the instincts and memory of the investigative journalist she'd once been, and she would remember Rod Bartlett's baby and the case that had begun Andrea's troubles with Mason Piers.

Her conversations with Miri Silverman had always been like this. Not so much flitting from one subject to another as getting to the bottom line with a minimum of fuss. Proving the nanny did it—or the proverbial butler—was more important than research and consulting for the Antiquities Foundation, or another greenhouse, or even a prime vineyard.

Refilling her watering can, Andrea turned to water the hanging plants—the not-so-creative excuse she needed to avoid Miriam's nit-picking glance.

"Dr. Piers was the M.E., Miriam. And my superior. He ordered me to confine my speculations to my areas of expertise—which did not include the improbability of spilled pills on the nursery floor." She poured the last of her water into a hanging fern and replaced the watering can on the shelf above the sink.

"And then the nanny conveniently died in a boating accident."

"Yes. Within a month of my leaving the M.E.'s office."

Andrea shrugged. How very convenient for Rod Bartlett. At least the drowned nanny wouldn't be killing any more babies. "Why don't you move back your flight reservations and come home with me for some gazpacho and homemade wine?"

Miriam sighed. Her sack lunches, Andrea knew, included a cucumber sandwich more often than not, and the chilled soup invitation was a guaranteed distraction from this conversation, just as Andrea intended.

"Cucumbers from your garden?"

"Where else?" she teased.

"I'd kill for some of your gazpacho—not to mention the wine. But if I don't make it home on this flight out, I'll never be ready in time."

Miriam talked about the PBS project back in New York while Andrea walked her to her rental car. Miriam ended with a promise of a rain check for gazpacho the next time they could get together. Andrea watched the car until her friend had disappeared into the landscape.

Returning to the silent and now deserted lab, Andrea headed for her desk to collect her purse and car keys from the drawer.

She sat down, compelled by Miriam's questions, to think about why she had accepted this position seven months ago. Miriam was still under the impression that it was over the nanny's case that Andrea had left.

The Bartlett child's murder had instigated tensions that the Solter homicide had only worsened. The atmosphere around the examiner's offices over Neil Caulfield's disappearance—

Oh my...

God. How could she have been so blind?

Suddenly chilled, Andrea stared at the book on her desk. The textbook stood amid half a dozen others grouped between her amethyst geode bookends—the book she'd so witlessly replaced when she restored her lab to its accustomed order.

Medicolegal Investigation. She reached for it. Paging through, she found within thirty seconds what she should have discovered an hour ago—a flesh-colored adhesive memo in the shape of a footprint from her stationery supplies. Placed carefully at the start of a chapter on forensic evidence, across the foot was scrawled a message: *The truth is where you find it.*

It confirmed for her the identity of the man who appeared to belong in her lab, but didn't.

His hair was longer than she remembered, wilder. And lighter. Sun-bleached maybe. His coloring was darker, more harsh, and he wore a beard now that magnified the impact of his strong, arrogant features.

Neil Caulfield. He'd been missing—a fugitive from justice—for many months, though in all that time, he had often been in the news reports, seemingly more sought after than a serial murderer.

The truth, he'd written, *is where you find it.*

Why had he come here—to leave this message for her? Why now? Why had he taken the chance of exposure at all?

She peeled the foot-shaped note from the textbook page, and then the top three blanks from the pad that would reveal the impress of his scrawl, and sat there staring at them. She was about to destroy them, to quash any evidence that the fugitive Neil Caulfield had ever been anywhere near her.

Her throat went as dry as the New Mexican desert.

As a deputy medical examiner, she had been an officer of the court, legally bound to preserve evidence. Yet she sat there not doubting for a minute that she would ditch these scraps of damning evidence.

Three thoughts came to her in rapid succession. One, if Neil Caulfield were guilty of murdering Ben Solter, he'd have gone underground so fast and far he'd never be found. Two, he had to believe he could trust her not to call the authorities.

And three, he'd put her in an impossible position. Not to report him was tantamount to aiding and abetting a criminal.

Andrea ripped up the little pages one by one, flushed them down the commode, then left and locked up the lab. She drove to the market with no memory of getting into her car. She'd have preferred Miriam's company. Now that she'd recognized Neil Caulfield as the stranger in her lab, she *needed* Miriam's company.

She intended to make her gazpacho with or without Miri, and she needed sour cream. But she didn't realize how angry she was until she dropped the container and sour cream splattered through the broken seal onto the checkout conveyor.

On her way out, near the bulletin board by the exit, where customers advertised rentals and used cars and litters of puppies and day-care homes, Andrea saw Caulfield again. This time it was only a photograph of him, printed squarely on a slick eleven-by-seventeen Wanted For Murder poster.

NEIL WONDERED AGAIN what in hell he'd been thinking. He knew to the day and the hour how long it had been since he'd jumped bail, and exactly what it had cost him. He wouldn't second-guess his decision to run, or its consequences now. There was simply no point in regrets.

The decision had been coming for months. He didn't want to live the rest of his life in shadowy holes in the wall. Or some lousy foreign dictatorship without U.S. extradition agreements.

Least of all in the New Mexico state penitentiary.

There had been two choices—turn himself in and cool his heels in prison while a conviction and then an appeal lumbered its way through the court system, or prove himself innocent from outside the system.

The first was no choice at all. The second required help.

That was why he'd gone to Andrea Vogel's lab, and why he'd sat here waiting on Vogel's back porch with her golden retriever, a sweetheart of a dog, graying in her muzzle and nearly deaf.

He'd let himself onto Vogel's property by a back gate, which led from the yard to a pasture to state forest behind that. There were no horses, and the retriever's bark had sounded as if she'd be happy to take off his leg. Both legs. For some unfathomable reason, the old girl had changed her mind about him quick.

A sweetheart. He'd been playing ball with her for hours now, and he had the dog to thank for taking his mind off what kind of reaction his presence would get from Andrea Vogel.

Now the dog dropped her toy far short of Neil's reach, then came up to him, ready to crawl into his lap. She rested her head on his thigh, added one front paw and then the other. Neil scratched her ears and began to talk to her.

"Tired, girl?" he crooned softly. "You got a name, honey?"

"It's Doodle."

Neil stiffened, recognizing Vogel's soft, sultry Louisiana drawl, then turned on the wooden porch toward the back door to her house. Doodle took the move as an invitation to sit in his lap. Neil had never known a mutt her size who thought she was a lapdog, but he didn't mind.

Her mistress stood at the screen door, fingers within reach of a latch. She wasn't making any moves to open the door. Then again, she wasn't holding a phone, dialing cops or 9-1-1 or some brawny, heroic neighbor.

Maybe she already had. Neil couldn't remember the last time he'd been caught off guard like that. He was so tired. But he didn't think he'd become so blatantly stupid as to fail to notice the presence of another human being.

"Doodle," he repeated.

"Her sister was called Dandy," Vogel replied. "They were born on the Fourth of July."

"Was?"

"Yes. Was."

Her eyes, vivid and darkly green, had never left his. Her tone was flat and concealing, merely providing information. Standing behind the screen door, she was smaller than Neil remembered, and she looked breakable, but the lack of emotion in her voice would stop a lava flow cold. He didn't know whether it was anger or fear or a deadly combination of both.

"What are you doing here, Caulfield?"

She had recognized him. Neil took a deep breath and retreated for a moment into the simple pleasure of Doodle's honest affection.

All his pleasures of late were simple.

"A fugitive has only so many options, Vogel. And fewer choices than a beggar." He stroked Doodle's brow with his thumb, then stretched out one long leg and shrugged. "I had to trust someone."

"Why me?" She leaned with her shoulder into the doorjamb. She'd asked the question, but her arms crossed in front of her like a woman unwilling to listen.

Even through the screen, even though his eyes were black as a starless desert night, Andrea saw them darken dangerously.

"I never underestimated you. Try not to mistake me, either."

"I haven't mistaken you, Mr. Caulfield. You need help. You want to be cleared of all charges. You must want more than anything to see your reputation restored. You believe I can help you. No mistakes so far?" she challenged.

The woman with all the answers, Neil thought. Andrea Vogel had a reputation to back up the rumors. If she'd ever been wrong, no one knew about it—which was why he wanted her on his side. Neil shook his head. No mistakes. "Please. Continue."

Andrea flipped the latch, swung open the screen door and stepped out onto the back stoop. She wore white sweats with a Taos ski area logo. Twilight in the Sangre de Cristo foothills where she lived got chilly, even in mid-July.

She sat on the edge of the stoop near to where Neil had Doodle sleeping in his lap. Folding her arms over her knees, she stared out toward the forest into the deepening twilight. In another half hour, Neil thought, he wouldn't be able to tell where her hair left off and the black of night began.

"So," she continued, as he had asked, proving that she hadn't misunderstood why he sought her out. "You had to come back, but how? You had friends, of course, but—"

"But now they don't know what to believe," Neil interrupted. "Does a man jump bail if he's innocent?"

Her eyes clashed with his. He wouldn't look away, wouldn't so much as blink first. He had to make her believe him.

"You should have stayed," she said, her voice low, magnolia-soft, insistent. "You should've trusted the system."

Neil laughed as if she'd made a joke. At least, that's what he'd intended. "Yeah, well, from where I sat, the system wasn't looking too trustworthy."

Andrea looked away. There wasn't a scrap of bitterness in his voice. Not when he acknowledged the doubts of old friends, nor in his manner to her now. No bitterness, but maybe...maybe a weariness.

"So go to your attorney," she suggested. "Or the D.A., or the cops. Or the judge on the case, for that matter. Medina is a fair man."

He ignored her warning that she couldn't help. "I'm the defendant in an aborted murder trial," he responded. "A fugitive from justice. The D.A., the cops, the judge—all of them are absolutely bound to report any knowledge of my whereabouts, to bring me to justice. And it'd be in chains this time, because I've jumped bail once and cannot be trusted."

"Which led you to me." A harsh ache took hold in Andrea's throat. He truly had no other choices. Why did she feel the need to remind herself that he'd cut off his own options the night he jumped bond? "I can't help you. Harboring a fugitive—"

"You can," Neil interrupted. "You are the perfect choice. You saw the evidence, you're familiar with forensic procedure. You know the case—you helped build it. But you resigned as deputy M.E. You're no longer an officer of the court.''

"Helping a fugitive evade justice is a crime. Period.''

Neil straightened, dislodging Doodle's head. The old retriever whined, then inched her way toward Andrea. The last rays of light gave way to nightfall. Tiny bats flitted through the chill and the darkness, and somewhere in the foothills a coyote bayed at the bright quarter moon. Neil figured he had only one shot at this, and it'd better be good. Damn good.

"If you think what happened in that courtroom was justice, Vogel,'' he answered carefully, "then go ahead. Call the cops. I'll sit right here and wait.''

Chapter Three

"You have no right to put me into this position." Andrea got to her feet in one quick motion and opened the screen door.

The door slammed shut behind her. In the same instant, the overhead light came on. Neil followed, and stood in the doorway, his shoulder against the jamb.

With the quick instincts of a wanted man, Neil assessed his surroundings. Her kitchen was done in Southwestern pastels—terra-cotta tiles and muted cobalt accents. The small dining area flowed into more open spaces. Hardwood floors stretched everywhere, covered with an occasional Navaho throw rug. There were floor-to-ceiling windows throughout, except in the loft which Neil assumed to be her bedroom. The house was shielded all around by sparse, towering evergreens; still, walls of glass made him feel exposed. Edgy.

An angry flush stained Vogel's cheeks. She picked a paring knife from a drawer and began cutting the rich green peel off a cucumber. If his hands had been as unsteady as hers were now, he'd sure as rain not be handling a knife.

It wasn't a great idea to goad a woman with a knife in her hand, either, and Andrea Vogel was already angry. Neil guessed why.

"Do you always run out on a moral dilemma, Vogel, or just this one?"

"I don't know what you're talking about."

"I think you do," he answered heatedly, angry for the first time. "I'm not asking for some textbook answer or even some intuitive leap of faith based on facts and figures you could take to the bank." Neil ran a hand through his hair and ended gripping wire-taut muscles in his neck. "What you have here, Vogel, is a choice. Call the cops, or don't. Hacking away at a pile of cucumbers is no answer."

Cubed vegetable piled up beneath her hands. "The choice isn't so simple as call the cops or don't—"

"Yeah, it is," he interrupted harshly. "Either you believe that justice was being served in that courtroom, or you don't. Yes or no. It's really very simple. But if it makes you nervous—"

"That's absurd—"

"I'll tell you what's absurd, *Doctor* Vogel. I've been framed, I've got a trumped-up murder indictment hanging over my head—not to mention flight to avoid prosecution—and you're afraid of an aiding-and-abetting charge."

He could tell by the way she opened her mouth to speak, then closed it, that he was right. In fairness, he understood her caution.

"People go to jail for less, Caulfield. This is no joke!"

"No. It isn't funny, is it?"

Andrea scraped her pile of diced cucumber into a bowl and swept the peels into the disposal. Maybe, she thought, there was a higher moral obligation here than to doggedly insist that the law was the law. But she hadn't failed Neil Caulfield; if anyone had, it was the system, yet he was holding her responsible.

Worse, she *felt* responsible. Which made her feel trapped and angry.

Andrea stared directly into Neil's eyes. "What is it that you want me to say?"

"That you'll help me." He needed too much, that was certain. Her support, her insight, her analytical skills. A quiet, private place to stay. Answers. A smile from her. Just one smile. But she must admit, especially to herself, she had never really believed that he had murdered Ben Solter.

"A yes or a no, Vogel." His voice scraped past something raw in him. "It isn't something to be analyzed. This decision has to come from the gut."

"You're asking me to ignore the law. To deliberately and knowingly act outside the *law*."

Neil crammed his hands deep in the pockets of his battered Levi's. "Yeah. That about covers it." He should have shut up then. Vogel wasn't stupid. She knew as well as he how helping him might ultimately hurt her.

So he should have kept his mouth shut. He couldn't. "Hear me out, Vogel. I don't think you believe that I murdered Solter."

"What I believe, as my former boss was quick to point out to me, means nothing."

"Then it's true you left your job in protest of the way he and Tyler handled the investigation?" His voice was low and strained, and he saw by her expression that he had guessed correctly.

He paced, unable to stand still and plead his case at the same time. He ended up across the tiled counter from her, reached out and touched her chin to bring her eyes to his. "Your boss was wrong, Vogel. What you believe means one hell of a lot to me."

Andrea felt a shiver pass through her. Neil Caulfield seemed to fill her kitchen, to overwhelm her with sheer conviction. The touch of his callused finger made her aware of her own vulnerability, and she fought not to flinch, to show any emotion. To answer his control with her own.

Her gaze met his.

"Am I wrong, Andrea?"

"No." His use of her Christian name had taken the question, and thus her answer, beyond the realm of professional disputes or opinion. "You weren't wrong."

Neil's hand fell away from her face. His head tipped forward in relief.

Andrea backed away from her side of the counter. She turned, opened the freezer and pulled out a steak wrapped in butcher paper. She tore open the package of meat, placed it in the microwave, touched the controls and turned back to him.

"I won't call the police. I'll fix you a decent meal and give you a place to sleep tonight."

Neil nodded, but before he could say a word, she held up a hand to prevent a response.

"Don't thank me, Caulfield. I will hear you out, but I can't imagine what I can do to improve your circumstances."

The relief he felt was nearly overwhelming. He'd gambled on her reputation for pursuing the truth. Now he understood it wasn't her principles he'd bet on, but her instincts. Her empathy.

He watched her preparing the rest of the cucumber-and-tomato concoction, and his eyes were drawn to the gold bracelet at her wrist. It charmed him, as did her small fingers, their nails well-kept, short and unpolished. She smelled of peach blossoms, and her onyx-black hair fell softly to her shoulders. For the first time, he became aware of her as a woman, and he hadn't expected that, either.

Now that he had her ear, he didn't know where to begin. She wasn't making it easy, either, fussing over her dinner preparations.

"Can I help?" he offered, nodding at the half-thawed steak she removed from the microwave.

"No, thanks." What she needed was space. A few moments to herself to consider what she'd agreed to do.

"Maybe you'd... If you want a hot shower, there's time before this will be done."

"A hot shower?" He looked at her as if she'd offered him his life back—free and clear of murder charges, no questions asked. "You wouldn't mind?"

"No. Should I?"

His gaze went from measuring the guardedness in her eyes to her lips. He was already grateful enough to kiss her. Hell, he *wanted* to kiss her. He couldn't remember the last time, the last place, he'd felt safe enough to entertain thoughts of making love to a woman. He grinned. "No."

She told him where he could find the bathroom and towels, just off her bedroom in the loft, and turned away from him to go light the gas grill on the back stoop. She stood there long moments after the gas had ignited into flame, each of her hands clasping the opposite elbow, her mind refusing to judge what she had just done. She heard Caulfield bang the shower door closed and turn on the water.

She liked his smile. And she refused to judge that, either.

She put on the steak and went about setting the table. More nights than she cared to count, she took a book and a carton of yogurt or cottage cheese or take-out Chinese to her massive easy chair, settled in and later washed up the one fork and glass she'd used.

It helped settle her mind to move about doing such ordinary, instinctive chores.

The steak was grilled and ready to serve when he returned, taking the circular loft staircase two steps at a time. He'd dressed in worn but clean cords and a brown plaid wool shirt. His thick brown hair was still damp and smelled of her shampoo. He smiled again, a bit awkwardly.

"You tend to forget about decent shower heads and enough hot water when you're... out there."

He noticed the fire then—its light reflected off the warm terra-cotta floor tiles—and the cordial table she'd set.

"Place mats," he murmured, shaking his head. "Goblets and cloth napkins."

She'd used a blooming cactus for a centerpiece, as well, and poured wine. None of her preparations were anything more or less than she'd have done had Miriam come to dinner. But Caulfield clearly hadn't seen anything half so gracious in a very long time.

She handed him a plate with the steak she'd broiled, a bowl of gazpacho and a thick slab of sourdough bread. "Out where?" she asked. "Where have you been all this time?"

Neil took the plate and sat down opposite her place. "Here and there. Two hundred and seventeen days of nowhere special. Nowhere I'd attract any notice." He wasn't going to tell her that twice he'd been backed into corners a nice man wouldn't have escaped.

He began to butter the bread, then looked up when he realized she hadn't joined him. Bread in one hand, his knife in the other, he waited until she sat before he went on. "Is this homemade?"

Andrea spooned chilled gazpacho into her bowl. "No, but the wine is. Try it."

"You made this?" He picked up the goblet and inhaled the fruity aroma. "Cabernet?"

"Mmm. You noticed the vines outdoors."

"Overtaking your stoop," he agreed. "That's where I hid my dirt bike." He took a drink of the wine, let it coat his tongue and then swallowed slowly. "This is fine, Vogel. Really. . . fine."

Andrea sipped at her own wine, letting the warmth and body of it drizzle through her. She was unaccountably warmer than the one drink of wine could cause. She'd never in her life seen such naked appreciation as that which Caulfield had shown for the dinner and the wine she had made, and it embarrassed her.

She wondered how he'd withstood the isolation, the fear of discovery, the certainty that the life he'd known would never again be the same.

"'Nowhere special' is not an answer, Caulfield," she said at length. "Where did you go? Why did it take you so many months to come back?"

"I had a great deal of money put aside—money-market funds, penny stocks that had gone through the roof. I had plans for a lab like nothing you've ever seen. And a house. I was in the process of buying some land." He gestured broadly. "A lot like you have here, in fact."

He put down his bread, the butter melting, and began cutting into his steak. He hadn't forgotten that Andrea Vogel had agreed only to hear him out and that he still had to convince her that he needed her help. He'd tell her almost anything she wanted to know.

"Anyway, when I knew there was nothing left to do but cut my losses and skip town, I planned to cash it all in—only to find out every crying dime I owned was frozen on court order."

"How did you manage?"

"I hawked a few things and considered myself lucky to get away with ten cents on the dollar from a pawnshop outside Albuquerque."

Andrea glanced at her gold bangle. Her mother's gold bangle. She couldn't imagine having to sell it for hand-to-mouth cash. "What things?"

"My watch. Some coins." The emerald he'd given his mother, before a lifetime of struggling and deprivation had finally taken their toll and killed her. But he didn't need or want the good doctor's sympathy.

"Anyway, I spent weeks just driving, trying to figure what I should do. I bought an off-road bike from a kid in Arizona, and when I ran out of money I hired on with a rock-crushing crew. If you can handle the job, they don't ask questions—or stick around one place very long, either."

The sort of occupation, Andrea thought, that resulted in the tanned, hardened look of him, and the workman's calluses on his hands. "Did you ever intend to come back?"

"No. I was never coming back. The life I'd built here, the work I'd done—all of it was history."

Far more than history, Andrea felt. "What changed that, Neil?"

He washed down another bite of steak with his wine, then took a deep breath and a moment to consider his answer. Survival had demanded every ounce of energy and concentration he had, but he'd been thinking about Andrea Vogel for weeks, about her ability to help him get at the truth. He tried to think now, to remember if there hadn't also been times when he'd thought of her as a man thinks about a woman.

"You did."

Her spoon stopped halfway to her lips. Her eyes flew to his as she spilled the chilled soup back into its bowl and put down her spoon. "You've lost me."

His admission had disarmed her. "You were the prosecution's star witness. You were the one with the reputation for getting to the truth. Your testimony may have clinched the case against me, but I didn't think you believed it."

She stared into her bowl. "You couldn't have known that."

"Instinct told me," he argued. "Then I found out you had left the M.E.'s office, and that Mason Piers wasn't saying why."

"When was that?"

"Two weeks ago tomorrow, on the twenty-third of July," he said. "I was working a crusher. The temperature was over a hundred degrees in the shade, and the dust was so thick the engine choked up. The foreman put the mechanics onto it. I went into the site trailer, washed off a pound or two of dirt, chugged down a quart of water and...I knew I'd had enough. I called your office."

"The examiner's office?"

"Yeah."

"And asked for me? What would you have said if I had answered?"

"I don't know. Right now I couldn't tell you what I was thinking. Calling you seemed like...like an option I'd stored up as a last resort. I would never have turned myself in, Andrea. *Never.*"

He saw her recoil from his bald *never* and the fierce implication. He meant it, but he didn't want to scare her off. "You're the one chance in a million that the truth will ever come out." He hesitated, gauging her willingness to grant him her assistance. "It's now or never, Vogel. You're in a position to help me get at the truth—if you will."

Andrea served herself another ladle of gazpacho. "What is the truth, Neil?"

He laughed. The harsh smile that remained made her shudder. "The truth is, I didn't kill Solter. I don't know who did. He was dead when I got there, though his body was still warm."

She knew that, of course. The time of death was instrumental. If the body had been cold, he'd never have been indicted, or even charged—even though he'd been caught, syringe in hand, over Solter.

She replaced the soupspoon on the dish beneath her bowl and pushed it to the side. "Why did you go to his house that night?"

"Solter phoned me about eight o'clock and asked for a meeting. No—*asked* isn't quite right." Neil had finished his dinner as well and folded his napkin haphazardly. "He *begged* me to come over. To resolve our differences. He said he'd been hearing things about Zolgen that led him to think he had come out 'prematurely and too vociferously'—his words—'against it.' 'And certainly,' he said, 'too severely against me personally.'"

"You had no doubt that the voice on the telephone was Solter's?"

Neil thought about that for a moment, then shook his head. "I never doubted it, never thought to question it. Solter didn't have a very distinctive voice, but..."

"He was very literate, very smooth," Andrea supplied. "He was an accomplished columnist, and his choice of words would have been very characteristic.... Did you believe him?"

Neil swore. "I told him to take a flying leap. I told him I didn't care what he thought or didn't think about Zolgen. But he insisted. Said he wasn't a man to muddy the waters and then not do what he could to rectify the situation—again, his words."

"So you went."

"So I went." Neil drank the last of his wine, then poured more from the jug for both of them. "My mistake."

"And now Brightmark Pharmaceuticals has come out with Zolgen."

His fingers twisted the stem of the wine goblet back and forth. He nodded. "Zolgen got to market so fast it broke industry records. Someone wanted it out—fast."

"Someone who knew what they were doing saw the potential profit margin—"

"And then worked out a scheme to frame me for Solter's murder. Killing two birds with one stone. Convicted of Solter's murder, I'd be in prison for life and Zolgen's loudest critic would be silenced—all in one fell swoop."

Andrea shook her head. "I'm missing something here. Why would it have been necessary to get rid of you in order to bring Zolgen to market?"

"It wasn't. I'd already begun negotiations with Brightmark—and a couple of others. But by taking me out of the picture, the profits on sales were up for grabs."

Unable to sit still and consider this possibility, Andrea rose, stacked their used dishes and carried them to the sink.

"As a convicted felon, would you have had to forfeit the patent?"

"No. Fetcher—my lawyer, Dale Fetcher—believed the government would have no trouble at all coming up with a precedent for revoking the patent of a convicted felon."

"But by disappearing," she speculated, "you removed even that necessity. From prison you could have filed suits to tie up the patent in the courts forever. But if the murderer produced a phony sales agreement, being a fugitive from justice, anyway, you could hardly protest. Meanwhile our murderer is free to take Zolgen, which had received the FDA approval, and negotiate a distribution contract."

"Exactly." Neil got up from the dinner table, tossed more piñon pine into the fireplace, then poked at the coals. "I was blindsided on this one," he reflected. "More concerned about other potentially explosive problems than I had ever been about Solter's objections."

"Like what?"

"Zolgen could have upset some very established, very nasty applecarts. If it cures addicts, there are fewer drug buyers. Fewer buyers means the loss of millions in street profits. Right now, though, only drug rehab centers are using Zolgen, and their patients aren't buying, anyway—which means no significant losses to the drug lords."

"So...your point is, none of your initial fears for the future of Zolgen ever materialized?"

"Yeah."

"Which leaves us back at square one," she mused. "The drug peddlers had no reason to kill Solter, or to frame you. So who did?"

"I don't know." He hadn't heard much past the word *us* and hadn't realized how much he'd wanted to hear that word until she'd said it. This was what he'd hoped for. He needed her interested. He needed her principled devotion to the truth captured to the point of no return, so that she would go after Solter's murderer with every resource she could muster.

He watched silently as she finished tidying the kitchen. She sat down in an unadorned antique rocker, one leg beneath her, the other extending only enough to allow her to set the chair into motion with a push of her toes.

He was on the verge of enlisting her to his cause, and only now did he think what a bad idea this was. What kind of man was he to drag her into this mess?

Also, she was smart and talented and intuitive and beautiful, and he was attracted to her. If the cops apprehended him right now, it would happen because he'd lost his concentration and his belief in avoiding glass houses.

He had to stay free and alive long enough to find Solter's murderer, and he couldn't afford hankering after Andrea Vogel.

He rose quickly from his place near the fire, picked up his pea jacket and battered army-surplus backpack. "Look, Andrea, I thought you could help, but—"

"Sit down, Neil," she said softly. "Please. I think you're right."

He stood there beside her rocker for a moment, trying to absorb her sudden change of heart and reconcile it with his.

"Please."

That one, softly accented plea robbed the starch from his determination to get out before his attraction to her became a real problem. His tongue locked into the bottom of his mouth. He was in the worst straits of his life, needing more than anything to clear himself, and all he wanted now was to not disappoint her.

Andrea saw the struggle going on in his eyes. He tossed his coat and backpack aside, then dragged his stiffened fingers across the tension-knotted tendons in the back of his neck.

"Right about what?" he asked at last.

"Please," she said, motioning for him to sit by the fire again. When he complied, she continued. "Whoever set up Solter's murder had an interest in seeing Zolgen get to the marketplace. Your disappearance must have seemed like an incredible piece of good luck."

"Yeah, followed by some incredible maneuvering. I don't think a week ever went by that there wasn't some disparaging mention of my name in the newspapers."

"Are you thinking there might have been some sort of conspiracy?"

Breaking up pieces of piñon, he focused on the elusive glimmer of collusion her question triggered. "Maybe. Have you seen the Wanted posters around town?"

Despite the warmth emanating from the fire, Andrea shivered. "Just this evening, at the grocery. Now I know I must have seen them for months on end.... Neil, that's crazy! The FBI doesn't post Wanteds in the grocery."

"Or use photos from a 35 mm camera, either. The photograph on those fliers is not from any photo the police took when they booked me for Solter's murder."

"Then . . . it had to come from some private source?"

On the track of some crucial link now, Neil nodded. "Then there's the constant hype in the press, taking the cops to task for failing to recapture me."

Andrea gripped her bracelet and twisted her wrist in acute concentration. The press had never let up in demanding that Neil Caulfield be brought back to justice. Had he been some psychopathic serial murderer, the papers couldn't have been more relentless. According to the criminal justice system, Neil had murdered Ben Solter, their most persuasive champion, and a posse hanging was too good for him.

"What if the press campaign is more smoke screen than substance?" Andrea suggested. "Suppose the whole crusade is meant to keep you from surfacing?"

"Yeah. What if." Neil got up again from his place by the fire and began to pace, a restless and immense predatory cat.

Andrea was struck again by the breadth of his shoulders, the size of his hands, the power of the legs confined beneath his cords. It was easier to imagine him taking Solter apart piece by piece with his bare hands than driving a syringe filled with a fatal potion into him. The image made her mouth go dry as dust.

"The whole operation smells, Vogel. Like rats following the piper to sea. How the hell could I miss it? I didn't kill Solter, but only the real murderer knows that. So he gets Zolgen to market, rakes in the bucks and keeps my face in front of the outraged law-and-order contingent. As long as I'm forced into hiding, he reasons, no one will ever have cause to doubt that I killed Solter, or start looking for *him*."

"It plays, Neil," Andrea agreed. And it represented the one reason she could see to convince him the authorities were still his best bet. She tilted the rocking chair forward and came to her feet as well. He had a dozen or more inches on her, and more than a hundred pounds, but she made her pitch to him as an equal. "Don't you see that you must go to the police now?"

"No."

She touched her hand to his forearm to prevent him from turning away, then drew it back when the heat of his body penetrated her.

"Neil, listen. I had nothing of any substance to back my demand that Mason Piers reopen the investigation, but this changes everything. If it makes sense that the real murderer is doing everything in his power to keep you from coming forward, it also follows that taking your story to the authorities is your best chance."

Neil swore and turned away. He planted the heels of both hands against the plaster-covered chimney to keep from railing at her babe-in-the-woods mentality.

It didn't work. "Forget it. Just . . . forget it." He turned back, grabbed up his pea jacket and his backpack again, and headed for the back way out.

"You don't do so well with a moral dilemma, either, is that it, Caulfield?"

"As in, the authorities represent the *moral* alternative?" He gave a hopeless shrug of his shoulders, then turned away. He stopped and turned three feet short of the screen door. The expression in his eyes was as hard and unrelenting as anything Andrea had ever in her life confronted.

"I don't have time for anything but staying alive, Vogel. I should've known better. I was always the street-smart survivor, and I'd bet my last nickel you were always the teacher's pet."

"You'd lose," she snapped. "And you're a fool if you leave here in this reckless mood. I know how tough you are. Don't mistake me, either, Caulfield. Not my soft voice or my intellect *or* my will."

Neil dropped his backpack to the tiled floor, hooked his thumbs in his jeans pockets and shook his head. "I'm not going to the cops, Andrea. I can't. You're going to have to make up your mind. You're either in or you're out. Which is it going to be?"

"In."

She turned on her heel and walked away from him, toward the loft stairs. She darted up the spiral staircase, yanked open the linen closet, pulled out a blanket and pillow and threw them over the railing to him. "The sofa pulls out into a bed. It's not the most comfortable thing, but it's all I can offer. If you're still here in the morning I'll see how else I can help you."

HER DECISION PLAGUED her sleep.

She listened to Caulfield prowling the glassed-in confines of her house. He poured himself another glass of her homemade wine, and she waited for a long time for the sounds that would tell her he'd made a bed of her sofa. After a while, she made excuses to herself about needing to know exactly where he was, and got out of bed to glance over the loft banister.

She saw that he had taken off his boots and unbuttoned his shirt. It hung loosely at his sides as he stood staring out into the darkness from one of the glass walls. Not until a thunderstorm moved in, blotting out the moon and sending violent, pounding waves of rain against the walls did he stretch out on the sofa.

She wasn't known for her lack of caution. She respected and paid heed to the tenets of etiquette and social intercourse every well-bred Louisiana daughter held dear. She believed in the law, and until recently, the criminal justice system. But Neil Caulfield had been at large for many months—time enough, with his survival instincts well-honed, to have invented the story he'd told her tonight.

She returned to her bed and lay motionless, staring up at the skylight, which was battered now with the force of the thunderstorm. Parts of his story were unassailable. Zolgen was on the market. Grocery stores didn't even post the pictures of missing children, never mind wanted criminals. The most intensive manhunts eventually lost the fickle attention of the press.

Neil Caulfield appeared to be an honorable man, horribly accused. Still, forensic literature and true-crime books teemed with accounts of brilliant murderers who, to all appearances, seemed charming and charismatic and utterly incapable of committing the crimes of which they'd been accused.

Andrea heard every hourly and half-hourly peep of the cuckoo from the miniature Swiss clock Miriam had sent for her last birthday. Moments after the cuckoo's 3:00 a.m. foray, Andrea got out of bed and went to the top of the spiral staircase again. She listened to Caulfield's deep, regular breathing for nearly an hour. He slept, aided by the wine, perhaps, like the dead.

She crept down the stairs and waited again. She observed no change in his position or breathing. His backpack leaned upright against the sofa, and she intended to get it. To see what an innocent man running for his life carried with him.

Or a guilty one.

She prepared to lift fifty pounds, possibly more. Caulfield's pack weighed no more than thirty, and it surprised her. Despite the awkward burden, she made her way soundlessly back up the narrow, winding staircase to her loft. She levered the pack gently onto her bed and lighted a couple of the dozen candles scattered about her bedroom.

The cuckoo sprang to life, announcing four o'clock. One cuckoo. Two. Between the second and the third, Andrea heard a muffled thud from downstairs. Three cuckoos. Four.

Andrea shivered, and then froze. The cuckoo retreated. Silence engulfed her. The candle flames were straight and eerily motionless. If Caulfield had been awakened by the cuckoo, or the instincts of a fugitive, he already knew that she'd taken his pack.

Chapter Four

Her own instincts came fully alert. Her mind ran through a thousand excuses. None adequately explained why she had resorted to this... this gesture of mistrust. She'd given Neil Caulfield a bed in her own home.

The dark, and the deep of night, had her second-guessing that decision. Self-preservation had her willing to violate his privacy in this way, and no matter how despicable her plan, she had to know more about Neil Caulfield than she was willing to ask.

She dared to exhale, and drew another breath. Her hands shook and her mouth was dry as bones interred for a thousand years. When the clamoring settled down in her mind, she guessed Neil hadn't wakened. Though she couldn't hear the measured breathing of his sleep, she heard no further movement, either.

Andrea swallowed and forced the primitive fight response from her body. Slowly the tension ebbed from her neck and shoulders. Dressed in a short satiny sleep shirt— more than she'd have worn had she been alone—she eased herself onto her antique cherrywood four-poster bed and set about unmasking Neil Caulfield by his possessions.

A small, zippered leather bag lay atop several layers of clothing. Worn jeans, T-shirts, long-sleeved cotton shirts. Black Jockey shorts, crew socks—clean, but no longer white. A pair of once-white athletic shoes, their leather brittle and nearly cracked. A couple of bandannas, neatly folded. The faded mauve Indian print intrigued her.

Had he worn the bandannas like cattle drovers a hundred years ago, covering his nose and mouth against the dust of the quarries where he claimed to have worked?

She sorted through the contents of the small, zippered leather bag. A double-edged razor, no shaving cream. He carried a cheap tube of shampoo, fingernail clippers, a toothbrush and a small tube of toothpaste. Nothing out of the ordinary. Nothing suspicious.

She dug a little further into the pack, and came up with a battered copy of *Zen and the Art of Motorcycle Maintenance,* its pages curling and worn. Again, the whimsy of it touched her. She came up next with a roll of toilet tissue, and stuck her fingers into the cardboard tube, where a folded paper had been tucked. It was a battered copy of the Wanted flier she had seen in the convenience and grocery stores.

The black-and-white picture didn't do the man justice. In person, the snapping black of his irises was different, more penetrating, seeing more than the photo would suggest. The flier conveyed none of his masculine presence, nor any hint of the ruthless survival attitude that marked him now.

There were no other pages identifying him as Neil Caulfield, escaped criminal or award-winning biochemist. He carried no false identification papers, either.

He had reduced himself to the level of a careless itinerant.

Andrea stretched her back, lifted the weight of her hair from her neck and cradled her head back against her hands for a moment. Tucking her legs Indian-style beneath her, she sighed. His possessions didn't justify her search. What had she expected? Syringes, maybe? Deadly toxins with which to murder again?

She began to repack his clothes. Though she'd conducted her search on her own bed by candlelight, old habits had guided her. As if preserving evidentiary integrity, she'd automatically noted and maintained the precise order of his scant belongings. He would never know by any carelessness on her part that she had rifled through his pack.

She restored his shabby athletic shoes, toes down and facing the front of the pack. Her knuckles knocked against something hard and concealed and not part of the internal pack frame.

Her insides felt suddenly cold.

She knew before her fingers explored its outlines that a side compartment of the pack concealed a weapon. A gun. Sharp disappointment rose in her, and Andrea admitted to herself that she hadn't wanted to find anything incriminating Neil Caulfield. She couldn't ignore a concealed weapon.

What she wanted had very little to do with what *was*. Clenching her hands, blinking away the tears along with hopes that had been so completely dashed, Andrea put off repacking his belongings. She withdrew her hand and slid it into the interior of the side pocket, where she encountered the cool metal barrel of the gun. It wouldn't take a side arms specialist to identify the .32 caliber automatic pistol.

The gun was common enough. Its ammunition wasn't. Expertly, though her hands were shaking, she spilled out brutal hollow-point bullets any forensic analysis expert could identify instantly. When they entered a soft tissue, bullets like these flattened, tearing a devastating path.

She felt angry, and betrayed by him. One hand cradled the weapon; her other tore through her hair distractedly. Damn him, damn it all!

But before she could get a grip, she felt herself respond at a gut level to the threat of an enormous shadow looming over her. Neil moved with deadly quiet and speed, and his hand clamped down on her wrist.

She cried out as the gun fell silently from her hand to her treasured old log-cabin-patterned quilt. She leaped off the bed and jerked her wrist free of his hold. He'd pulled on his corduroys without taking the time to zip them. His naked torso was covered with darkly curling hair and was heavily muscled. He looked as dangerous as the weapon on her quilt.

She wouldn't be caught sitting down.

Unconsciously she moistened her lips, and darted a glance at the stairwell, assessing her chances of getting away from him.

"What good would it do me to kill you, Dr. Vogel," he asked, his voice low and rough with outright anger, "when you're the only hope I've got?"

"I'm no hope to you at all," she returned. "No rational, innocent man carries a concealed weapon—or ammunition this inhuman, Caulfield."

"Like no *innocent* man skips bail?"

"Exactly!"

His eyes flashed, and sinew strained at his neck. "For God's sake, grow up, Vogel. This is the real world, complete with real guns and nasty bullets."

He took one angry step toward her. Andrea jerked backward. "Stop it!"

"You ought to know the good guys don't always wear white hats or carry badges, and the bad guys sure as *hell* don't fight bears with a peashooter."

"This," she cried, waving disjointedly at the weapon on her bed cover, "makes you no better than them!"

She stepped back to put space between them, but the back of her calf jolted the nightstand. For a moment the candle-light flickered crazily. Her glance darted again to the stairs behind him.

"You just don't get it, do you?"

"What? Am I missing something here? You're in very serious straits, Neil—"

"Serious straits!" He took her by the shoulders, forcing her to look at him, and bit off a string of epithets meant to level her naïveté.

He smelled clean and wholesome, but that was probably the scent of her shampoo. His eyes were black as midnight, and sexy, but her impression was out of kilter and ill-timed and she blamed him. No man had ever invaded her bedroom or dared hold her like this against her will.

"No one is trying to... to *kill* you, Neil!"

His fingers pressed too hard into her shoulders. "What makes you so sure?"

"Because this isn't the Dark Ages," she snapped. She couldn't think clearly with his immense hands controlling her. She feared the fierce, snarling survivor in him. "And there is no mob waiting to string you up!"

He would have laughed, but there was nothing funny about her naïveté. He supposed it didn't happen often, but when she was wrong, she was dead wrong.

She tried to duck out of his hold on her, but nothing worked. "Let me go."

"No." His *life* depended upon what Andrea Vogel believed, and he damned well wasn't letting loose of her until he could trust her not to bolt. "No."

"Now. I mean it." He towered over her, but she wasn't defenseless. She put her hands on his forearms like a child fending off a stranger, levering her body to land a kick to the groin.

He knew instinctively what she intended. She was afraid of him, and he hated her for that. He had damn little to convince her of his innocence, and any caution left in him went up in smoke.

He trapped her head between his hands and brought his lips down hard on hers. He felt her startled, disbelieving breath, and then the exquisite softness of her bow-shaped lips.

She stiffened, fighting his violation of her defenses with all her might. "Neil, don't!" she pleaded. This scared her more than if he'd aimed the Colt Special at her heart, because no matter how hard he kissed her, his tenderness, his *humanity* besieged her.

"I won't hurt you. You know that." But he pressed her against his body and bit at her lips. His thumb stroked stray wisps of hair from her brow. His kiss demanded she give in, that she listen to him, and he wanted to pretend, for one solitary moment, that he didn't have to convince her of anything.

Her fingers inadvertently touched his bare back. He flinched and withdrew, but not before Andrea's fingers discovered the scar.

I don't have time for anything but staying alive, Andrea....

The blood rushed from her head, and she reached out to him. "What happened to you?"

He backed away and began stuffing his belongings haphazardly into his pack, admitting to himself that he'd never have kissed her if he hadn't half-intended her to find the scars. Proof of his words. "Like I said, Vogel. The bad guys aren't packing peashooters."

"You were...you were shot?" Nausea swept through her. It didn't seem to matter that she'd done hundreds of grisly postmortems, that she should have been able to distance herself. That long welt of scar tissue on his body enraged her. "In the back?"

"Yeah." He picked up the Colt Special. "And the first thing I did—when I knew I wouldn't die—was to buy myself some nasty protection."

He caught the horror in her eyes, and something else, something...tender. "Don't even think it, Dr. Vogel. I need your help, not your pity."

He spilled the ammunition into his hand and held the bullets out to her. If he had to disarm himself to gain her faith, he'd do it. "Here. Take them."

Andrea shook her head. "Put them away, Neil. I'd rather you replace them with something less...brutal. But I won't be the reason you can't defend yourself. Do you... Did you ever see a doctor about—"

"No." His biting, cynical glance cut short her question. Watching her, he reloaded the gun, checked the safety and replaced it in the side pocket of his pack. She knew the answer to that as well as he did. Doctors are required by law to report gunshot wounds. "I never saw a doctor."

She lifted her chin. "That was a stupid question. I'm sorry."

He nodded and dragged a hand through his hair. He stared at the rough-hewn beams across the ceiling of her bedroom.

"What?" she demanded, forcing him out of his silence.

The memory of a bullet—two bullets—exploding into his back nearly brought Neil to his knees. The scent of his own seared flesh. The sound, like a thump on the head, but a thousand times more sickening. The pain. Oh, God, the pain.

He reached for a cotton work shirt and shoved his arms in. "I want to get at the truth, Vogel, but I don't know how I'd live with myself if you were to get hurt." Things had gone too far, too fast. A week ago—an hour ago—he'd never intended her to know. "I wasn't going to tell you."

Because a careful woman wouldn't knowingly put her own life in jeopardy? But she was ashamed of attributing selfish motives to him. "Why did you, then?"

He shrugged and did up the bottom buttons on the worn plaid shirt. Picking up the ragged Wanted flier, he stared at it for a moment. In the candlelight, Andrea saw small muscles in his jaw bunch. "You'd better understand what you're getting into, Vogel. That's all."

Straightening the old-fashioned quilt, she sat on the bed and leaned back against the headboard. A cautious woman would understand. Clearly.

"Will you do me a favor, Neil?" He nodded. "I have a first name. Use it."

Wearily, he slouched down at the other end of her bed. His pack occupied the space between them. "Okay. Andrea."

For the first time, she was aware of the skimpy satin nightshirt she wore. The end of her bed sagged under his weight, and she became aware, too, of him as a man. She couldn't keep her eyes from returning again and again to his lips.

But Miri was right. All a man ever wanted of her was not *her*, but what he could get from her. Her help. Neil Caulfield was different, but the same. "Tell me, then. What am I getting into?"

He plied his left thumb against the heel of his other hand, easing some ache. "I don't want to insult your intelligence. You must have seen a thousand very ugly ways to die. You can't be... You can't see those deaths and not know how the real world works."

Andrea nodded, but though her memory could conjure grisly case histories to mind, she avoided the images. The one she couldn't avoid was the tactile sense of ungodly scar tissue. Neil's scars. "So. Would it help you to know what I think I'm getting myself into if I help you?"

"Yeah."

She drew a deep breath and let it all go. "Okay. Someone killed Solter and framed you for the murder. Solter was a law-and-order fanatic. He was powerful and persuasive and influential, and he had hundreds of thousands of readers, so his murder is especially sensational. It only requires a few true believers to take the law into their own hands. You're the target. They'll take you any way they can, even if it means shooting you in the back.''

"And anyone else who gets in their way." His lips curved in a half smile, a cynical smile. Appreciating her grasp of the situation, he knew she still hadn't the flimsiest notion what it was like to *live* his outlaw existence.

"So which part of this do you think I don't understand?"

His gaze fell away from hers, and he picked at calluses on his hands. "The part about eating beans out of a tin can, Boo."

Her chin went up like a shot. "That's a private thing, between Miri and me."

"And me, now." His eyes bored into her, beyond her objection. "I'm not afraid—of you or your answers."

Andrea combed her hair back with her fingers. She would have to think, later when he wasn't so near, if she minded his calling her Boo. "What about eating beans from a can?"

"You're a smart woman, Andrea. Figure it out." He could have told her plenty, but he didn't see much point. He sat quietly for a moment, then reached across to her and took her icy fingers into his hands.

"Andrea, there's one hell of a difference between chucking your position at the M.E.'s office out of principles, and throwing in with me. Whoever killed Solter isn't done yet." He looked down at their hands joined together, and deliberately let go of her.

She understood. The danger in joining hands with him against such hidden and overwhelming forces numbed her. But she thought of her mother, of the legacy Lillian Vogel had left, of taking on evil with so much at stake and so little to fight back with.

Andrea Vogel was her mother's daughter. "There's also a difference between sending a man to jail and shooting him in the back, Neil." This time she joined their hands, but he pulled away and rose from her bed.

The dilemma tore at him. He needed her help in the worst way. He believed that his life depended upon her help. But he had no business making her a target. He gave one last stab at dissuading her. Maybe if she understood how savagely he regarded his own survival, she'd take a clue and get out before she ever got in.

"I won't be taken alive, Vogel."

"'I won't be taken alive, *Andrea,*'" she corrected coolly. "Don't make the mistake of underestimating me, Neil. I want to live every bit as much as you do."

"The difference is, you're not prepared to die."

"I don't intend to die."

He let his eyes caress her crudely, assessing every curve, her shoulders, her breasts, every soft part that made her unequal in fighting for her own survival, much less his. "I'd hate for it to take a bullet ripping into your delicate flesh to convince you that you shouldn't have gotten involved."

"In my professional experience," she said, "a woman's flesh is no less vulnerable to bullets than a man's."

He slung his pack strap over his shoulder. His gaze touched her again, in all the places he'd looked before. Andrea watched him, and this time felt something quite different than the scorn of his last perusal. Like a man looking at a woman he could make love to. Her heart began unexpectedly to hammer.

"I won't forgive either of us if you get shot up, Andrea."

She felt curiously... thrilled. She smiled to cover the bittersweet notion that he cared and that he wanted to protect her. He would, but for just as long as he needed her ability to get at the truth. Until he was free to come and go as he chose.

"A real moral dilemma, isn't it?" she teased gently. He would owe her his life. But he'd already been shot, and it occurred to her that if she'd taken her objections to Mason Piers weeks earlier, the case against Neil Caulfield would have been dismissed in time to prevent all of this.

"I'm in, Neil."

He rose from her bed, lifted the pack and nodded curtly. Why on God's green earth had he felt so compelled to warn her off? Because, he knew now, he'd save her skin as quickly as his own, no matter how he had to do it, which made his situation worse, not better.

Having to look out for her, too, was sheer folly. But he hadn't felt half so hopeful in a very long time.

ANDREA WOKE WHEN THE SUN broke over the eastern horizon. Her bedroom windows faced west. Clouds in the distance tinged with gold began to scatter, and sunlight bounced off the sugar-water feeders she'd set out for the hummers on the small deck extending from her loft. The scent of pine permeated the air, as it did every morning, strongest at dawn.

This morning the impression of Neil Caulfield's body remained at the end of her feather mattress where he'd sat a few hours before. And she was more aware of the memory of his scent than of the pine bouquet.

She tossed back her covers and chided herself while she showered. Yes, he had eyes to make any woman's heart throb. Yes, he'd kissed her. Admittedly a harsh, demanding kiss that her memory colored fine and rare.

Neil Caulfield was unlikely to ever invade her bedroom again. The smart thing would be to put her bothersome recollections far, far away. No one had ever accused Andrea Vogel of lacking in smarts.

She stepped from the shower, dried herself, applied a dusting of powder and dab of perfume and took care to pull back her wet hair in a flattering chignon. She was a woman, a Southern woman raised on a certain awareness of herself and attention to genteel grooming. Surely she could perform all those feminine rituals as on every other morning of her life. She wouldn't go to any special effort for Neil Caulfield.

To prove it, she chose a soft, well-worn periwinkle T-shirt and jeans, then went barefoot down the stairs. Her guest slept soundly, one arm flung up over his head, one leg trailing over the edge of the sofa.

He appealed to her even in sleep. A brilliant scientist, he was no one to cross. Male and dangerous and smart and hard. All man. If she trusted him not to hurt her, she didn't trust him not to take advantage of any of those qualities or her attraction to them. He needed her.

She turned and went into her east-facing kitchen. Sunlight streamed in. She measured out coffee into the filter, enough for both of them, and watched Doodle giving chase to a squirrel. She added a pot of water to the coffeemaker, then picked up her cordless phone and punched in the recall digit to reach Miriam's place in New York.

She was sitting on the back porch by the time Miriam answered. "Boo! Isn't it terribly early out there?"

"Two time zones, Miri. The sun is up."

Miriam groaned. "That late! I didn't expect to hear from you again so soon, anyway."

Andrea laughed softly. "I didn't expect to be needing your help, either. Something has come up, and I could use your input."

"Name it."

"Would you mind dusting off your old investigative reporter skills?"

"Lord, no! Once a reporter, always a reporter. Especially if it's in a juicy cause. What's up?"

"Do you remember the brouhaha surrounding the Solter murder?"

"Well, let me think. The defendant—Caulfield, wasn't it?—was in the final stages of licensing Zolgen for retail sales through the Food and Drug Administration. As I recall, Ben Solter took exception on his usual law-and-order high horse."

"Exception?" Andrea laughed. "You've managed to raise understatement to an art form, Miri."

"Naturally. Understatement is at the soul of the finest in journalism, you know. Why? What gives?"

"Well, the really odd thing is, I never understood how Zolgen got to market after Caulfield skipped. I mean, how did they get around his patent? Who got around it?"

"Hmm. Have you considered calling a patent attorney?"

"Yes. I thought of that." And immediately discarded an attorney as a possible resource. There didn't seem any way to put her questions in general enough terms that they wouldn't raise unnecessary suspicion. On the other hand, Andrea didn't want to make an accomplice of Miriam in abetting a fugitive from the law. The less her friend knew, the better.

"The problem is, I need to keep a low profile on this," she continued. "I'm not supposed to have the least interest in any case I handled while in the M.E.'s office."

Miriam was silent far longer than Andrea would have liked. She could almost hear her old friend's mental wheels turning, making connections.

"Are you going to tell me why you're interested, given that you're not supposed to be?"

"I always thought this case involved a lot more—"

"Come on, Boo," Miri interrupted. "Something has set off your curiosity. Caulfield is back, isn't he?"

Neil picked that moment to appear at Andrea's side. He'd pulled on a fresh pair of jeans and a T-shirt, and he brought with him two mugs of coffee. He sat down next to Andrea on the back porch and handed her one of the mugs.

Andrea gave him a grateful glance. But what to do about Miri's assumption? She trusted no one in this life more than Miri. And she couldn't see lying to her. Not even in this. "Yes. He's here."

"Here?" Miri cried. "Here, as in at your place right this minute?"

Andrea met Neil's glance and sipped at her coffee, relishing the wealth of aroma more than the scalding brew. "Yes."

"And he knows you're talking to me?"

"Yes. Miri, I—"

"Andrea, you must be certifiable! Or is he...is he threatening you, Boo? Is he—"

"Miri, will you shut up for a minute, please? He's innocent." Andrea watched Neil's eyes darken and his jaw muscles clench. He drew a deep breath and stared into his coffee mug. She knew Miri's reaction was typical, and she could see how tired of it he must be.

Funny, she thought, how she failed to remember from one time to the next what a large man he was, or how shadowed his eyes were with his solitary outrage at having been framed for a murder he hadn't committed. She smiled to encourage him. Miriam wasn't done with her vehement objections.

"I don't give a fig whether he's innocent or not! The fact that you've even seen him puts you in an impossible position. Boo, you cannot—"

"Miri, I didn't ask you what I can or cannot do—or even what I *should* do," she interrupted. "I'm asking for a favor. Period. I want to know how Zolgen was put on the market, what the production and vending arrangements were with the pharmaceutical house, and who the parties to the deal were. All that should be a matter of public record, shouldn't it?"

"Yes," Miriam snapped, clearly unhappy with Andrea's decision-making. "That information should be available."

Her retriever, Doodle, had come bounding out of her doghouse, bringing Neil her toy bone. Setting his coffee aside, Neil hurled the bone to the far reaches of the fence separating her land from the forest.

Though Andrea let the condemning silence build, Miri didn't volunteer to go after the information. At last she said, "Miriam, I need you to trust me on this one." She smiled, and tried to make her friend laugh. "I'm never wrong, you know."

"Don't I know it?" Miri returned. She hesitated, and concern replaced her trenchant tone. "This would be one very bad time to make an unwitting exception, Boo."

Chapter Five

Andrea pressed the on/off button and set the phone aside. Miriam had quietly broken the connection. They understood each other well enough. Miriam might not approve, but she would do what Andrea had asked.

Neil side-armed Doodle's bone again. Andrea sensed tension coming from him like heated rays off the early-morning sun. "She'll help, Neil. We have to start somewhere."

"Yeah. Somewhere." He kicked at a clump of weeds and leaned back, resting on his elbows. Someone else knowing his whereabouts bothered him, but he knew it was inevitable. "I gather she wasn't happy about it."

Doodle fetched the bone and nudged Neil's knee. Andrea ordered her old pet to lie down, then looked at Neil. "I can't fault Miri for caring what happens to me, but she doesn't usually second-guess me like that."

"She has good reason, I'd say."

His look told her she was a woman he wanted to protect. She lifted her chin, wondering where her resolve had gone. If he felt compelled to protect her, it stemmed from his own conscience at having put her in danger—nothing else. *Get a grip, Boo,* she chided herself. Falling for Caulfield's haunted good looks, or even his intelligence, would be all wrong.

"Let's not get off on that tangent again," she warned. "I'm already involved, like it or not, and if you walked out of here this morning I'd still want that information. You didn't kill Solter, but *someone* did. I shouldn't have let go of it in the first place."

"Because you're never wrong?"

Andrea smiled and sipped at her coffee. "Yeah. Because I'm never wrong."

NEIL RINSED THEIR breakfast dishes and stacked them in the dishwasher, then finished dressing. He wore a plaid work shirt tucked into jeans that concealed the holster strapped low on his leg. He put on athletic shoes, then added a University of New Mexico baseball cap and a pair of horn-rimmed glasses.

Between the short beard he'd grown, which looked more as if he simply hadn't shaved in a while, and the clothes, he no longer resembled his own photo on the Wanted fliers—or the clean-cut scientist he'd been, on trial for the murder of Ben Solter.

Andrea left on her jeans and T-shirt and slipped into a pair of sandals. Over waffles with raspberry sauce, they'd concluded that she had to get at her files on the Solter murder case. She called the Antiquities research department secretary, advising the girl that she'd be taking a few unscheduled days off. One major advantage of her position was that there were very few obligations that couldn't be postponed.

She planned to ask Mason Piers, still the chief medical examiner, for access to the morgue archives, and her casual, unprofessional garb was deliberate. Neil took one look at her, and his brow furrowed doubtfully.

Andrea grabbed up her shoulder bag and tossed in a legal pad for notes. "Piers will be a lot less likely to refuse than if I came in looking serious and official. Don't you think?"

He scraped the heel of his hand over an itch beneath his beard. "Depends on your strategy. I didn't mean to question—"

"Yes, you did." She lifted the shoulder bag into place and headed out the front door. Her blue Taurus wagon sat in the graveled circular driveway.

"Okay," Neil conceded, following her out. He checked the brass handle on the front door to make sure it was locked, then let himself in the passenger door of the car. "Okay, I *did* mean to question. Are you saying Piers will feel threatened by you, by your request?"

Andrea started the car and pulled out. "It really doesn't matter, Neil. I'm legally entitled to examine the records of my work."

"What if he refuses?"

"He could, temporarily, but I don't think he will. He may put me off, but he knows I won't have to go far to get permission anyway."

"Whose permission?"

She glanced in her rearview mirror at the cloud of dust behind her car, then at Neil's profile. Her eyes lingered. "It would take a court order, if he wanted to throw roadblocks in my way." She understood how reluctant he must be to have the slightest attention drawn to either one of them. Or to give up his control of the situation. "You'll have to trust me to handle this, Neil. There is no other way, and you know it."

He let out a frustrated breath and stared out his passenger window at the passing landscape. "What's your reason?"

"Simply that I'm compiling case histories for my résumé. Mason never believed I would stay out of forensic pathology, anyway, so he'll believe it. Besides," she joked, sensing a need to unravel Neil's tension, "the man believes I'm constitutionally unable to lie."

Neil laughed.

"So. Any other questions?"

"Yeah. When did you earn 'Boo' for a nickname?"

Andrea gave him a half smile. "Almost the instant I walked onto the Tulane campus. Miri and I were in the same English-lit class, otherwise our paths would probably never have crossed."

She hesitated for a moment, remembering. "Miri's very observant. She had this theory that men believe a woman with brains can't possibly be any good in bed." She laughed softly, because the memories were more bitter than sweet, then gave him a challenging glance. "Ever since I was a little girl, Neil, I knew things and understood more than anybody thought I should. And I think Miri was right. It scared off more men than you can imagine."

"Better men than me?" he asked. He delivered the question straight-faced, but she could hear the humor, the innate confidence in himself.

"Yes…well." She reached the highway and turned south toward Santa Fe. "I wouldn't know about that." She doubted there were much better men than Neil Caulfield in the overall scheme of things. But he must know that he had her respect, or she wouldn't be jeopardizing herself to help him. "Have you decided what you're going to do while I'm there?"

"Goodwill, I guess." He had to have more clothes—not new. Used, worn, but wearable. The soles were about to crack away from his athletic shoes, too. "If Piers agrees to let you go through your files, what will you do? Take notes right there?"

Andrea shook her head. "I want you to be able to see the file, Neil. You can go over what evidence there was, and maybe find something no one else would look for. Besides, I don't want to open your file right under Mason's nose. I'll ask to check them out overnight and in batches, starting with my last five or ten cases."

"You won't be long, then. Drop me at the Goodwill. I'll pick up some clothes and meet you at that little cantina up the street. José's. Do you know the place?"

"Headed away from town, you mean?"

"Yeah."

Andrea nodded and exited the highway, heading for the Goodwill location. A few minutes later, after he'd pointed out the cantina to be sure she knew where to meet him, she dropped him off and took his thumbs-up sign with a smile of gratitude.

The truth was, she would need all the luck she could get.

FOR A FRIDAY MORNING, the associated hospital parking lots were predictably full. Andrea opted for an Official space right in front of the wing occupied by the office of the medical examiner, Mason Piers's domain. Her stomach churned as she pulled into the space. Two things caused the upset. First, despite her calm assurances to Neil, she didn't know if she could pull off this charade with Piers. She hadn't ever tried anything remotely like it.

The second had to do with the van parked directly in front of her Taurus. Its logo read McGowan Security Corporation. She'd heard of the company. She'd signed off on an invoice herself when McGowan Security had designed and installed the updated Antiquities lab alarm system.

Somehow, the appearance of a security team at the very moment she planned to raid the medical examiner's files didn't bode well for her success. Andrea gave herself a mental shake and turned off the car. She had every ethical and legal argument on her side. She was entitled to access to the records of her work in this office.

She got out, locked the doors and glanced at the security guard who looked up from his newspaper as she entered. Murmuring a distracted greeting, she signed in as A. K. Vogel, M.D., and dropped the pen back onto the logbook. "Where is the McGowan team?"

"Working in the basement," the guard answered. "Testing the electrical."

She nodded and turned toward the stairwell door as she had a thousand other times. She suspected the guard, overtly bored, overweight and almost certainly an ex-cop without much in the way of ambition or a curious nature, wouldn't challenge her. He didn't.

Piers's secretary was gone from her desk. Andrea crossed the expansive reception area quickly, knocked on Mason's door, then let herself in. Except for the calendar, nothing in his office had changed, including his ability to tune out the rest of the world. Piers sat poring over the morning newspaper, his concentration unbroken by her entrance.

"Hello, Mason."

His attention snapped at the sound of her voice, and his head came up instantly.

"Vogel?" She'd surprised him, and he clearly didn't like it. "What are you doing here?"

She gave him her most disarming smile and searched for something helplessly female to say, anything to defuse his instant suspicions. "Would you believe looking for a job?"

He sat back and folded his hands across his lean middle. "Come off it, Vogel. You haven't even been off the job a year yet."

This wasn't going to be an easy sell. But she wasn't half-done. Let him underestimate her. Just as her mother might have done to get her way, she shrugged in a feminine and vulnerable manner. "Even half a year has been enough to convince me, Mason. I need to get back into a real pathology lab before I forget everything you taught me."

"Well, well, well. The prodigal daughter." He turned in his executive swivel chair and snapped open the blinds. "I find your change of heart very unconvincing, Doctor."

She rubbed the back of one hand with her thumb and envisioned a complicated game of chess. She'd learned the game at her father's sickbed; he'd died before Andrea turned twelve, but not before he'd taught her the advantages of strategy and daring. She met Piers's challenging stare head-on. "I'm sorry that we disagreed in the end, Mason, but I'm quite sincere."

"Well, I'm at full staff, Vogel. I don't have anything to offer you—and I bet you knew I wouldn't."

Andrea nodded as though disheartened. "I suspected as much, of course. Naturally, I'd prefer to return here, but I was fairly certain that would be impossible."

"A phone call would have told you that much. So why don't you tell me what you really want?"

She damned the flood of alarm that threatened to break loose in her. He couldn't know what she was after, and she had to play this right. "I'm putting together a résumé, Mason. I need to review my case files in order to accurately report my experience."

"No, you don't. You're a board-certified forensic pathologist and your employment record here will suffice for any application."

So, yes. He *was* going to throw roadblocks in her way. "Suffice, maybe. But to be competitive, I need to document my experience. Mason, you *know* that. Especially since I've been out of the field for a while."

"That's not my problem."

"No," she agreed, "it's mine. But I'm asking you as a friend and former colleague to help me by granting access to my files. Call it professional courtesy."

He appeared to be somewhat touched by her appeal, but his telephone rang just as he seemed ready to concede. Annoyed with the interruption, he reached for the receiver. "Piers." He was on his feet before he'd hung up. "I'll be there in a minute." To her, he said, "I'm needed in the lab. Walk with me."

She followed him out of his office. His secretary was still absent from her desk.

He opened the stairwell door and waited for Andrea to go through. Down one story, he followed her through the next door and stopped at the security entrance to the lab.

"So just exactly what do you want to do?"

Carefully now. She was almost there. Almost. She shouldered her bag and slid her hands into her pockets as she stopped next to him. "I'd like to check out the files overnight, five or ten at a time, and work backward."

"Including the Caulfield case?"

Check. Inside, Andrea swore.

It took every resource within her to stand there and agree that she wanted the Caulfield case file. "Well, yes. All of them."

"I think the D.A.'s office would take a very dim view of that."

"Why?" Andrea countered. "The case—"

"Is *still* a political bombshell. Whatever else I may or may not agree to, Vogel, the Solter file is out of the question."

Checkmate. Her frustration soared. Still, she managed to act as if any one case were hardly important enough to argue over. "Fine. May I take some with me now, then?"

Piers shook his head. "See me tomorrow, after I've had a chance to run this by some legal beagle." He laughed at his own small joke, but his laughter seemed strained, tinged with anxiety.

Tomorrow would be too late. Instinctively she knew that twenty-four hours from now—even six hours—the Solter case file would be missing from the records room, probably under lock and key in Piers's office. She had to act now, do something to insure she had a chance at that file before Piers or the D.A. made it impossible.

"Look, Mason. If it would make life easier for you—until you can put my request to legal counsel—I'll work here for a while, starting with the oldest cases first."

"What would make my life easier, Vogel, is for you to come back."

Andrea smiled sympathetically. "I know, Mason. I never made life easier for you, did I? But this is very important to me, and someday I'll—"

"Someday you'll make it all up to me. I know. I know." He waved off any further pleas and barked "Jericho!" into the voice-activated door mechanism. The bullet-proof glass door swept open before him. Holding out his left arm impatiently, he waited for her to pass through the secured entrance first.

Relief drizzled through Andrea, and she passed through the door before he could change his mind. "Mason, I can't thank you enough, really."

"No," he returned, following her through, "you can't. I'm warning you, Vogel, no more. Hit the archives, and don't go past 1990 accessions. You've got one hour. And I'll call *you* when—and if—I get approval on the rest." He paused when a technologist rushed up to him with the test results Andrea assumed he'd been called to review. He started to walk off with the tech, then turned back and made his parting shot over his shoulder.

"Don't count on the Solter file, Dr. Vogel. Not in your lifetime."

NEIL SAT IN THE CANTINA up the street from the Goodwill. If he'd had his preference, he'd have sat in the corner booth where there was nothing but several inches of adobe wall behind him and a smoke-hazed window to the side through which he could watch all passersby. But he knew from unpleasant experience all the subtle ways a man could draw attention to himself.

A man on his own in a place like this sat at the bar, not in a booth.

He'd chosen the stool up against the wall at the far end of the bar, directly under a television tuned to a sports channel. The bartender slopped a few glasses around in the sink half-full of dirty water. Half a dozen other barflies, four crusty men and two tired women, sat scattered around the cantina. Five of the six sucked on long-necked beer bottles. The sixth had passed out beside his bottle of Jack Daniel's.

Neil regretted suggesting Andrea meet him here. The place had turned into a real dive.

A couple of years ago, under other ownership, José's had been a great place, frequented by respectable patrons privy to the best-kept secret in Santa Fe. Green chili like nowhere else on earth.

Now the place smelled of burned fat and stale beer. The voice of the sports announcer rose in decibels and pitch at the end of a hotly contested futurity race as Andrea walked through the door.

She stood silhouetted against the bright sunlight of the outdoors, peering uncertainly around the dark interior of the cantina. She looked small and fragile, her shoulders narrow, her waist tiny, her hips flaring gently, leggy in her jeans, and Neil felt suddenly very possessive of her.

He waited, unmoving, for the space of several heartbeats, then more, to see if she could pick him out. He saw that she was about ready to give up looking and turn away. He slid lazily off the stool and stood, then picked up his bottle of beer and moved toward her.

She let the door close behind her, and the barflies and the bartender blatantly stared. She drew attention without trying in this miserable excuse for a watering hole. Neil was suddenly glad that she'd only worn jeans and a T-shirt this morning.

He ambled around the corner of the bar and gestured for Andrea to join him in the back booth. Her eyes darted from him to the old, falling-down Cinco de Mayo banner to the half-drunk men letting out wolf whistles.

Neil stared a couple of them down and let his body language clue them in. In their language, she was his property. He slung an arm around her shoulders and pulled her along with him to the booth.

Andrea slid in and settled her bag beside her. "Nice place, Caulfield. You won't mind if I pick our next rendezvous point."

"All part of a low-profile existence," he answered. "But feel free next time."

"Ya wanna drink over there, lady? Some nachos, maybe?"

"Um ... wine, perhaps—"

"A ginger ale, in the can," Neil ordered, delivering the barkeep a cut-you-off-at-the-knees look. "Trust me on this one, Boo. You wouldn't want anything out of a glass."

She laughed and agreed to his suggestion. It disturbed her that she almost hadn't recognized him, although she knew that he was safer that way. Still she took the time to truly look at him, memorizing him while he had the camouflaging horn-rimmed glasses pushed up high on his head.

Under thick, broadly arching eyebrows, his brown eyes were set wider apart than in most men, and his cheekbones were less prominent. Deep dimples carved a furrows that extended nearly to his jaw beneath the thick layer of whiskers several shades lighter than his hair. She'd known men more classically handsome, but none so compelling as Neil Caulfield.

If seven months passed before she saw him again, or even seven years, she wouldn't fail to recognize him. In her experience with witness identifications, she knew most people never truly looked at other people—particularly strangers. Most of the time Neil was probably quite safe, despite the fliers posted in every public nook and cranny.

He took a pull on his beer and searched her eyes. "So tell me. What happened with Piers?"

The barkeep delivered Andrea's can of ginger ale, and she handed him a dollar bill. "It was a mess, Neil. He'd really rather I disappear through some cosmic trapdoor, never to be heard from again."

Neil swore under his breath, succinctly and straight to the point. "So that's out."

"No, not exactly. He finally agreed. He even let me into the archives. But he made sure I knew, absolutely certain, that he'd never consent to my seeing the Solter file." She popped the tab on her can and leaned toward Neil. "If he were anyone else, I'd wonder if he had something to hide."

"*What* he has to hide, Boo, not if," Neil chided. "There may be nothing in that file that would clear me, but a man with a clean conscience doesn't bury the truth ten feet under." He drew an aggravated breath and leaned back, planting the heels of his hands against the edge of the table. "Sorry."

Andrea nodded. He had no outlet for his futile anger, no ears but hers to burn. For a moment she sat in silence, aware that his apologies always took her off her guard. She was also aware that she liked him.

And that she was very attracted to him.

"I think there is something in that file, Neil. I don't believe Piers has a clue as to what it is, but if I know the man, he's been through the entire file with a fine-tooth comb. He doesn't know what to look for. None of us did. But between us, we might hit on exactly the right thing."

"Maybe. Can you modem into the file and download somewhere else?"

Andrea sipped at her soda and smiled. "Well, it wasn't easy, but I got lucky. The medical librarian had to take a rather complicated question over the phone. The computer was up under the librarian's access codes. I didn't think I had time to transmit the entire file, but there were three updates to the Solter file that I sent to my hard drive for storage—and I switched the contents of your file box with the contents of another one from 1988."

Neil shoved at the damp edge of the label on his now-empty beer bottle and frowned. "But you still have to get back in."

Andrea nodded. "Later this evening, when most of the staff has knocked off for the weekend."

"I'm going with you."

"That would be really stupid, Neil."

"Maybe," he said. "But that's the way it's going to be. I go with you, or you don't go at all."

"Caulfield," she blurted, "I can't believe you would be so feebleminded as to—"

"Shhh!" With a lightning movement, his hand darted out and he grabbed her wrist.

Andrea lowered her voice to an angry whisper. "No. You are not—"

"Shut up and listen to me, *Boo*." His eyes went black and unyielding as cold lava. "If you get caught, and I think the likelihood is strong, you're going to need me."

She tried to jerk her wrist loose and only got a tightened grip for her trouble. "For some macho escape? Spare me, Neil!"

"For a scapegoat, Vogel. Someone to blame. You're not going to flush your reputation down the toilet because you want to call the shots." He let her go and called for another beer, but his eyes never left hers.

Andrea switched tactics. "Neil, I'd be far more likely to get caught if you're with me than if I go alone. Please reconsider. I'm a big girl, and I've been making my own choices for a very long time. I know what the consequences are, and I'm willing to take the gamble. I couldn't stand it if you wound up back in jail over this."

"Couldn't you?" Suddenly he wanted her to care that much, wanted to think she would pine away if he were sent up. He reached for her again, gently this time, and took her hand. His thumb stroked her delicate, feminine fingers. He'd kissed her last night, too.

A ploy to force her discovery of the nasty, ill-healed scars on his back.

And for one second there, he'd allowed himself the luxury of believing he could hold Andrea Vogel and kiss her for no reason other than that he wanted her.

His eyes passed over her heart-shaped face, her widow's peak and sweet, pointed chin. His gaze caught on her raven's-wing-black hair, caught up in a braid, and he wished with all his might that he hadn't had to drag her into this. That he could take her home and take her to bed and forget the world.

Andrea saw longing in his eyes and wondered if the look had anything to do with her. But that was silly, she knew. Hopeful and reckless and silly. He needed his life back, nothing more. "What are you thinking, Neil?"

"That I don't want to end up back in the slammer. I'd probably be safer in jail than on the streets, but I won't set you up to take the flak alone, Andrea. Believe me. It won't happen."

NEIL REPLACED HIS GLASSES. They went to the movies to kill the remaining hours before they could return to the medical examiner's. Andrea had a death grip on her gold bangle for most of the ninety-minute movie. She just couldn't relax. Near the end, Neil unfolded her fingers and let them tighten again around his own.

When it was over, he volunteered to drive. Andrea nodded, got in on the passenger side and pulled her seat belt into place as Neil turned on the ignition.

He pulled out of the parking lot and onto a southbound one-way boulevard. "So. Tell me how this is going to work."

Andrea pictured the layout of the building in her mind's eye and tried to forget about the half-dozen ways it could all go wrong. "The guard at the main entrance will have gone home. All the offices are locked after 5:00 p.m., and the lab has a voice-activated security mechanism. Anyone coming in or out after hours is supposed to sign in on the logbook. I'll sign in."

"There are no surveillance cameras?"

Andrea shook her head. "Piers was allocated the money for that kind of surveillance a couple of times, but he always spent the money inside the lab instead."

"So then what?"

"We'll take the fire-escape stairs to the second floor. Piers used the word *Jericho* this morning to get through the security door. It shouldn't change until midnight."

"Then it's a simple matter of retrieving the file box with the Solter case?"

Warming up after the chill she'd taken in the air-conditioned theater, Andrea pushed back her hair and nodded. "There's a high speed fax machine in the records room. Thankfully, there's an automatic door that keeps the archives closed off. We'll send everything to my computer at Antiquities. The incoming line feeds onto the hard drive, where everything is stored until it can be downloaded to a printer."

Neil applied the brakes and downshifted to first gear as the intersection light turned yellow. "Why not send it to your computer at home?"

"I've got a modem at home, but no ability to receive a fax. Besides, my printer is dot matrix. For some of the things in that file, Neil, I'll need near-perfect reproduction. The Antiquities printer is the only way to go."

Piers's '91 blue Buick Century was missing from the staff parking, as was his secretary's car. Only one of the other assigned spaces was filled. Andrea didn't recognize the car. Neil followed Andrea's instructions to the hospital parking lot where her car would least likely be noticed, then held her door and handed her the keys.

He took a deep breath. Yellow fall leaves scraped along the walkways, and he watched one cling to a crack in the concrete, then get caught and swirled away in the brisk evening breeze. He didn't want to think about the leaf being a portent of any kind, good or evil.

Dr. Andrea Vogel was on the case. The lady, it seemed, had all the answers, the means to the only end he could abide.

He shoved his workman's hands into the pockets of his jacket and gave her an encouraging smile. But he couldn't deny the tightness in his chest, or escape the chilling hunch. Nothing was ever quite as it seemed.

Chapter Six

She felt the first real crack in Neil's composure—a tension in the way he walked, in the way his fists plunged into his jacket pockets. Oddly, it bolstered her own confidence, making her more determined than ever to succeed.

"We'll be fine, Neil." She tucked her hand into the crook of his arm. He wasn't recognizable, and she had an innate faith in herself that she tried to convey to him. "Just act like you own the place."

"Have you ever done anything like this before?"

"All the time." She laughed. They climbed the stairs, and she let him open the front door to the building for her. She let go of his arm and crossed the foyer, then picked up the pen and bent over the logbook.

Neil folded his arms and leaned against a display case of antique lab equipment. He appreciated the curve of her bottom as she bent over the desk. He appreciated her attempt at putting him more at ease. Oddly, it was working.

"*When* have you ever done anything like this?" he encouraged, only half joking.

Straightening, she turned back toward him. "I remember my first day at Tulane—the first class, in fact. I'd tested out of a prerequisite biology, so I signed up for a junior-level genetics course. I was only sixteen, Neil. I *looked* sixteen, and I shouldn't have been there."

Indicating the doorway to the stairs, Andrea took the lead. She wasn't done with her story, but Neil thought if this adolescent crisis was an example of the worst Andrea Vogel had ever encountered, they could be in far deeper trouble than she knew.

"Anyway," she continued, climbing the stairs ahead of Neil, "this poor, homeless little mutt followed me into the classroom. The instructor was— Well, I'm sure you know the type. A grad student, full of himself. He promised an automatic *A* on the midterm for the person or persons who would put the mangy little freshman out to pee."

"Meaning you, not the dog?"

"Meaning me," she agreed.

"Come on, Andrea. I'm talking about more than a little college hazing."

She turned as she reached the second-floor landing, preventing him from taking the last two steps, and they stood eye to eye. "If they'd have left it at that, I'd have taken it. But these guys literally picked me up and carried me outside. Seventeen straight days of it."

"Oh." He felt like a heel. She stood there smiling as if it hadn't hurt. He'd been sixteen once, and in far worse straits, but he understood. She knew exactly what it was to be where she shouldn't have been. "What happened?"

"It was the first time in my life that I quit."

He was perversely glad to know Andrea Vogel had given up at least once in her life. He wished, suddenly, that he'd be around her long enough to merit sharing other painful memories. But it was an idle wish. The best he could do now was to believe in her. "It was their loss, Andrea."

"Yes. Their loss," she said lightly. The kindness in him always surprised her, and she still couldn't accept it. "Let's go."

She swung open the door and moved purposefully through. Neil followed, their steps echoing in the well-lighted, abandoned hallway until they reached the set of double glass doors labeled Lab—Restricted Access.

"Jericho," she commanded, directing her voice toward the speaker.

She expected the door to activate. But the door did not open to her command. Nothing in her careful, simple plan had prepared her for this one possibility.

Through the double glass doors she watched a technologist moving among the aisles, and Andrea could not believe that the door would not open.

"Andrea." He had to touch her cheek to interrupt her disbelief. "Come back tomorrow. There's no point—"

"Neil..." Her voice strained. "I don't know.... I... There has to be a way! You try it."

"We're getting out of here." He took her by the arm, prepared to march her straight out of the building.

She pulled away. "I may not get in tomorrow, Neil! Piers could change his mind at any time.... Try 'Jericho.' Maybe your voice—"

"Jericho!" he snapped, but he didn't expect it to work, and it didn't. He was ready to throw her over his shoulder and carry her out bodily. She couldn't handle being wrong about this. Given enough time, he knew, she'd find a way to circumvent the system.

Given enough time, they'd be discovered, and Neil couldn't afford that.

Instinct told him there wasn't another soul on the floor besides the ones on the other side of the glass door, but the longer he had to stand there the edgier he got.

"Give it up, Andrea," he ordered, his body towering over her. "Sometimes—" he took her by the shoulders, forcing her to face facts "—you just have to give it up."

"No. Not—"

"Hey, there!" a voice boomed down the length of the hall. "State your business!"

Neil stiffened. The voice had come from behind him, at his back, and the nerves he'd thought blunted by scars screamed. Andrea watched the raw fear of being shot in the back again crawl all over Neil, and it galvanized her out of her confusion.

She stepped between Neil and the uniformed security guard. "Officer, I... Bill? Bill Gantry?"

"Doc Vogel?" Gantry pulled up short and let his side-arm slip back into the holster at his hip. A big man, though shorter than Neil, he approached her with a marked limp from an injury that had cut short his career on the police force. "What are you doing here?"

Andrea swallowed and forced an easy, unconcerned response. She could handle Officer Gantry. "Bill, am I ever glad to see you! I was in this morning and Dr. Piers—"

"I thought you resigned," he interrupted, suspicious, she thought, more by nature than of her specifically.

"Actually, I did—but I couldn't stay away." She smiled and shrugged, as if Gantry himself had known all along that she'd be back.

"Who's your friend?"

"John," she answered, stupidly unprepared for this question. "A colleague of mine from the university. Bill Gantry, John Brice."

"Pleased." Neil stepped forward and offered his hand. He'd been about to take back all his unkind thoughts until Andrea spouted off the name of some colleague Gantry could check. She might have all the answers, and she might think fast on her feet, but she was damned inept at intrigue.

Gantry sized Neil up one end and down the other. Andrea's mouth went dry as a wad of Georgia cotton. Please, God...she thought, searching desperately for something to say, anything to divert Gantry's attention from Neil.

"So, Bill. Did you and Eleanor ever find a specialist for Davey's asthma?"

Falling Stars

Gantry broke off his handshake with Neil. If there had been a glimmer of recognition, he let it go. "We did. Eleanor's been living up in Denver so Davey could get treatment at a special clinic. But here, what's the problem?"

Andrea shook her head forlornly, and her Louisiana drawl had never been sweeter. "Well, I can't fathom what the problem is! Dr. Piers gave me the code word, you know, Jericho, but—"

Gantry smirked. "Leave it to the brain trust to forget how their fancy system works... Overkill if you ask me. Who the hell would break into a morgue? Sure as I'm standing here, nobody's breaking out." He chuckled. "The stiffs are already... stiff. Know what I mean?"

She smiled appreciatively, indicating that she'd gotten it. "Shall I come back tomorrow, Bill?" From the corner of her eye, she saw Neil shifting his weight. Her own heart raced with the incredible nerve of the chance she'd taken, acting as though tomorrow would be good enough. "What shall I do?"

"Nah. No need. You just have to get your voiceprint into the system. See, the code word don't mean diddly if your voice isn't on the tapes." He turned away and bellowed "Jericho" into the speaker.

The door swished open, and Andrea smiled brilliantly. "Open sesame. Just like that. Bill, I can't thank you enough—"

"No need, Doc." Gantry stuck his thumbs in his holster belt and bounced on his toes, then gave Neil another dubious glance. "Piers know your friend here was coming along?"

"Of course." Andrea fought off a telltale shiver, willing Gantry to accept her assurances.

He stood there seeming to vacillate for several seconds, then at last nodded. "Just remember to get Dr. Piers's secretary to set you up for voiceprints—both of you—for next time.''

With the last dregs of her nerve, certain that her knees would buckle beneath her, Andrea thanked Gantry again, walked through the door, turned left and strolled the distance to the archives entry. Neil followed right on her heels, anticipating the moment she'd come crashing down off the adrenaline rush her performance had required. His own relief over the close call nearly hobbled his lungs.

She was trembling violently by the time the archives door closed behind Neil. He reached for her and pulled her with him as he sank back against the door.

''Easy, Boo.'' She came like a rag doll into his arms, shaky in the knees and breathing fast enough to hyperventilate. No stranger to this paralyzing fear, he knew he had to stop her.

The need distracted him from his own alarm. ''Take it easy. It's done now.''

But it wasn't. He stroked her back over and over again, but she was beyond simple words of comfort. She'd managed to pull off her lies, but the threat to Neil, the chance that Gantry might eventually remember him, exacted a toll from her system unlike anything she'd ever endured. She couldn't stop her shuddering or force her lungs to inhale air faster than blowing it out.

Neil could think of only one remedy, and he didn't give a damn about the consequences. He took her chin in his fingers, lifted her precious face and brought his lips down on hers, hard. His kiss was fierce and pitiless, and he meant it to be. He could handle his own anxiety. He'd had weeks, months, to perfect his control.

He couldn't handle hers.

His lips locked onto hers as his arms bound her to him, and Andrea struggled like a rabbit caught in a hunter's snare. She fought the need for this, for his kiss, his control of her, but his arms only tightened around her, and his tongue touched her lips. Pleasure raced through her on nerves already drawn unbearably taut.

She lost the will to escape him and simply reacted to the pleasure. Her fingers molded to his pectorals, then strayed to his shoulders. He groaned and shifted his legs, pulling her closer, and his kiss deepened immeasurably.

Her panic eased, giving way to languorous aftereffects of her body's flight-or-fight responses. He knew that if he let go of her now, her breathing would return to normal. And so would her composure.

A fierce arousal thrummed through his body, displacing his own anxiety. He wanted to shape his hands to her gently rounded hips. To ribs he could count because she was so thin. Or to her breasts, fuller by far than a slender woman ought to have. Damn, but he wanted to touch her.

He took his arms from around her and put his hands on her shoulders, gently easing her away from him. She felt him retreating, backing away emotionally from that kiss. She dragged in one unsteady breath and then another, forcing herself to regard his kiss as nothing more than a tactic meant to arrest her reaction.

The ploy worked, and she owed whatever equilibrium she'd regained to him. His own grave circumstances had brought him calling on her, nothing more. And nothing had changed, except to worsen the situation.

"Andrea, who is John Brice?"

"John is a forensics and law enforcement professor at the university." She backed away and rubbed her hands together, willing warmth into her chilled fingers. "He really is a colleague—" She broke off at the rueful twist of Neil's lips. "Oh, no..." Her folly hit Andrea like a bucket of cold water in the face. "If anyone ever checked with John, if anyone ever asked—"

Still leaning against the door, Neil ran a hand over the back of his neck. "Miss Intrigue," he teased. He had an unblemished faith in her ability to get at the truth of Solter's murder, but what she knew about survival—a fugitive's school of hard knocks—could be summed up in one word.

Zip.

The last thing she needed was anymore pressure from him. She didn't stand a snowball's chance in hell of becoming adept at intrigue. Her attempts would only draw attention instead of deflecting it. Hanging out with her made him crazy, but he couldn't live with the alternative. "Chances are," he reassured her, "no one will ever ask John Brice if he came here with you."

Andrea nodded. "You're right. But I am sorry. It won't happen again." She squared her shoulders and pointed out the high-speed fax machine, which sat on a table across from the librarian's desk, then went to the stacks to pull the file box she'd substituted with the Solter case.

She dialed the number necessary to access the Antiquities computer's fax, confirmed the connection, then pushed up her sleeves. They worked in silence, the only sound being the whirring noise made by the machine itself. Andrea fed in document after document while Neil placed the originals into a stack, preserving the original order.

The process took nearly an hour. Andrea replaced the stack of documents generated months ago in the file labeled with the Solter accession number. 92-A/WD-432—the four hundred and thirty-second case in 1992, with the autopsy and wrongful death designations.

She then proceeded with the contents of four of her own cases from 1989—old files she chose simply because they held significantly less material to be faxed.

The fax machine worked flawlessly and at top speed, and by the time she'd finished, Andrea allowed herself a tiny measure of elation to counter the exhaustion.

Refiling the last case file, 89-A/WD-217, she dusted off her hands. "Put *that* in your pipe and smoke it, Dr. Piers."

Neil smiled. He could have told her this was far too soon for even minor declarations of victory, but decided to spare her his chronic skepticism. Instead he gave her an optimistic thumbs-up gesture.

"What do you say we get out of here?" He broke the connection to the Antiquities computer, and the fax machine generated a confirmation of 2006 transmitted pages. He took the sheet, folded it carefully into a tiny square and stuck it into his jeans pocket.

Andrea followed his actions with her eyes, then stared up at him, wide-eyed and innocent. "Isn't it the norm in intrigue circles to swallow the incriminating evidence?"

Taking her by the collar of her T-shirt, he headed her in the direction of the door, yanked once at her French braid, then gave her a small shove. "A little respect for the master, if you please. Get going."

Andrea was still laughing when she ran smack into Edward Gresham, coming in the double glass doors as she exited. Gresham was the staff pathologist who'd taken such exception to the assistant district attorney's insistence on calling Andrea the rising star of the medical examiner's office.

As usual, his eyes pinched the moment he recognized her. "Vogel! What are you doing here? Is Piers out of his everloving mind, letting you in here like this?"

Gresham failed to notice Neil, who broke off as though he hadn't been with her and passed through the door to the outer hallway. If she had learned anything, it was that Neil knew when and how to disappear.

"Nice to see you, too, Ed," she responded, reminded so forcefully of the daily aggravations she'd faced working in this environment. "I'm merely researching case files to flesh out my résumé. Nothing to get excited about. With any luck, I'll get a pathology position hundreds of miles away, and we'll never meet again."

"To God's ears," Gresham snapped. "But don't think I believe for a minute that Piers should have let you back in here—for any trumped-up reason." He glared at her, then jerked his head in the direction of the lab, from where he was being summoned. "You'll have to excuse me. I've got a body coming in."

Only too grateful to excuse him, she passed by Gresham and through the controlled glass doors. Once outside, she walked beneath streetlights to her car, spotting Neil waiting unobtrusively under the eaves of the main hospital building.

With a nod of his head toward the street, he took off, walking along the back of the medical complex. She unlocked her car and got in, then drove out of the parking lot and circled back. Neil jumped in, and Andrea pulled back into traffic.

She took Cerrillos Road where 2nd Street intersected across from Ashbaugh Park, then north on St. Francis. She'd have to backtrack later to get to the Antiquities campus off Bishop's Lodge, but driving the long way around would restore her nerves.

Headlights from oncoming traffic shone occasionally on Andrea's face. Struck by the tension evident in her compressed lips, Neil stretched an arm across the seat and kneaded the muscles in her shoulders.

He wanted to ask about the guy they'd passed on the way out. Whether he represented a threat. Neil's gut was reacting badly, always a warning, and he popped an antacid, but he refrained from asking what couldn't be helped anyway. "So. We print the file and then head back to your place?"

Andrea nodded. She pulled into her usual space at the abandoned Antiquities parking lot several minutes later and hurried out of the car. Driving hadn't eased her anxiety in the least. All she wanted now was to get the damn file and drive home.

She wanted a glass of her homemade wine in the worst way. If Neil lived with this level of stress every hour of every day, she couldn't see how he'd managed to survive this long at all.

Locking the door behind them, she pocketed her keys and switched on the lights, then the computer and laser printer in their climate-controlled anteroom.

Within moments she'd started the printer humming, and it churned out page after page of the Solter murder file. She fled to the bathroom, convincing herself every step of the way that she wouldn't throw up.

The text pages were, of course, flawless. Photos and graphic lab reports printed with a clarity Neil hadn't begun to expect. He stared at one crime scene photo until his eyes blurred. Solter, lying there, unquestionably dead.

A gallon of pH-neutral antacid wouldn't have helped the upset roiling in Neil's stomach as he examined those photos. The printer ran out of paper and the small but strident alarm made him break into a cold sweat.

He cracked new reams of paper, placed them in the deep feeder bin, then pushed the Ready button. The printer began again, turning out the M.E.'s report, evidence collected to convict him. Neil turned away and strode to the door to keep an eye on the parking lot.

He was in the middle of chiding himself over his constant paranoia when a set of headlights arced from due east to south, into the Antiquities lot, which was lit only by a million stars in the autumn New Mexico sky. Then another, and finally a third set of headlights swung in, directly toward Neil. Two of them were state police cars, the last, civilian.

He couldn't believe this stream of ill-gotten luck, and he swore. A part of him denied this off-chance of discovery turned too real. The chances that the cops outside had nothing to do with him were laughable.

The survivor in him backed away from the door. He had Andrea's welfare to consider, and in that moment he knew what he had to do.

He pulled the .32 caliber automatic from his concealed holster and called out to her quietly, urgently. "Andrea. Better get out here. We've got company."

Dripping cold water she'd splashed on her face, Andrea jerked a paper towel out of the holder, pulled open the bathroom door and rushed back into her office area. At the same moment that the cops pounded on the door, ordering her to open up, the whine of the printer faded.

And Andrea found herself facing the barrel of Neil's automatic handgun. She understood his intent right away. He thought he could protect her from an aiding-and-abetting charge. If she appeared to be his hostage, forced into her illegal actions, she couldn't be charged.

"Save the theatrics," she hissed. "Maybe someone else will appreciate them." She'd never been more angry in her life. Men could be so blindingly stupid, and Caulfield was king of the mountain. Neither one of them had to be sacrificed. She turned her back on him, dug into her pocket for her keys and raced to the printer.

The cops banged on the door and bellowed another warning. "This is the state police, Dr. Vogel. Open up *now!*"

Andrea defied them, scooping up papers with no intention of opening the door until Neil Caulfield was successfully concealed.

Neil followed her and grabbed her by the arm. "Vogel, consider yourself my hostage. Damn it—"

She ignored his trumped-up threat and heaved the papers into his arms, then broke away from him. Unlocking the door to the scanning electron microscope room, she ordered him inside.

"Andrea, this doesn't have a prayer of working—"

"Get in, Neil. I won't play hostage, so you'll just drag me down with you if you insist—"

"Dr. Vogel, this is the state police. You're on State of New Mexico property and if you don't open this door in the next sixty seconds, we're going to break it down!"

Chapter Seven

Andrea stood toe-to-toe with Neil, neither of them moving. Precious seconds ticked by. Neil refused to budge, to hide. Even if it cost him his life, he wouldn't endanger this generous, naive woman by accepting her protection.

"Neil, please, for God's sake!" Tears welled in her eyes. He blamed them on her exhaustion, then took the responsibility on himself. She wanted his freedom more than he did. If push came to shove, he'd make the cops believe he'd forced her cooperation.

"Thirty seconds!"

"If you get into trouble—"

"Fine, Neil," she said dismissively. "Please. Get in." She walked away and stood over the computer long enough to begin printing the fax files of the other four cases.

Neil closed himself into the microscope room a heartbeat before she opened the door to half a dozen state officers.

"Dr. Vogel? Andrea K. Vogel?"

"Yes, I am Dr. Andrea Vogel." In the sum total of her life, she hadn't experienced so much raw fear as in this one day. She still felt the fear—at a profound level on Neil's behalf—but she wasn't about to cave in now.

She took a deep breath, smiled ingratiatingly and spilled the exact truth on the spot. "Gentlemen. Forgive me. I was in the powder room—upchucking my dinner, I'm afraid."

But there weren't only men. Entering ahead of the last officer was Chief Assistant District Attorney Janine Tyler, laughing gratingly.

"Interesting story, Dr. Vogel. Whatever would cause you to... *upchuck* your dinner, as you so quaintly put it? Breaking the law? Would that do it, Dr. Vogel?"

"Yes, I suppose it would—though I wouldn't know from personal experience." Andrea smiled faintly, wondering why she'd never quite trusted Janine Tyler. They should have been friends, two women working hard for their respective places in male-dominated professions. But even with that powerful common bond, she'd never clicked with Tyler. "I'm sure it must only be something I ate."

"Or, perhaps, your encounter with Dr. Gresham?"

"Possibly." She'd underestimated Ed Gresham this time. He *had* carried through on his threat to call Piers, who in turn reached Janine Tyler almost immediately. "Ed doesn't care for me. But then, he doesn't like you, either, Janine."

Tyler ignored the bait. "There was a man with you earlier. Who was he?"

"A friend. May I ask what all this is about?"

"You know perfectly well what this is all about, Andrea. You've misappropriated documents properly belonging to the city and county. I'm advising you that I intend to prosecute. I want the records you're printing turned back to me immediately." She nodded toward the officers, as if directing them to search the premises.

"Prosecute? Am I under arrest?" Andrea stepped back and spread her hands wide, intercepting the search. "You haven't Mirandized me, Janine, and none of this will be admissible."

"Read her her rights," Tyler snapped to one of the officers, a small fellow nervous to be under the eyes of an assistant district attorney. He pulled out his card and began reading her Miranda decision rights verbatim.

"I waive the reading. And to be perfectly clear, the New Mexico Antiquities Foundation is *not* property of the state, but privately held and privately funded—not one dime of taxpayers' money supports us. Produce a search warrant, Janine, or take your officers and get out."

Tyler walked over and examined a few pages as they were reproduced by the printer. "These," she said, waving a few sheets at Andrea, "constitute probable cause for a search. I don't need a warrant, Vogel." She seemed to hesitate, as if mired in circumstances beyond her control. "I wonder if you understand how serious this is?"

"I understand a great deal more than you might think, Janine."

"Dr. Piers told me he had agreed to allow you access to your files—with the exception of the Solter murder."

"Yes, he did. And he made that exception very clear."

"But Piers believes the only reason that you would proceed in this underhanded manner is that you have had contact with Neil Caulfield himself. That you are either conspiring with an escaped murderer—"

Andrea willed Neil to stay concealed, to let her play this one out to the end.

"—or acting in his behalf against your will. Is that true?"

"No." The worst possible outcome had unfolded. Despite the care she and Neil had taken, Piers and Tyler had now associated Andrea with Neil. But it made no sense that a seemingly harmless request for access to old records should merit the posse that Piers's call to Janine Tyler had produced. She couldn't help wondering if Piers and Tyler themselves had something to hide.

"I have never been coerced, my life isn't in any danger, and I would not willingly aid or abet a murderer." She walked a very thin semantic line here, but every word was the truth. Neil Caulfield hadn't killed Ben Solter.

"Then what are you doing, Andrea?" Tyler asked almost plaintively.

The officers accompanying Tyler stood there uncomfortably, shifting weight from one foot to the other, waiting for Tyler to fish or cut bait. The time had come to call her bluff.

"Compiling case histories for a résumé." Andrea keyed in the commands to abort the printing, then put a disk in the E drive and directed the computer to copy 89-A/WD-37, 89-A/WD-126, 89-A/WD-177 and 89-A/WD-303. Tyler watched over her shoulder as she executed an erasure of all A/WD files, which included the 1992 Solter case.

"Why four cases?" she asked, ignorant of the coup Andrea had just pulled off. "Why not five, or an even ten?"

"Nothing mysterious. These are all the wrongful-death autopsies I performed in the first half of 1989." She unlocked the drive, took out the disk, and together with the pile of printed material, handed them to the assistant district attorney. "Press criminal charges if you choose, Janine, but I'm afraid you'll look very foolish if you do."

Tyler flushed. "Why don't you let *me* worry about what will make me look foolish?" She directed the officer in charge to take his men outside to wait for her, then turned back to Andrea. "I'll take this under consideration, Dr. Vogel, but let me assure you of this. There will be swift and extremely unpleasant consequences if you *ever* pull a stunt like this again."

"I'll try to remember that." Andrea felt the tiny thrill of the chase, the small triumph of a fox escaping the hounds. She switched off the power strip to the computer and printer, then walked the assistant district attorney to the door.

Tyler got in the parting volley. "I'll have a squad car escort you home. I'd hate for things to turn out badly for you, Andrea."

THE FUNNY THING WAS, Andrea almost believed that Janine Tyler wished her no ill. On the other hand, it would be the height of folly to trust her. After all, Tyler had prosecuted Neil's case with a vengeance, as though her career depended upon the jury returning a guilty verdict, though clearly it hadn't.

Sometimes the assistant district attorneys were called upon to proceed with cases that were a good deal less than open and shut. She didn't believe the Solter murder had been one of those in Tyler's estimation.

Something *had* to turn up in the Solter file that would give her a place to begin absolving Neil. But the drive home, particularly with the trooper escort behind her, left Andrea skittish and fearful for Neil. She'd managed to leave a key in the delivery door of the Antiquities facility. Neil would find it, be able to let himself out and get cleanly away, but a sleeting rain had begun over the Sangre de Cristo mountains, and she had no notion what he would do or where he would go after that.

She had to believe he'd somehow make his way back to her house. Where else could he go?

She waved into her rearview mirror to her escort when she drove into her attached garage and activated the door to close behind her. Letting herself into the house by the door off the mudroom, which in turn led into the family room, she dumped her bag into her easy chair and headed for her bedroom loft.

She lit a few candles and turned on the lights in the loft. If her escort had been ordered to stake out her house, the only lights she wanted on were the ones in the loft, where surveillance was impossible.

She returned downstairs in her robe. Working in the dark, she put on a kettle of water for hot tea but also poured herself a healthy measure of homemade wine. She lit a fire in the fireplace, stoked it with plenty of hardwood, then sank into her rocker with her wine.

The wine went straight to her head. She'd had no dinner, nor had Neil, only a handful or two of popcorn in the movie theater.

She dozed, dreaming fitfully, and woke only when the fire had died down and the chill returned.

Her cuckoo announced the hour of 3:00 a.m.

She got up, stretched her cramped muscles, checked the doors and peered out into the darkness, searching for a sign of Neil.

Doodle whined to be let in, and Andrea opened the door. She discovered Neil, sitting hunched up beside the back door, so breathless and soaked through by the sleet that he couldn't speak or move.

He warned her with a forefinger to his lips to keep still, and dragged in one ragged breath after another.

"Come on, Doodle, girl. Are you all right?" She crooned to the old retriever, but Neil understood that she was questioning him, and he nodded.

"Yes," Andrea comforted, and she bent to stroke the old dog. "That's my girl. Are the bad guys out tonight?"

"Yeah," Neil croaked softly. "In front. The guy'll wake up with a kink in his neck."

"Is that why we're being so quiet, huh?"

He'd thought the prettiest thing he'd seen on this sleet-ridden, godforsaken night was Andrea Vogel's back stoop, but he'd been wrong. The prettiest sight was of her cobalt-blue silk robe parting over her breasts as she bent low, crooning over Doodle. He felt incredibly warmed by seeing her, but his chilled flesh made him shiver violently.

He dragged his eyes off her, wishing he hadn't seen anything, because the awful irony was, he wasn't going to be crawling into her bed to ward off the cold.

"Can you make it inside?"

He had to. Another five minutes in the cold, soaked through to the bone, and he'd pass out. Andrea offered him a hand, which he reached for.

"Neil, you're frozen," she cried as their hands met.

He ached in every joint, every muscle. The hike from her office would have been grueling enough without the weather, or cops to evade. His teeth began chattering the instant he stepped inside, and he clamped his jaw shut.

"You've got to get out of those wet clothes, Neil."

"Y-you f-first," he cracked, staring pointedly at her chest. But the beginning of a smile only hurt his stiff cheeks, and his teeth began to chatter again.

Tears sprang to her eyes, mostly because he was so miserably cold, but also because he'd stolen her breath away as he stared at her breasts.

"Me first," she muttered, scolding. "I thought *you,* at least, had more than a one-track mind." She urged him up the stairs where she could check his extremities for frostbite. Violent shivers shook him, and it was all she could do to help him up the winding stairs.

She draped his head with a towel, then examined his face—forehead and nose—then his fingers for the telltale white spots. Finding none, she turned to run a hot bath. "Get out of those wet clothes, Caulfield."

But when she returned, having stopped the bathtub and adjusted the water temperature, he hadn't removed a thing. Dazed, he stood there, his fingers too cold and stiff to work snaps or buttons or zippers.

"Neil, snap out of it," she begged, jerking open his jacket. The packet of papers from the Solter murder file fell to the floor.

Distractedly, Andrea shoved them away and helped him get out of his jacket and shirt, then his boots. She automatically set aside the handgun she discovered hidden there and pulled off first one sock, then the other.

Crusts of ice fell off his jeans as she worked to strip them away. Worry saved her from embarrassment, but every dark hair on his lean, well-muscled body stood out, and a ripple of sexual awareness washed through her, anyway. His body racked with yet another shudder, Neil was too physically impaired to make anything of her stripping him, or even to notice her.

Andrea stopped at his shorts and stood to leave the bathroom.

"Get in the tub, Neil. Now."

She hurried downstairs to put together some hot soup, trusting that he would find the stamina to get himself into the tub. She dumped a package of soup mix into a pan, then half the already steaming water from the teakettle.

Letting the soup come to a boil, she strived to get a grip on herself, to forget that she'd looked at Neil and seen a man. That she'd felt a pinch deep within her at the sight of his near-naked body. There was no place in all of this for needing him to make her feel like a woman, she berated herself. None.

She transferred the soup to a mug, picked up a spoon and returned to find him, eyes closed, covered to his shoulders in the hot bathwater. Tenderness welled up in her, and she fought that off, as well. She reached for a couple of bath towels and tossed them on the floor for her knees, then brought one of the candles in for a bit of light.

Kneeling next to the bath, she held a spoonful of the soup to his lips. The scent of it made him open his eyes. He smiled, then allowed her to spoon in the soup. He consumed it as fast as she could deliver it.

For the first time in long, tedious hours, he felt half-human again. "What is this stuff? Homemade?"

She shook her head and set aside the empty cup. "Just packaged soup. What else can I get for you?"

"Nothing." He scooted up in the tub and turned on the hot water. When he did, Andrea glimpsed in the faint flickering of the candlelight the still-pink, shiny flesh healing over his gunshot wound.

"Oh, Neil! These are... This is awful." She couldn't prevent herself from running her fingers over the ugly welts.

He stiffened. "Don't." Then he leaned back in the water until his knees came out and his head submerged. When had he gotten so careless that he would allow this woman a glimpse of his mangled flesh?

He hated it, hated the stinking son of a bitch that'd fired on him, and hated her for making it an issue. But when he came up for air, he couldn't ignore the stricken look in her wide green eyes or the witless quivering of her lower lip. Or the splotch of water on her breast, dripped there from her fingers after she touched him.

"Forget it, Boo," he told her. "It's history."

She returned his intense gaze. "No, it's not, Neil. Not yet."

His eyes returned again to the spot of water, to her lips, to her eyes, and he reached for her, catching her at the nape. He pulled gently, and she came willingly, and his eyes followed her lips until he felt them next to his mouth.

He felt himself becoming hard and his heart beginning to thud. He splayed his hand over her raven-dark hair and ran his lips over her sweet bow-shaped lips, over and over again, light as could be, until no sensation would do but to open his mouth and take her in.

Warm and dark and wet, with only the light of the flickering, vanilla-scented candle, his kiss made Andrea believe there had never been such a one as this. Her heart seemed to have no rhythm, her mind no thought, her body no being apart from his lips, caressing her.

His hand trailed down, and down even more, past her collarbone, until his fingers found her breast, and then his kiss wasn't be-all anymore. He stroked her, passing over her tender, swelling nipple again and again, creating sensations too exquisite to bear. Muscles deep within her clenched as though he had entered her, and she became suddenly frightened of her own wildly intense need.

She backed away from him and tore his hand from her breast. Helpless to prevent her, Neil let her go.

It hurt him more than any parting he'd ever in his life imagined.

Unable to meet his eyes, she pulled the wet silk from her breast and reached for the empty mug. "I'll get you some dry clothes."

"Andrea—"

But she'd already gone in search of his backpack. Neil eased out of the tub and reached for a towel.

By the time he emerged from the bathroom, warm, dry and dressed in gray sweatpants and a T-shirt, Andrea had dressed in worn jeans and an oversize kelly-green sweater. She sat in the midst of her bed, sorting the faxed Solter case files into various piles, a bottle of her homemade wine and two glasses on a tray near her.

Neil sat cross-legged on the foot of the bed and poured the wine. Andrea forced herself to meet his gaze. She had to remind herself that she'd never once thought to put *unshaven* and *sexy* in the same category. His appeal—and what had happened between them over a hot bath—needed to be put behind them. Forgotten.

"I can't get over Janine backing off her threat to press charges," she said, accepting her wineglass.

"She hasn't. Yet."

"I think she has, Neil. I think she's covering every bet. She can always go forward with a criminal prosecution. But if she and Mason really believe you've contacted me—" she set down her wineglass and began sorting again "—then the only course of action that makes sense for them is to lie low and hope that you'll contact me again, and hope they can nab you when you do."

Neil swallowed a healthy swig of wine. It warmed him. Precious little else about this conversation did. "How long do you think we have before they show up at your door with a search warrant? Or a full-blown stakeout?"

"I think it'll take them a while to decide they're onto something, Neil. I could be wrong, but it's the weekend now. Say, twenty-four hours? Forty-eight?"

Neil thought both estimates optimistic. "Better get on with this, huh?"

Andrea nodded and began explaining the piles she'd created, touching each in turn. "Reports of physical evidence here—copies of police reports, our investigator's summary. Autopsy in these three piles—actual test results including lab reports, my observations and measurements at the actual postmortem, and my notes from the crime scene."

Neil leafed through the small separate stack of updates made to the Solter file. Two were simply memos reiterating the disposition of the case—fancy legal terms for limbo. The third, he couldn't believe.

"What's this?"

Andrea took the sheet of computer paper—it had no logo or letterhead—and read the memo through. It appeared to have been generated in the district attorney's office and copied to several law enforcement agencies, the medical examiner's office being only one. The content reconfirmed that the crime scene would remain sealed until final disposition of the case, and the memo was dated just three weeks before.

"This is crazy. It just advises all concerned agencies that the crime scene is still under criminal jurisdiction."

"Since when?"

"When Judge Medina was forced to call a mistrial, Janine petitioned the court to order Solter's home sealed until you were apprehended and retried."

"Why?"

Andrea nodded. "Exactly. Why? Procedurally, the house ought to have been released to Solter's estate, or probate, as soon as the investigation was closed—particularly in a case as open-and-shut as this was supposed to have been."

"You'd think Solter's estate administrators would be coming unglued, wouldn't you?"

Andrea agreed. "There must be a couple hundred thousand dollars tied up in that house."

They sat combing through the remaining files for a couple of hours. Neil perused the biochemical studies last and found nothing unexpected. Zolgen B was clearly and cleanly identified chromatographically, and proven to be the cause of death.

He wasn't intimidated or confused by the contents of the technical reports, but by the time he'd made a second pass through them all, he felt as if he'd missed something. Or that the report itself was incomplete.

He picked out a sheet on which the likeness of a human skull was rendered from five different angles—face up, facing left, right, forward and facedown. Andrea had nearly thirty individual measurements inked in. At the bottom were Solter's name, accession number, age at demise, height, weight and cause of death.

"Is all this routine for an autopsy?"

Andrea glanced at the sheet Neil held. "Not at all. As a forensic pathology fellow, I was required to have some work published. I wrote my paper on comparative craniofacial landmarks. I did these—" she gestured at the sheet he held "—on every postmortem. Habit, I guess."

"So what does this tell you?"

"Well, lots of things. Look." She pointed to a side view. "Here is the glabella—it lies more or less beneath your eyebrows. If you measure from this point to the very back of the cranium, you have what we call the 'maximal cranial length.' Or here. Cheekbone to cheekbone. That's the bizygomatic breadth."

Neil studied the illustration comparing it to Andrea's face. He looked first at one, then the other, and back, then touched the very tip of her chin with his forefinger and smiled. "A very pointy menton, Dr. Vogel."

Andrea nodded and turned to give him a side view, then touched the sharp curve of her jaw right below her ear. "Pointy gonion, too."

Neil leaned back, away from her, and swallowed. He found the sight of her neck, tilted and stretched to show him her bone structure, erotic. But maybe it was his own response that was indecent. His mouth watered and his eyes darted to her breasts, and he'd as soon have kissed her pointy places as look at them, and for a moment, awareness like sharp hunger pangs flashed between them.

"Andrea, I—" Sitting cross-legged with a pile of papers separating him from her, he couldn't think of a single thing to say that would ease the impact of his hunger.

"Neil, don't worry about it, okay?" She felt hopelessly flattered. Oddly, she was pleased that he had looked at her. Pleased that she had . . . preened.

He stared at her for another moment, then swallowed and dragged his gaze back to the illustrations. "So, do these measurements tell you anything about Solter?"

She drew a deep breath and exhaled carefully while she reviewed her measurements. "Only that he had very typical Caucasian features. A head size in the median range, though at the larger limits. Eye sockets set closely. Things like that."

"But no dental records or—"

"No. If Solter had been a John Doe, then evidence to identify the body would have been essential. But he wasn't. He died in his own home, he was a widely recognizable local celebrity, he had identifying jewelry—"

"Lieutenant Columbo always collects hair samples, Boo." Half teasing, he still didn't see why there seemed so little physical evidence. And he still had to make an effort to keep his eyes off her. "They never took a sample of my hair, for instance."

Andrea nodded. Back in territory familiar to her, she regretted the passing of that sensual moment between them. "Columbo is a bulldog. At the time, Neil, I was frustrated by the fact that the investigation was called complete at so early a stage. The thing was, nobody else thought it was odd at all."

"Shouldn't they have collected hair samples or looked for my skin under Solter's fingernails?"

"Under any other circumstances, yes."

"What the hell *other* circumstances?" Neil demanded. At fifteen, he'd had one hell of a bent for being in the wrong place at the wrong time under the wrong circumstances. Twenty years ago he'd been a know-nothing street kid.

A grown man ought to have seen through the bait. He should never have agreed to meet Solter. He'd dug his own grave, and he knew it, but he couldn't understand or excuse the criminal justice system's failure to get at the truth.

"Let's go with hair samples," she answered. "In other circumstances, every hair at the scene would have been collected. That's because, according to what is known in forensics as the theory of interchange, the perpetrator will leave evidence of his presence."

"Fingerprints, for example."

"Yes. Or maybe powder if the perpetrator uses gloves, or clothing fibers. Or, as you suggested, hair or his own blood or skin if the victim fights back. The interchange happens because he'll also take something of the crime scene away with him. Paint chips from a car wreck. Carpet fibers and so forth."

"So, suppose there had been evidence of the real assailant? Come on, Andrea! Why did the system break down? Who was looking out for the hallowed rules of the theory of interchange then?"

"In *this case*, Neil . . ." She hesitated for a moment, sick of making excuses for what seemed—now more than ever— a shoddy, short-shrifted job. "You'd become embroiled in a very ugly, very *public* controversy. Then you were discovered hovering over the body, and you had the syringe in your hand." She spread her own hands wide, palms up. "Motive, opportunity and method on a silver platter. Case closed."

Chapter Eight

"Andrea?"

Neil rubbed his eyes, blinked and stared at the red numbers glowing in the dark. The digital clock read 5:17. Sometime during the night, exhausted and emotionally spent, they'd cleared the bed of the Solter files and fallen asleep. Sprawled across her bed, he pulled himself up into a sitting position.

Andrea stood fully dressed at her window, staring out. In the darkest part of the night, maybe an hour before dawn, the moon shone brightly and glinted off the chrome of a squad car parked out on the road.

"Are you up for a morning jog?" she asked softly.

"Spare me," he groaned, flopping back, covering his head with a pillow. Life on the lam made jogging for recreation laughable. But he pulled the pillow away and saw that she wasn't fooling.

"I've been thinking this through, Neil, and I—"

"You should have been sleeping, Andrea. You can't run yourself into the ground over this." On the other hand, he knew why her mind wouldn't let go.

"I couldn't. There may not have been anything concrete in the files, but so many things don't add up."

"Okay." He lay there watching her silhouette, and the way the indirect moonlight made her a wraithlike beauty. It seemed to him that he had known her for all time, that he'd been seeking her forever. "Tell me."

"Piers's attitude. Janine Tyler threatening prosecution and then backing off—which doesn't ring true given her law-and-order stance. I don't know if you ever paid much attention to local politics, but Solter endorsed her every chance he got.

"Most of all—the length of time that house has been sealed off," she continued. "I never imagined they'd get away with that kind of overzealous decree this long. The more I think about that, Neil, the harder it is to believe."

Listening to her, Neil was struck again by the slow, enticing Southern cadence of her speech. By the paradox of the way her voice soothed and seduced while *what* she said set him on edge.

Stretching, he got off the bed and went to stand by her near the window. He'd missed some vital link in her train of thought. "Does this have anything to do with a morning jog?"

"Yes." Distracted by her efforts to fit random pieces together, Andrea pulled her attention back. "Solter's place is no more than five miles over the foothills toward Santa Fe. I think we have to get into his house." She inclined her head toward the police squad car parked out on the road. "He's still there. We don't know if he'll be replaced, but I don't think we have a lot of time, Neil. If that house is still sealed, there has to be a reason."

The idea of returning to Solter's place didn't sit well with Neil, and tension made his back knot. He dragged a hand through his hair and massaged the muscles in his neck. He had to respect her intuition. To go with it. If he'd had any useful ideas of his own, he wouldn't have involved her in the first place.

Staring out at the squad car, he saw the headlights come on, then do a slow U-turn before the car sped off in the direction of the highway. "Lucky break. He's leaving."

"So much the better. Shall we go, as well?"

"Betteh?" he teased.

She cast him a scornful but playful look. "Damn Yankee."

He took a quick shower, dressed, then sat in her rocking chair downstairs reading his copy of *Zen and the Art of Motorcycle Maintenance* while dressed for a hike—for no reason but to keep his mind off how threatened he felt by the idea of returning to the scene of the crime he hadn't committed.

Andrea defrosted and warmed a bag of miniature bagels from her freezer. Neil spent a few minutes in her garage gathering some rudimentary tools, a flashlight and screwdriver. They left her place through the pasture in back, leading to state management forest land, leaving a very unhappy Doodle shut into the pasture. They covered the first two miles over the rugged terrain in an hour. The sky turned a spectacular blend of peach and yellow and mauve hues as dawn broke.

They sat on the rounded top of a boulder barely protruding from the earth. Neil doled out the bagels and canned juices Andrea had put into his day pack. Blanketed in a bun warmer, the bagels were still warm.

Munching hers, Andrea sat transfixed by the sunrise. "I should get up for this more often. It's . . . life-giving."

Neil polished off his bagel, washed it down with juice and reached for another. "I can live without it."

"Really?"

The planes of his face hardened. "The promise of a new day is pretty much a joke to me, Andrea."

His remark hit her wrong. "Then what am I doing out here, Neil? Marching off on yet another illegal entry for the hell of it?"

He knew his attitude got to her. Until now, he'd never heard the mildest profanity from her. "Don't get your panties in a knot, Vogel. I just—"

"Don't patronize *me,* Caulfield," she snapped. "If you're stuck in the past—"

He crumpled a grapefruit juice can with one hand. "That's what they call it when you've got no future."

"Don't you think I'm aware of that, Neil?" she asked, her temper flaring. "*I'm* the one breaking all the rules to put things right for you. I won't be your punching bag, too."

Neil swore and turned away from her. For long moments he sat there thinking. He ripped a bagel to shreds and pitched the pieces around for birds too wild to come after them. He'd put things right for himself once. Bad, juvenile, crazy things that could easily have ruined his whole life. He resented the hell out of needing Andrea Vogel to rescue him now, but he did need her.

He wanted her, too. Every minute he spent with her, he knew he wanted her, man to woman. But an accused murderer, a fugitive from every law enforcement operation in the country, had no business even making eyes at a woman like her.

Maybe if he told her where he'd come from, she could understand what made him so bitter. He popped the tab on another grapefruit juice, drank it, then packed up the trash and stood.

"Come on. I'll tell you a story." He offered her a hand getting up, and they started off again as the sun broke fully over the horizon. He held her hand while they traversed a small meadow.

"When I was a kid, we lived in a pretty rough neighborhood in north Denver—my mom and sister and I. I don't remember my old man. I was fifteen, and my sister Tammy was...fourteen, I guess, when she got a job waiting tables. One night she came home with a black eye, and her clothes were all bloody because her lip was split open."

They came to an especially steep incline, and Neil broke off. Andrea took the lead, and they made their way to the top of the ridge in silence.

"She said she'd been mugged on her way home, so I decided the next night that I'd go walk her back from this greasy spoon where she worked. She wasn't there. I found out she hadn't been there for several weeks. It took me three nights to find out where she was going every night. She was hooking." His voice roughened. "She was a fourteen-year-old addict and she needed the money for her habit as much as she needed to bring money home."

Breathing deeply to keep up with him, Andrea felt the depths of Neil's adolescent rage in her own heart. There was so much he didn't say, so much agony and loss and fear that she had to read between the lines, but that wasn't hard.

No forensic pathologist was spared the shock of the lurid, grotesque, *cruel* suffering human beings inflicted on themselves and each other. If she'd done one postmortem on a girl who might have been Neil's little sister, she'd done twenty.

Only the pain and suffering couldn't be measured.

Andrea shivered and clung to his hand as he paced down the mountainside. "What happened to her, Neil?"

"She disappeared. Six days after I found her, she left for school and never came back. She was classified a runaway. We never saw her again."

Andrea didn't know if she could stand hearing what had become of Neil then, but she asked. He hadn't told her this much without meaning to come to some point. "What did you do?"

"I hit every pimp and drug dealer, every runner, every *supplier* I could find. I set booby traps and slashed tires and broke store windows and even stole deliveries from drop points. Anything I could think of to get even with those bastards. I made a career of it for a while. And then I got caught and sent up to juvenile detention. It didn't matter that I'd been busy taking out the *real* bad guys."

In all his adult life, he'd never uttered one word of this to another human being. He guessed it must be a true measure of how much he'd come to trust Andrea Vogel.

Visually gauging her steps to avoid a tangle of tree root on the forest floor, Andrea looked up at Neil. Sunlight passing through age-old pines glinted off his rich, mahogany-colored hair and put into silhouette the determined set of his lips.

No wonder he'd devoted himself to finding a medical solution to substance addiction. She knew instinctively that telling her this story was difficult for him, and she squeezed his hand. "How long were you in jail?" she asked finally.

"Three years." And he'd spent more than a few hours during those years in prison picking up skills you didn't talk about in polite company. What it took to strip or hot-wire a car, to pick locks or blow them to kingdom come, to disarm burglar alarms or turn them into time bombs. And things far worse. Which made him curious whether Andrea had the least idea how they were going to get into Solter's house.

Fifty yards down a steep, wooded slope they could see the roof of the house they'd set out to find. A valley meadow extended as far as the eye could see beyond the house. Both of them stopped dead in their tracks.

"Got a plan, Boo?"

"Oh, gee." It suddenly occurred to her that she didn't exactly have a plan. "I guess, I mean I thought we'd just—"

"Break a window?" he offered, draping an arm over her shoulders. "There's a security system, you know."

The edge of humor in his voice irritated her. "How would you know that? Or remember?"

"Once a delinquent, always," he said. The differences between them only seemed to become more pronounced, not less. She'd obviously grown up believing that good things lasted and bad experiences were temporary. Knowing she'd find what she needed, expecting things to turn out right.

He'd grown up in the real world, where goodness and mercy didn't often overcome the bad, where nothing much turned out right and optimistic expectations were Pollyanna schlock. "I can't help it, Boo. I notice things like that."

She frowned. "So what *are* we going to do?"

"Find a way." Luckily, he probably could. He started off down the slope, slide-stepping sideways, alert to Andrea's movements above him. Within five minutes they stood at the side of the house. It was a large, modernistic two-story, covered in stone and elaborate patterns of cedar shake shingles. Police tape still crisscrossed the front door.

A paved, circular drive split in two places—to the garage and down the slope behind the house. There were no other houses around for two or three miles.

Expecting the worst, Neil searched the perimeter of the house for surveillance cameras. There were none, but what he spotted while looking for them made his blood chill. He stopped Andrea short and pointed near the ground toward something Andrea couldn't seem to pick out.

"What? Neil, I don't see—" He pulled her closer to his side, his arm around her shoulders, and then dropped low. From that vantage she saw sunlight streaking along a length of wire no thicker than a single human hair, staked no more than six inches from the ground.

Andrea turned toward Neil. "A trip wire?"

"Yeah. Probably sets off a silent alarm."

"Could it be electrically charged?"

"Sure it could, but it wouldn't stop a jackrabbit."

Andrea nodded. "Of course."

Neil guided them over that perimeter wire and another, then Andrea examined the yellow strips of tape in a large *X* over the front door. They appeared unweathered, almost new. But the burnished brass of the door fixture snagged her attention.

"Neil, come look at this. I've never seen anything like it."

"The doorknob? You don't remember the security system, but you remember a doorknob?" But she was right to have noticed. This was new hardware.

"I wouldn't have, but look." Vertically oriented, its outline curved, the hardware had no keyhole, only an electronic keypad combination lock. "The police would have had no reason to change locks—and even if they had, the existing hardware could have been rekeyed."

"Unless it was broken," Neil agreed.

"But if the house had been broken into, there would be no point in trying to maintain evidentiary integrity by keeping the house sealed."

Neil swallowed hard. Clearly the house had not been sitting abandoned all these months, and he didn't like any of it. His more primitive instincts had already begun churning out signals of profound evil and danger lurking in this place.

He exchanged glances with Andrea and knew that she meant to get to the meaning of a changed lock and perimeter wires.

With Andrea trailing along, he followed the alarm system wiring to the housing on the elaborate fuse box, and opened it. He dug some electrical wiring from the pocket of his jeans and began shaping and twisting its wires to those in the fuse box.

"Where did you get that?" she demanded.

He grinned. "Out of the middle of the wiring on your electric garage door opener." God knew the acid in his stomach right now would eat through tempered steel. A sense of humor was all he had to fight back with at the moment. "One of us, Ms. Intrigue, has to think about these things."

"Why, I'm in charge of ideas, sir," she protested. "*You* are in charge of plans."

"A damn good thing," he muttered. Twisting wire around one final switch, he replaced it, then banged shut the housing on the fuse box. "We're as good as in."

With a pocketknife he stripped the plastic from one last piece of wire that had formerly conveyed power to her garage door, then knelt at the back door and plied the wire carefully into the keyhole.

"I guess I don't have to ask you how you know these things," Andrea said.

He gave her a short-lived smile. "It's a no-brainer. You just have to have seen how it works. A ten-year-old could figure it out." The tumblers fell to Neil's wire manipulations, and he opened the door.

He searched immediately for the alarm box, which, if the system were still working and not short-circuited, should flash until an operator keyed in the combination of numbers to abort the alarm. He found the box on the entry wall and saw that it wasn't flashing.

His shoulders drooped with relief, and he took one very deep breath. "So. What are we looking for?"

"Anything and everything, Neil. Whatever is inconsistent. Whatever doesn't fit. Whoever murdered Solter had a motive—not only to kill him, but to frame you. That took some careful planning. God willing, we'll find something."

"Even unwilling. I don't have many options left."

To the left of the back door was another door, which led to the basement of the house; to the right lay the kitchen and dining room. In the forward part of the house, where Solter had been murdered, the living room was wall-to-wall with a dusty rose thick pile carpeting.

Solter's study, set off by immense sliding doors—of bleached oak—sat to the right of the front entry, where the chalky outline of Solter's body could still be detected. A massive curved stairwell, its banister made of the same oak and varnished to a high sheen, led upstairs. Here they found a thick layer of dust, dulling the finish.

No one had been upstairs in a long time. At least, no one who had touched the handrail.

"Let's start upstairs and work our way down."

Nothing escaped their scrutiny. Since they wouldn't know what they needed till they saw it, they couldn't afford to overlook anything. The second and third bedrooms upstairs were large, comfortably furnished and yielded nothing but a few wasted minutes.

"Solter's room won't be so easy." Andrea looked around the master bedroom, feeling overwhelmed before they even started. Mementos of every sort adorned the walls. Photos of Solter with celebrities, framed columns from his early years in the newspaper business, collector signatures in gold-leaf frames.

"Get a load of this," Neil said, giving a low, disbelieving whistle. One entire wall was covered with wine labels. Hundreds of them. Solter had written on each of them the date, the occasion and who he'd been with. He had shelf upon shelf of books of every variety, and every one Andrea pulled out was an autographed copy.

The hardwood floor was covered by an antique Persian carpet. A huge four-poster bed was flanked by a nightstand, and to either side of the walk-in closet stood enormous, matching armoires. Neil began with them, while Andrea took the closet.

She found that Solter hadn't possessed a shirt that wasn't tailored silk, or a silk blend. His suits were mostly wool, of impeccable tailoring, and were arranged by color. She went through hats, ties, coats and slacks by the dozens, finding nothing remotely remarkable.

But in a dry cleaner's bag cast into a corner she discovered a suit coat. Crafted from a heavy, quality cotton blend material, it was cut in a Western style unlike anything else in Solter's closet.

"Andrea?" Neil called to her from the bathroom.

"Neil, look at this." She carried the suit coat to the bathroom door. "Can you picture Solter in this? Everything in his closet is straight out of *GQ*, and it's all from New York or Santa Fe. This one says Falsbury of Amarillo."

But Neil stood absorbed by something he'd discovered in the elaborate wooden medicine cabinet. "Amarillo? Explain this."

Taped to the inner door of the cabinet was an amateurish mock-up with "Separated at Birth" made from magazine letters glued to the top. The tape was transparent but yellowed with age and cracked. The crude mock-up had been there a long time. Two grainy photos, each of one man, were pasted side by side.

"Either of these guys could be Solter, but look..." One appeared to be a newspaper file photo of Ben Solter. The other subject wore plain garb, and the background was clearly a prison yard. Scrawled in a distinctive, overblown handwriting below the picture was "Fondly, your cousin and Brother in Crime... back home in Amarillo."

"Unbelievable," Andrea murmured, stunned by the likeness of a cousin to Benjamin Solter, in prison no less. "'Brothers in crime'? Solter was *the* voice of law and order. He can't have been amused by this."

Neil gave a short, harsh laugh. "No. He wouldn't have been amused." Staring at the bizarre display, he ran a finger along one brittle edge. "Guys in the slammer do things like this, Andrea." His voice grew low and harsh, and his dark eyes seemed to focus inward on memories too terrible for words. "They're consumed with hate, and they do these things to remind themselves every waking moment of who they despise and how they'll get even if they ever get out."

Transfixed by his intense otherworldly focus, Andrea reached out to Neil. She was scared for him, scared of the power of such memories. He'd survived untold hardship, and somehow, with some prowess or strength of character or sheer will, he'd managed to overcome the rage and the trap of believing only revenge would do.

Andrea discovered that she was more than half in love with this man, and her heart tightened painfully in her chest. If he asked her, though she knew he wouldn't, she'd turn her back on all this and follow him to the ends of the earth.

Her touch brought them both back to this moment. "Solter was never in prison."

"No," Neil agreed. "He was even more obsessed. He played on everyone's worst fears of crazed addicts and rapists and murderers. He was a snake-oil salesman, a Jim Jones wrapped in a law-and-order banner."

All of it was true, though Solter had been clever enough not to appear so fanatical as Neil had described him. But her thoughts returned to the "Separated at Birth" mock-up. Would Ben Solter, internationally acclaimed columnist, punish himself by confronting this thing day after day?

"We're missing something, Neil. What else could this be?"

Neil shrugged and closed the medicine-cabinet door. "Blackmail?"

Blackmail. The possibility played in her mind. She stepped back, and Neil left the bathroom to begin sorting through framed photos on Solter's nightstand.

"Well, blackmail would explain the 'brothers in crime' bit." Leaning into the doorjamb, she ran through another possibility. "Suppose Solter did commit some terrible crime, and this cousin found out about it. It would have to be a murder to matter after so many years."

Neil replaced one photograph and picked up another, taking care not to disturb the dust. Seeing the logic in Andrea's scenario, he carried it one step further. "Then the law-and-order reputation Solter built so carefully over the years would be protection against an accusation by his lunatic cousin—and eventually, protection against the blackmail itself."

Andrea agreed. "No one would believe for two seconds that the nationally syndicated crime spoiler Ben Solter had ever committed a crime of his own. Which—especially if Solter had been paying hush money—cut the cousin off at the knees. No leverage, no blackmail, no money."

"So," Neil reasoned, "Solter's cousin knows the guy is worth millions and that he's just been cut off without a crying dime. Does he find a fall guy and plan a murder?" The scheme left its own unanswered questions. "Sure. But how does he get hold of the Zolgen B variant?"

"Oh, my God. The variant came first, Neil!" And for a moment, she didn't dare breathe.

Chapter Nine

Excitement streamed through her, and the anxiety of pinning down viable answers, real possibilities.

He felt her tumult. "Talk to me, Andrea."

"Neil, didn't you once say it was possible that Solter himself could have stolen an aliquot of the B variant?"

"Possible, yeah. I'd agreed to an in-lab interview with a national news broadcast team—supposedly to set the record straight on Zolgen after Solter had taken his potshots."

"But Solter turned up halfway through the interview—"

"Right in the middle of the crowd," Neil confirmed. "Technicians were working, the refrigerators weren't ever locked.... Yeah. It was possible. If Solter had the guts to filch the B variant right out of the lab, he had the opportunity."

"And no one would have noticed it missing?"

"It was one compound out of fifty discarded possibilities. I kept most of them around for later testing, but we didn't inventory that stuff regularly at all."

"Then Solter could as easily have picked up some entirely different precursor to Zolgen," Andrea guessed, "but he didn't. Suppose he got the variant home, got it tested— just a few drops, because he wouldn't trust any lab completely. He learns his sample is a useless derivative. But he still has the stuff sitting around—maybe in his own refrigerator.''

"Enter Solter's cousin." Neil thought he knew where Andrea was headed. "Somehow he learns of the Zolgen variant in Solter's possession—maybe he eavesdrops, or maybe Solter goes into a temper when he finds he hasn't got the right stuff.''

Andrea nodded. "And if the blackmail theory holds water, when Solter got tired of paying up, he cut his cousin off with nothing.''

"Yes. Cousin is left with nothing. His life-style is in jeopardy so he figures he'll just snatch Solter's whole estate. He plans a murder. He has to pick his time and place, and he has to come up with a means. Then he thinks about the Zolgen variant, and he has his answer. Death by lethal injection, with the added advantage of an obvious scapegoat. Me.''

"This could be it, Neil!''

"Or a figment." He stared down at the old black-and-white photo in the expensive gold frame. He knew Andrea was elated. He should have been, too. The possibilities for a jury to find reasonable doubt that he had killed Solter were there now, where they hadn't been just hours ago.

But he couldn't conjure up any pleasure. He couldn't forgive his own stupidity in picking up that syringe. He couldn't forget all those Wanted posters with his face on them, or getting shot in the back, or perimeter trip wires surrounding a supposedly unused house in the boondocks outside Santa Fe.

The little black-and-white photo fell out of the frame, fluttering to the floor. Andrea picked the picture up and examined it. In small block letters the date 1936 and the name Dierdre were written by hand near the legend Potter County Photographers, Amarillo, Texas.

"Solter's mother?" Andrea suggested.

Neil shrugged. "That's as good a guess as any.''

Andrea put a hand to his upper arm. Her hand wouldn't span his biceps. "Aren't you even a little encouraged, Neil?"

He covered her hand with his and gave her a brief smile. He felt one hell of a lot better with her than without her, and a thousand times more encouraged than he'd been two days ago. But the notion that Andrea was a far cry from safe with him made him sick. "Better get on with it, Boo. We haven't touched the study or the basement."

The study was another full day's project. The file cabinets were locked, but Neil had no trouble opening them. Solter had an extensive portfolio, all concentrated in a Santa Fe bank and a New York investment firm to which Solter had made quarterly installments of nearly ten thousand dollars.

Andrea searched through two years' worth of check registers without coming upon anything that smacked of blackmail hush money.

Waiting on Andrea, increasingly on edge, Neil compared one investment firm statement to another. The figures didn't add up, unless Solter was losing money hand over fist playing the market. He reached for a pencil and leaned back into the navy blue brass-studded leather chair across the desk from Andrea. A fistful of statements later, he saw the pattern.

"Look at this. Up until last March, the Sandusky Trust Company in New Jersey received monthly payouts of twenty-five-hundred dollars."

Andrea frowned. "Should I recognize the name?"

"Nope. But look at the fine print here. The First Continental Bank of Amarillo is its largest subsidiary."

WHEN NEIL SAW the basement, he finally understood the necessity of perimeter trip wires.

There was only one basement room. Outfitted with a bomb shelter straight out of the sixties, the room had walls two feet thick, made of concrete blocks cemented together.

The floor was almost certainly concrete as well, though it was covered in a thick carpeting. A massive oak conference table took up the central area, surrounded by eight chairs. Along the concrete brick walls were state-of-the-art duplicating and video technologies, half a dozen 486 computers and towers, and seven three-drawer file cabinets, each filled with file dossiers.

In contrast to the upstairs, there was no dust here.

The most cursory inspection left Andrea shaking. "Neil, look at this. Files on car dealers, theater owners, franchisers, discount houses . . . priests!"

Neil opened another drawer, a couple of cabinets away, and examined file labels in ever-increasing alarm. "A who's who in publishing, right here. Newspapers, magazines, *TV Guide*."

Andrea moved to another file cabinet. "Oh, Neil! This one is vintage Solter. There are judges in here, lawyers, key senators, governors. Look at this—an entire cabinet devoted to the American Civil Liberties Union lawyers."

Dossiers crossed all lines. Some were quite scant, containing only some cryptic note Solter had scribbled to himself. Others fell open on stacks of embarrassingly personal, intimate information, details and allegations so petty and sordid and damaging that Andrea couldn't believe what she was seeing.

"So this was Solter's stock-in-trade." The place made his skin crawl, spurring every nerve, every muscle, every *cell* in him to a terrible pitch. "He made one hell of a living writing informed opinion columns."

Andrea agreed. No one should be so *informed*. No one should have access like this to the most intimate details of another person's life. Names, dates, places and photos the

Inquirer would drool over. Information people would kill to keep private.

"So what did Solter have on our assistant district attorney, Janine Tyler?" Neil asked cynically, flipping open a file he'd pulled.

Andrea went back to the drawer containing the names of judicial establishment. Tyler should have come between Triegel, Martin, Federal District Court, and Ulibarri, Kathleen, staff of the state bar association. The drawer contained files on Julio Medina, the judge on Neil's case, and on Tyler's immediate superior, the district attorney himself. On assistant district attorney Janine Tyler there was nothing.

"Nothing on Mason Piers, either." His elbow perched atop a cabinet, Neil let the file folder he held fall shut, then handed it across to Andrea. "But you're in here."

Stunned to silence, Andrea paged through the dossier labeled with her name. It held a photo, her Tulane transcripts, her medical and pathology registries, the name of a therapist she'd briefly seen a few years ago for sleep dysfunction.

Then there were photos of Andrea's mother, and of the scathing comments scribbled to the sides, "bloodsucking idle rich, bleeding heart liberal" was the kindest. Andrea discovered an ability to despise another human being. Ben Solter earned the honors.

Neil picked up a carousel of slides and settled it onto a slide viewer, then switched the mechanism on. Controlled by that one switch, the overhead lights dimmed, a viewing screen descended in such a way that every position at the conference table had clear and direct view, and the slides clicked past in relentless procession.

Photos of convicts appeared in turn, they were all from the FBI most wanted file and they were all identified by the name and date of disappearance. But the last three were of

Neil himself. He recognized one which must have been used to create the Wanted fliers.

He thought he'd have been immune by now, but he wasn't. His scalp prickled and his stomach heaved. He felt like smashing something. He needed to vent his blinding anger. Instead he reached for Andrea and took her into his arms and buried his face in her raven-colored hair. The warmth of her body against his was the only thing keeping him on an even keel at all, the only reason he had to hold on to his own humanity.

Andrea clung to him, instinctively seeking assurance that good might still triumph. What went on in this forty-by-sixty-foot room was evil and twisted and monstrously corrupt—an outright full-scale vigilante operation, served by the electronic combination lock and the trip wires and the hundreds of files Solter could never have used solely for his columns.

And the whole operation was safeguarded by the wickedly clever ruse of protecting the integrity of a crime scene seven months old. Tyler and Piers, and God alone knew who else, had to be involved, functionaries at worst, unwilling accomplices at best.

Swallowing the rising bile, Neil parted from Andrea, switched off the slide projector, then slammed the carousel back into its place and grabbed her hand.

More lives than his were at stake, and he had to get out before he could commit any one of the five or six ways he might have destroyed Solter's house along with every menacing scrap of ill-gotten information it contained.

NEIL TOOK THE TREK BACK over the foothills at a killing pace, and staying with him demanded everything Andrea had. She'd had to remind him to undo the wiring that had short-circuited the alarm system on Solter's house. It had rattled him that he had forgotten the fuse box.

She suspected that Neil would rather have left the back door wide open, or the trip wires yanked off the ground, butchered into half-inch lengths, or his own sabotage of the fuse box intact. Any one of those actions would have left the unmistakable message that the vigilante operation was no longer a secret network accountable to no one, but a wide-open target.

Just past the ridge overlooking Andrea's property, Neil stopped and hunkered down, scanning the landscape for men or cars that would indicate her place was under surveillance. Andrea sat on a fallen tree trunk and fought to catch her breath. She'd been a long-distance swimmer in college. She hiked these hills often with Doodle. But she wasn't prepared to keep the pace Neil had set.

"See anything?"

"No, but anyone could be parked in front."

Andrea hugged her arms to her body. Despite the bright midmorning sunshine, she was cold. "Shall I go down first and make sure no one is around? Maybe I should take Doodle in with me, and when I know the coast is clear, I'll put her back out."

His conscience wanted to know what kind of man let a woman spring the traps ahead of him. Realistically, he knew the likelihood of her encountering trouble was very slim. His choices were few, and Andrea's plan made sense.

Nodding, he patted her knee. "Be careful."

"Of course." She picked up her bag of clues—the dry cleaner's bag with the Western-cut jacket, the names and numbers she'd gathered from Solter's study along with the ancient photograph of Dierdre from Potter County Photographers—and started for home. "Come in when you see Doodle back outside."

Again Neil nodded. He watched her take off down the mountainside with her bag of clues in hand.

Not *if* Doodle was put out, but *when.*

Andrea never doubted that things would turn out all right. Had nothing in her life ever happened to prove otherwise? He didn't know how she could come out of that nightmarish experience in Solter's house and, an hour later, still *believe* everything would be fine.

She wasn't suited to this. She wouldn't last two days on the run, and despite her background there was a misplaced trustfulness about her that scared him. But he envied her faith. She had this upbeat, enduring belief in life and goodness and herself that Neil found endlessly appealing. Seductive.

In the two days he'd known her, he'd discovered his own greatest shortcoming. He trusted himself, but he didn't trust anyone or anything around him. If he ever had, he couldn't remember it. He wanted her brand of optimism for himself, and if he couldn't attain that, then he wanted a woman in his life who inspired it. A woman like Andrea Kathleen Vogel.

He watched her open the back gate to her property and greet Doodle with a hug. He watched her until she and the retriever entered her back door. Four minutes later he watched Doodle return to the outdoors, an enormous, brand-new chew bone in her mouth.

Neil kept to the trees and made his way back to Andrea's property. Despite her faith, and his own great need for it, he couldn't afford to drop his guard.

He found her listening to a message on her answering machine from her friend Miri Silverman.

Andrea pushed the stop button, and gestured for Neil to come listen. Her phone sat on a bookcase near the spiral stairs. "You should hear this."

Neil closed and locked the screen door behind him, then stood by Andrea. Folding his arms, he waited while she rewound the tape, then played it from the beginning.

"Boo, hi. Here's the scoop—for what it's worth. FDA licensing of Zolgen went to one Peripeteia Enterprises. That's P-e-r-i-p-e-t-e-i-a. Interesting word. Look it up. Anyway, Peripeteia is the client party of the first part— joke, Boo, laugh here."

Miri left a considerable space for the requested laugh. Andrea smiled. "Miri's a frustrated stand-up comedienne. We used to spend our free time planning our alternate lives."

"Are you laughing?"

Neil couldn't help his chuckle. Miri Silverman's long-distance silliness charmed it out of him. "So what was *your* alternative life, Boo?"

"I wanted a greenhouse devoted entirely to succulents. I love them. They're such survivors."

Neil thought he should appeal to her then, but he didn't get the chance to say so because Miri's message continued.

"Anyway, Brightmark Pharmaceuticals vends for Peripeteia which, unfortunately, seems mired in some terribly complex subsidiary scheme. Its incorporation papers are in Texas. Hope that's of some use to you. I'll call if I ever get a name. And, Boo? Be very, very careful. I won't last out another year without some of your gazpacho.... Take care."

"Texas again," Neil said. "Amarillo tailors. Amarillo banks. Potter County, Texas, photographers."

Andrea erased the tape. "Don't they say all roads lead to Texas?"

"Until Texans want to come skiing in Taos or Telluride," Neil joked. "You want to come along for the ride?"

"Interestingly put," Andrea tossed over her shoulder, climbing the stairs to her loft, "when it's my car we're talking about."

She was tirelessly naive, Neil thought, reaching for a glass of water. "We won't get to the city limits without being spotted in your car," he called after her.

Something distracted her, a car she thought, barreling down her road. "Neil, grab your stuff and get up here. Quick!"

Neil grabbed his day pack and took the stairs by twos. Andrea ran to her bedroom window, and between the trees spotted the approach of a later model gold-and-brown pickup. When the truck turned off at her drive, she recognized the man driving it.

"Oh, great. I don't believe this, Neil!"

The color had drained from her face. He took her by the shoulders and gave her a gentle shake. "Who is it?"

"John Brice."

"Who the hell is—" But Neil remembered. She'd introduced him as John Brice to the security guard at the medical examiner's labs.

Andrea drew a deep breath and straightened her shoulders. She'd handled Piers, she could handle John Brice. She glanced out the window. In another thirty seconds, John would be at her door. "I'll meet him outside. You can...you can stay up here, or go out the back."

Neil wasted precious seconds not letting her go, holding her shoulders. It wasn't his style to cower in a corner. It wasn't in his nature to abandon her to her own devices, either. "I'll stay.... Be careful, okay?"

Andrea gave a quick nod and darted from the loft. Two-thirds of the way down the spiral staircase, she popped back up one stair riser, so that all he could see was her sweet face.

"It helps, you know," she said, "knowing that you're here."

Her face disappeared and Neil swore. She was beautiful and clever and smart and gutsy, but she was a babe in the woods. A *blind* babe in the woods, and he'd put her there.

He pulled his pistol from his backpack, heard Andrea open and shut the front door, and the next time he saw her he was standing to the side of her loft window, and she was greeting a man who seemed to be twice her size.

SHE STEPPED OUT OF DOORS and called a greeting as she walked out to his truck. "John. Hello."

"Andrea." Brice nodded and closed his truck cab door with a shove. A criminologist at the university, he'd often invited Andrea to speak to his classes. He was a burly man in his middling forties, stood around five-eleven and looked strong as an ox. He wore his scant mousy brown hair conservatively cut, and he had odd yellow-hued green eyes. He clearly wasn't happy with her.

Andrea stuck her hands into her jacket pockets. They were shaking, and she didn't want Brice to know that. "What can I do for you?"

He crammed his own meaty fists into jacket pockets and rocked back on the heels of his boots. "For starters, you can leave off the 'little ol' me?' act. You dropped my name to the wrong folk, Missy, and I want to know why."

Until that moment she hadn't had the faintest idea how she would respond to John Brice, what she would say to him. The truth wasn't an option, and the fact that he'd shown up at her door was proof positive that she couldn't lie to save her soul.

Being treated like a naughty preadolescent made her quite angry enough to stonewall him into next week.

She gave him a cherubic smile. "Would you like to come in, John?" She turned and opened the front door and beckoned John Brice inside. He came like a fly suspicious of a spider's web. He didn't trust her cordial invitation in response to his hostility, and it pleased Andrea to have knocked him off balance.

Neil had to be wondering if she had even two brain cells devoted to common sense, but inviting Brice in seemed to her the clearest message she could send. *I have nothing to hide, John Brice. See for yourself.* She poured them both an ice tea, then sat on a stool at her kitchen counter, letting Brice fend for himself for a place to sit or stand.

But he wasn't stupid, or defenseless, and he went straight for the jugular. "Where's Caulfield, Andrea?"

She nearly choked on a sip of her tea. "Where's Caulfield?" she repeated. "You're asking *me?*"

Brice propped an elbow on her hearth mantel and gave her a taunting smile. "Yeah, I'm asking you. We know all about your little escapade last night—"

"*We,* John?" Andrea felt a chill take hold of her whole body. She could believe Ed Gresham had called Mason Piers who had in turn called Janine Tyler the night before.

She could even belief that Piers had questioned the security guard, Bill Gantry, who must have recalled her introducing her colleague with John Brice's name.

What she couldn't believe was the lightninglike speed with which this had all come back to John Brice himself, or that he'd say, *we know...* Not unless he was also involved in the vigilante network. "Who exactly is 'we,' John?"

He saw the trap in her question and deftly sidestepped it. "May I speak frankly, Andrea?"

She poked at the ice in her glass. "Please do, John. Why don't you start by answering my question? Who were you talking about when you said 'we know'?"

Brice sat down at one end of her dining table. "Everyone involved last night is all. No need to suspect a conspiracy where none exists." He set aside his empty glass and leaned forward, planting his hands on his knees. "What you did last night was wrong, Missy. If you know where Caulfield is but you're not saying, you're breaking the law."

She despised his calling her Missy, but it wasn't worth her wasted breath. "I've never had any trouble telling right from wrong, John. I don't need your help deciphering the difference now, either."

A flush began at his collar. "Well, maybe you do and you just don't know it. We've tried like hell to figure out why you'd be willing to break the law six ways from Sunday, and the only thing that makes any sense is that you're being coerced. Would you tell me if that were it, Andrea? Is that murdering—"

"If I needed your help, I would ask for it, John."

The angry flush spread to his cheeks. "You know the term 'unresponsive,' Andrea?"

"Of course I do." Andrea sipped at her ice tea and gave Brice a cool stare. "Similar to stonewalling, a noble Southern tradition. But I'm not on trial, or a sworn witness—and if I'm acting 'unresponsive' it's because I think you're way out of line."

He glared at her as if he could intimidate the truth out of her. "Why don't you just admit it was Caulfield with you last night?"

"Did Gresham tell you that?" she asked, wide-eyed. She knew perfectly well Gresham hadn't paid Neil the least attention.

Brice gave an aggravated wave of his hand "Gresham wouldn't recognize his hand in front of his face, but—"

"Oh," Andrea interrupted. "Then it must have been Bill Gantry."

Brice's jaw snapped shut, and he cast her a brittle look. "I didn't say—"

"Then what you're telling me, John—" she let her Southern drawl intensify with subtle disdain "—is that you've all leaped to a farfetched notion of what I was doing and who I was with based on absolutely nothing concrete."

"Humor me!" he snarled, coming out of his chair with his arm flung wide. He cuffed his ice-tea glass off the table and halfway across the room where it fell and shattered on the terra-cotta tiles. Brice ignored the mess. "*Suppose* it was

Caulfield! Then, Missy, you've bought yourself a boatload of obstruction charges!''

Andrea felt the blood rush from her face, and her hands started shaking again. She could handle Brice's tantrum. The glass shattering on the tiles shook her.

But what touched off her panic was spotting Neil's copy of *Zen and the Art of Motorcycle Maintenance* resting open on the hearth, not two feet from the mess Brice had caused.

Chapter Ten

"Answer me that one, Missy!"

Please God, don't let him look at what he's done. Desperate not to give him any reason, or to push him too far, Andrea dragged her eyes from Neil's book and stared into her glass of ice tea. "I can't give you any answer you want to hear, John." She looked up then and met his anger head-on. "Do you really think after this, or after Janine's little power play last night, that Caulfield will come anywhere near me?"

Her reasoning took the wind from Brice's sails. Her point was well made—Caulfield was lost to them because they'd hassled her. Brice must have decided that his hostile demands only entrenched her resolve to oppose him. Scrubbing the insides of his wrists against his slacks, he changed tactics.

"Andrea, look. How can I make this any more clear to you? The man is a menace. He's a murderer, no different than a hundred others running rampant, terrorizing good, ordinary people, opening fire on some grade-school playground in California or a family diner in Texas!"

"John, you can't be serious! You would honestly put Caulfield in the same—"

Brice shook his head vigorously. "It doesn't matter! I'm telling you, *now* is the time to act! *Now* is the time we in our country must put an end to this era of wild upheaval, and it will take the efforts of every man, woman and child of good conscience—women such as yourself, Andrea. Starting now, with Caulfield. *Right* now.''

But it mattered very much to her. She believed in what was right and fair and just, but Brice's words sickened her. They sounded rehearsed, memorized. Ingrained, like so much brainwashing, as if he could no longer separate what he believed from what really was. God help them, he believed Neil was no better than Son of Sam or Charles Manson or any other psychopathic criminal.

She wanted to challenge him. It killed her to hold her peace. *What's next, John? Sever the hands of every thief and the tongue of every liar? Pillory every disrespectful wife? Strap every naughty child?* So help her, if Neil hadn't been waiting upstairs, she'd have dared to push Brice, to ask him those questions.

She didn't care. Nothing she could say would change Brice's closed-minded attitude, but Lord, he scared her. Brice and everyone like him who believed in such a misguided perception of justice.

''I'll do the right thing, John. I promise you that.''

He knew her ability to sidestep the issue, and he eyed her mistrustfully. ''How can I believe you?''

''You're just going to have to trust me, aren't you?''

SHE WATCHED UNTIL Brice stormed out, slamming her front door, then grabbed Neil's book and ran upstairs. She'd never felt more shrill, more aggravated and angry in her life.

Neil saw his book in her hand and knew how close the call had been. He tossed his gun on her old, tattered quilt and took her in his arms. Relief spread through him. She'd handled Brice like a champ, standing her ground. He'd never known anyone like her, so sure of what was right, so determined. She was quaking like a leaf in a strong, corrupt wind. His respect for her soared.

He'd been a hairbreadth away from coming to her rescue, from hurling caution to the same evil gale. She'd saved him from revealing himself twice, and he swore she wouldn't have to do it again.

He held her and stroked her hair until her trembling ended, and then he eased off. It was Andrea who lifted her head, who met his eyes, then stared at his lips. And Andrea who kissed him, pressing her lips to his, her chin touching the whiskers in the furrow beneath his lower lip.

"Andrea."

He returned her kiss. The tenderness, the possession, the fierceness reminded her what his kiss was like. His breath mingled with hers, warm and damp. His lips brushed, then bruised, and she couldn't get enough of either sensation.

She tasted the manliness of him. She loved the velvety stabbing of his careless beard. His mouth distracted her wholly from the frightening scene she'd just endured, and if she'd needed anything else, she couldn't think anymore what it might have been.

When he touched her breast she felt the tug deep within herself, the pinch and the heat he aroused in her with only his hand cupping her, caressing her tender, aching nipple.

She'd never felt more a woman, or more afraid of her own emotions. She broke off the kiss and buried her head against his chest. She clung to his hand, holding it to her breast. She could so easily be in love with this man, so easily snared in emotions that weren't real, feelings born of fear and danger. But his hand on her breast felt so good.

Neil sensed her withdrawal. He wanted to take her hand and mold it to him, as his was molded to her. But the only place to take the raging ache in him was deep inside her, and he respected her too much to push her any further.

He dragged in a labored breath and held her, filling his hand with her.

He had more reason, now than ever, to clear his name and whatever shred remained of his reputation.

He took one more deep, determined breath and parted from her. There was only one way. "I don't know about you, Ms. Intrigue, but I say we blow this pop stand."

His small joke pleased her, and she laughed shakily. He pleased her with his humor in odd moments, and with his courage and his faith in her. The last thing she wanted was to put this precious moment behind her.

"Soon," she responded. "Before we get any more unexpected company. But..." She stared up at him and blinked a little helplessly. "I— Typically, I don't have a plan."

Neil cut off his smirk and cuffed her gently on her sweetly pointed little chin. "Fortunately for us, I do. Tucumcari by four, Amarillo by dark."

He figured the best way to throw off anyone keeping an eye on Andrea was for the two of them to take his motorcycle as far as some fly-by-night used-car lot, then head west in the cheapest functioning car they could find.

"With what money?"

"I've got a couple thousand dollars hidden in my belt."

"We couldn't do something simple, like renting a car—"

"Leaves a paper trail," Neil answered, shaking his head. He picked his pistol up off her bed and tucked it carefully into the holster, then crammed his paperback copy of *Zen* among his clothes.

"So when we get to Amarillo, we'll trade in one clunker car for another?"

"You're coming along, Boo." He gave her an approving smile. "By morning we can start following up on Solter's past. Will Doodle be okay on her own for a couple of days?"

Doodle's days were declining, and Andrea hated to leave her, but she hated the kennel even more. "If we leave her enough food and water, she will."

Andrea packed a shoulder bag of her own, including the things she'd taken from Solter's house, then threw together a few sandwiches while Neil doled out a couple of pans full of dry food for Doodle. Neil pushed the cycle up the hill to the end of the pasture to safeguard against anyone hearing the engine revving up.

He started the Honda engine. Standing astride the thrumming bike, he settled his helmet on her head, adjusting the chin strap as best he could for her much smaller size.

"What about your head, Caulfield?"

"Too tough to crack," he said. He kissed her quickly, then instructed her in the finer points of riding a bike not meant for two.

In the end, he took the bike over Glorieta Pass, and they wound up buying an old Ford Fairlane and a six-pack of canned ice tea in Las Vegas, New Mexico.

He took state highway 104. By Trujillo they'd polished off the sandwiches and in Variadero he bought her a couple of Mars bars. They made Tucumcari by four-thirty, returned to interstate 40. It was just a little past dark when the lights of Amarillo glowed across the panhandle prairie.

They stopped to eat a massive steak he couldn't believe she finished. In a matter of an hour he traded the Ford in on a '73 maroon-colored LTD off another used-car lot.

The transaction took longer than Neil wanted, or liked. He was dealing in cash, and he thought the salesman absented himself too long, running the trade Neil had offered past his boss. Months of living on the edge had given him a keen sense of trouble, and he mistrusted unnecessary delays. The salesman came a hairbreadth from losing the deal. Neil was nervous.

A man who'd been shot in the back even once was entitled. The encounter left him short-tempered, and Andrea steered clear of idle conversation.

At last Neil rented a room with cash and no questions asked in a broken-down motel on the west side of town.

They sat cross-legged on the hard motel double and played canasta with dog-eared cards, but Neil wasn't demonstrating any grasp of the game's subtleties. "If you discard that ace, sir, I'll have a natural and the game faster than you can blink.''

Neil tossed in his cards. Impressed with her playing, charmed by her genteel *sir,* he was still unnerved by the undue stalling of a used-car salesman. He'd ditched the bike in an alley in Las Vegas, and he didn't think he'd been spotted, but he'd been out in public too much for comfort. It would take an observant person only one phone call to set the vigilance committee on his trail.

Andrea folded her own hand, then scooped up the cards and set them aside. She reached out to Neil and cupped his face in her hands. ''Are you going to be okay?''

''Yeah.'' In another time, another place. The concern in her eyes touched him. Her hands smoothing his whiskers made his breath catch and he grew instantly hard. He touched her sweet, pointed little chin. ''What's this called again?''

''Menton,'' she said.

''Yeah. Menton.'' He wanted her, but he sure as hell wouldn't take her in this seedy Amarillo motel.

Instead, with monklike behavior made necessary by the raw need in him, he tucked her into one half the bed and forced himself to rest, facing away from her, on the other.

Andrea let him. She was neither stupid nor blind to his condition, and she respected his restraint, his greater need not to cheapen what might happen between them.

Still her breasts ached all night, not for any usual reason. Perversely, the more buttoned up he became, and the more restraint he showed, the more consumed she became with wanting him.

BY MORNING, SHE'D ONLY managed a scant few hours' sleep. She climbed out of bed and struggled under a shower with pathetic water pressure for a little renewed energy.

The first thing she saw stepping out of the shower was Neil's bare muscled shoulder poking out from beneath the covers. She dressed as fast as she could and pulled harder on her wet hair than she needed to make the French braid. She was sitting on her edge of the bed searching through a battered phone directory when he awoke.

"Once, just one time," he muttered for her benefit, "I'd like to be the first one awake." But that was a joke, because he'd known the moment she was up and about. A man learned to be alert to everything going on around him, even during what passed for sleep. He scowled when she laughed, and rolled over, dragging the worn, olive-green bedspread up over his chest. "Find anything?"

"Not Potter County Photographers. No such place—but then, half the pages are missing from this little jewel."

"Nobody said this was going to be easy." He rolled out and flexed the stiffness from his back, then headed for the shower. "Give me ten, okay?"

Andrea nodded. "Take twenty. Nothing is likely to be open for another couple of hours."

Ten minutes in that shower was more than he could stand. They left the room key on the sink, drove to a mom-and-pop restaurant for breakfast and spent a precious idle hour sharing the Amarillo *News-Globe*.

They were waiting outside the main branch of the county library when it opened. Andrea approached the information desk clerk about an Amarillo telephone directory from 1936. The clerk directed Andrea to the research librarian, a lady who barely stood four feet in her sensible black walking shoes and who clucked when she heard the request.

"You all might want to check with the phone company, but if you ask me, you're looking for a pig in a poke! Nineteen-thirty-six? Hah? Why, I wouldn't h'been ten years old."

Mildly amused, Andrea made up a story as she went, explaining enough of what they were after to catch the old librarian's interest.

"I have a photograph taken in 1936 of my great-great-aunt, by Potter County Photography. I know it's crazy, but I'd like to find more, only there is no such establishment anymore, and I was hoping to find—"

"You thought about the morgue?" Again the old lady chuckled. "The newspaper morgue, that is. Y'might find an old advertisement, y'know."

Andrea nodded. It was a long shot, but maybe one of the shops in town now had once been Potter County Photographers. "Wouldn't you have those old papers here, on microfiche?"

"I would," she agreed, a twinkle of orneriness gleaming in her faded hazel-blue eyes, "but heaven's sake, I've got to take care of things around here. Open up the windows, y'know, dust the shelves and sharpen the pencils and—"

"Miss Ruby?" Neil interrupted gently, taking his cue from her ID badge. "If you wouldn't mind looking, I'd be pleased to sharpen pencils for you." He flashed her a smile meant to charm her socks off, and it worked.

Andrea rolled her eyes disgustedly at his shamelessness, but cranky and eccentric or not, Miss Ruby knew exactly what she was doing. In short order she had selected the May 1936 roll—"graduation and June weddings, y'know"—and spun expertly through to not one but two photographers' advertisements. The second was Potter County Photographers.

Andrea compared the address to the photographers listed in the 1992 Amarillo directory and came up with a match. "This is it, Miss Maupin! Camera One. Same location for fifty years. Imagine that."

Neil gave Miss Ruby a sinful wink and promised her a bouquet of flowers before the day was done.

"Now don't y'go doing that," she scolded Neil halfway out to the main entrance. "No tellin' what some folks'll make of such a thing."

"But now let me tell you, the other thing is, my friend Ida Happelsmith—now, Ida would h'been ten years old in '36—lives in a nursing home across from the park. Ida's collected *volumes* on local folks' history. Why, if it weren't for her there wouldn't h'been any Historical Society, I can assure you."

Neil heaped on more words of thanks, but Andrea thought he didn't have a fickle bone in his body. He meant every word. He took down directions to the residence where Ida Happelsmith lived while Andrea consulted a city map. The first thing he looked for outside the library was a florist shop.

He picked an arrangement with daylilies and orchids and baby's breath, laid out thirty bucks and directed the delivery to the library. Miss Ruby Maupin got quite a bit more than a little bouquet of roses.

"You're absolutely shameless, Caulfield," Andrea accused, getting back into the '73 LTD.

He turned on the car and gave her the oddest, somehow smoldering, look. "Jealous?"

Heaven help her, yes. "Over a cranky little old librarian who's sixty-five if she's a day? Don't flatter yourself."

Neil squelched a grin. "No, I won't. You're right. I'd rather you do it."

She aimed for a scathing look, but probably only got to smoldering. "Drive, Caulfield." Somehow, every moment with him seemed more precious than the one before. "But not too fast."

UNLIKE MISS RUBY, the counter help at Camera One that morning was a gum-snapping teenager who acted brain-dead—and who couldn't have found his way out of a paper sack before Neil flashed a hundred-dollar bill. The kid found plenty of motivation then, and took them down to the building basement through half a dozen spiderwebs that looked as though they'd been transported whole from the *Arachnophobia* barn.

Andrea couldn't handle it. Spiders terrified her. She returned to the storefront and brushed every square inch of her clothing while she waited. Neil and the boy found the 1930's box of Amarillo high school yearbook photos and carted it up the ancient, creaking wooden stairs.

The final indexes must have been compiled sometime after the pages containing photographs, and they had nothing but the first name of Dierdre to go on. Andrea saw no choice but to look through pictures and names on every page.

All the way through to the *G*'s, the dust made Andrea sneeze, and she wished Miss Ruby, who would know what she was doing, were here now. But Andrea found the picture matching the one they'd taken from Solter's home near the top of the *H*'s in the class of 1936. The name beside it read Didi Hartsell. Neil flipped quickly through to the *H* pages in two more books and found Eugenie Hartsell in the class of '38.

Neil turned back to the teenager, who'd put on Walkman headphones and sat silently lip-synching the music. Neil lifted an earphone when the boy didn't hear him the first time. "You got a phone book I can look at?"

"You got another bill, mister?" But the boy didn't last half a second under Neil's threatening glare, and he produced a phone book from a drawer under the counter without moving off his stool.

Neil thumbed through to the directory's *H*'s. "Great," he muttered. "No Hartsells. Not even one."

Andrea looped her arm through Neil's. "So whoever said this was going to be easy, Caulfield?"

He scowled at her for mimicking his earlier warning, but it wasn't much of a sulk. "I hate it when that happens."

Andrea loved it when that happened, when she teased and he teased back. "Well. We have a name now."

"And Miss Ida Happelsmith's got the goods. Why didn't we think about a bouquet for her, too?"

Andrea shrugged. "So we'll go back and get her some flowers, too." She wanted to know why she herself didn't deserve at least a dandelion by now, but she kept her mouth shut.

Neil asked Andrea to drive, and had her circle the block while he went into the florist's again to buy Ida Happelsmith a bouquet the equal of Miss Ruby's—just in case the two later exchanged details. But he was really after the Christmas cactus he'd wanted to buy ever since Andrea got jealous over an old lady's bouquet.

Andrea took one look at the blooming cactus, a gorgeous succulent, and couldn't find a thing to say. She ran her finger along the length of thick stem, and a tear spilled over onto her cheek.

She hadn't had flowers from a man in a very long time. "I wish I hadn't just been thinking what an insensitive lout you were, buying two old ladies some flowers, and nothing for me. I'd have been happy with a dandelion, you know."

"Drive, Vogel." Her tear almost undid him. Her chronic honesty polished him off. "Not too fast."

THE CORNERSTONE ON the nursing home where Ida Happelsmith resided read Glen Haven, Dedicated this First day of June, Year of our Lord, 1951. They found Ida puttering around her room with a dust rag, and exchanged glances. Ruby and Ida were two of a kind.

There were differences, though. Where Ruby had been sparrowlike, Ida was round as a dove. Her ankles had thickened to the width of her calves, and her ample bosom interfered with her reach.

She was hard of hearing, wore drugstore spectacles, and she sniffed when she saw Neil's bouquet—clearly skeptical of strangers bearing gifts. But when she understood that

Ruby had sent them, and that they needed some of her prized historical information, Ida beamed.

This time Andrea had her story prepared. "Ida— May I call you Ida?" The elderly woman nodded, and Andrea continued. "Ida, I'm representing a client who is looking into her family tree. She was adopted and, well, I'm sure you can imagine how important it is to her to know about her birth family."

Ida went to a closet that in any other room would have contained clothing. Ida must have kept all her clothes in her chest of drawers because her closet had been modified to deep bookshelves.

"What's the family name, dearie?"

"Hartsell. The only two family members we were able to get names for were—"

"Hartsell?" Ida interrupted. "Did you say Hartsell?"

Andrea nodded, wondering at the consternation in Ida's expression. "Yes. Dierdre—Didi, maybe—and Eugenie."

Ida shut the closet door firmly and crossed her arms over her bosom. "Might as well tell your young lady that you couldn't find a single piece of the story as tell her a blessed thing about any Hartsell relatives. Only heartache up that tree."

Gesturing his deference to Andrea, Neil stayed out of this one. He might have gotten past Ida's reluctance to talk about Didi and Eugenie Hartsell, but he sensed from her impatience that she wouldn't deal well with more than one of them at a time.

"My client isn't a woman whose sensibilities will be easily hurt, Ida. And I think she's entitled to whatever history there is on these women. Ruby told us if it weren't for you—"

"Oh, hush a minute and let me think," Ida interrupted. Andrea didn't take offense. Like Ruby, Ida was a smart, quick-witted woman, and she saw where Andrea was going with that argument. History wasn't anything to be lost, no matter what the truth was.

Ida made up her mind as quickly, opened the door and asked Neil to pull down an oversize journal from one of the upper shelves. "That one. There."

She took the heavy volume from Neil and went to her table, indicating which chairs Andrea and Neil should use. Paging through the book, she seemed to get caught up in other lives several times before she got to the Hartsell girls.

"Absolutely nothing of any historical significance about this family at all. I seem to remember their papa was a dirt farmer from way back—though I suppose it was to the old man's credit that he sent those girls to school. Of course, they were both a few years older than me. I knew the younger one—Eugenie. She was quite the gadabout when I first started on the society column."

"You were a journalist?" Neil asked.

Ida glanced again at the flowers Neil had brought her, and looked on him more gently this time. "Not because I wrote that altogether too-precious society column," she answered. "But, yes. I did have some pieces appear in some fairly important syndications, and a short story or two." She hesitated for a moment, then went on.

"Funny you should ask about that. The newspapers is where this Hartsell story ends up."

Neil took Andrea's hand under the table. They were getting very close now.

"Why don't you start at the beginning, Ida?" Andrea urged her gently.

"Yes. Well. See here. This is as much as I ever pieced together about the Hartsell family—dirt farmers in all three generations." She pointed out Dierdre and Eugenie's grandfather, married to a woman named Inez. Their father was one of three sons. Didi and Eugenie had apparently had three older sisters die before reaching the age of eighteen.

"Abigail, Beatrice, Constance, Dierdre and Eugenie.

Right down the alphabet. But this is when it gets...
interesting." Ida flipped to another section of the journal,
where she'd begun with the advent of a family named Elbertson in Potter County.

Ida Happelsmith shuddered with distaste. "Mind you,
I've made it a point of honor in my life to record the history of this county without judging."

She turned the journal around and Andrea studied the
page written in Ida's careful script.

FAMILY ELBERTSON

GUNNER ELBERTSON, Sundries
    m. 1900
Sadie Prescott
        b. 1906
    ROLPH ELBERTSON, Druggist
    m. 1938
    Eugenie Marie Hartsell, b. 1922
            Anna, b. 1940 (m. Billow; last known,
            Poughkeepsie, NY)
            Truda, b. 1941 (m. Kline; last known: Hous-
            ton, Tex)
            Bethany, b. 1942, deceased 1951
            LEIF W., b. 1943 (Sept.), Pharmacist
          m. 1963
                Charlotte Paison, b. 1946
                  b. 1946
                  Beth Ann
          m. 1967
                Janice Morrow
          m. 1971
                Hillary Smithers
no m. (Dierdre Susan Hartsell)   (deceased 1960)
                b. 1943, Dec.; Journalist
                (BEN SOLTER)

"You'll notice," Ida said, "that young Ben's name was an anagram of the family moniker."

Ben Solter... Elbertson.

Neil hung over Andrea's shoulders, as she stared at the raw information contained in Ida's notations. Her eyes were drawn naturally to Ben Solter's name, then to Dierdre's. Interpreting them took little imagination or skill, but the implications forced her to make sure she understood correctly.

"Ida, does this mean that Rolph Elbertson had children with both Dierdre and Eugenie Hartsell?"

"Indeed."

Solter was the illegitimate son of Rolph Elbertson and Dierdre Hartsell, making Leif and Ben Solter both brothers and cousins.

Chapter Eleven

Ida pointed to the entry on Leif's daughter. "Beth Ann, I imagine, would most likely be your girl's birth mother."

Andrea murmured as if this might be true. "I see what you meant, Ida, about the heartache of belonging to this family."

Miss Happelsmith scowled. "Doesn't tell the sordid story by half."

"It must have been a terrible scandal."

Ida nodded, distaste all over her face. "Eugenie was pretty as a picture. Dierdre was plain as a fence post. But that didn't stop that philandering husband of Eugenie's from fathering a bastard child on her sister. Eugenie was mortified, *mortified,* I can tell you."

Andrea and Neil exchanged glances. The "Separated at Birth" mock-up hanging in Solter's medicine cabinet made perfect sense now. At least the cousin/brother aspect.

"Were they raised together?" Andrea asked.

"In no way." Ida sniffed. "Eugenie raised her son in the family home—a mansion, have no doubt. Dierdre lived on Rolph's leftovers."

"On the wrong side of the tracks," Andrea murmured.

"So to speak," Ida continued. "Rolph inherited the family business—a druggist shop, you know—and everyone in the county knew he kept one sister in style while he invented a diagnosis of rheumatoid arthritis for Didi."

Neil couldn't stand it anymore. "A druggist? Elbertson was a druggist?"

"Yes, and the elder, Rolph, was quite successful. Leif ran the business straight into the ground."

A man tailor-made to understand just how valuable Zolgen might become. Andrea exchanged a quick glance with Neil.

"Why the lie that Didi suffered rheumatoid arthritis?"

"So's to keep that poor woman drugged and quiet. All her life, mind you, trying to raise Rolph's bastard son half-crocked on morphine."

Andrea sat stunned by the implications and saw that none of them were lost on Neil, either. Rolph was a druggist, his legitimate son Leif was a pharmacist, and his plain-faced sister-in-law mistress, the ill-fated Dierdre, he made into an addict.

Neil went pale as paste, and his hands balled into fists. He shoved off the back of Andrea's chair and went to stand at the sliding glass door to Ida's small patio.

She knew the idea of deliberately addicting another human being pushed every button Neil had. To her, his tension scorched the very air, but it mustn't have been so obvious, because Ida just continued, clucking her tongue.

"Leif was no better than his father, certainly. Married three times, a wife-beater to boot. Lost his pharmacist license and got sent up in, oh, 1966. Yes, 1966. Some prescription fraud or other.

"Word had it," she continued, "that the old man repented after a while, felt real bad about Dierdre. But no matter what they tried, what other medicines, Didi couldn't ever make it off the morphine. Wasted away to nothing. She died right here in Glen Haven."

Ida went silent. Andrea didn't think her story was over, just that Ida needed a little time to rest. Her recollections seemed clear and lucid, the scandal of it all having provided her journalistic instincts ample reason to remember the smallest details.

"What became of Leif, Ida?"

"Went loony tunes," she answered promptly. "Didn't have two nickels to rub together. He'd already mismanaged the drugstore to the point of no return by the time he went to prison. So, he had no visible means of support—"

"None?" Andrea asked.

"Not so's you'd notice." Ida ran her thumb over the embossed lettering on the cover of the journal. "Still, he must have found some. Most homegrown Texas boys do when push comes to shove. He built a house out on the north side—a fortress, to hear folks talk. Kept to himself mostly, but when he came into town, he was always dressed to the teeth in hand-tooled boots and fancy suits."

"What kind of suits, Ida?" Andrea asked, thinking as well of ways a disgraced pharmacist, homegrown Texas boy had of getting money. Designer drugs. The black market. Blackmail.

"Oh, a Western cut, always. Texas to the core, and tailored, if I had to guess. The boy was brought up on the finer things."

Andrea gave Neil a glance, but he just stood rigidly, staring out over Ida's patio. There might be half a dozen reasons why a Falsbury of Amarillo, Western-cut suit jacket should be stuffed into the laundry bag she'd found on the floor of Ben Solter's bedroom closet. Only one made sense. Leif Elbertson had been to his brother's house. To his brother's bedroom.

"Did you ever hear what became of Beth Ann?" Andrea asked, trying to give credence to her story of an adopted client.

Ida shook her head. "Nary a word."

Andrea sat back. "Or anything of Ben Solter?"

Ida took a deep breath. "I never liked him much. He made me nervous. He could've sold an Eskimo an icebox."

"Persuasive?"

"More," Ida said, turning her attention to Neil. "Far more... Charismatic, you might say. You must have read his newspaper columns. He was syndicated all over the country, a law-and-order soapbox. I didn't often agree with him, but to give the man his due, he stood by his mother to the bitter end."

"He was with Dierdre when she died?" Neil asked.

"Some say it was him put her out of her misery."

NEIL PULLED OUT of the Glen Haven parking lot and drove, staying off the interstates, taking access roads leading to county roads leading to roads that were no more than cow paths.

Suppose Solter did commit some terrible crime, and this cousin found out about it.

Solter *had* committed some terrible crime, only nothing in Neil's experience could make him condemn the man. Neil's own little sister had been addicted, and that one fact had changed the course of his life.

He couldn't imagine what it must have been like for Solter to grow up with a junkie for a mother. What it must have been like to be a powerless kid watching his father condemn Dierdre and himself to a lifetime of destitution and ridicule, powerless to change any of it.

He had only to remember his own bitterness over Tammy's loss to imagine Solter's rage. The wonder was he hadn't killed his father and his cousin—his *brother*—as well.

Andrea sat curled up on the bench seat of the LTD beside Neil. She understood his black mood, his white-knuckled grip on the steering wheel, the dark emotion that mottled the skin beneath his light beard, and her heart went out to him.

For half an hour she sat silently, letting Neil vent his outrage on the desolate backwater-Texas roads. She ached for him, for everyone like him, even for Solter, but especially for Neil.

Truthfully, she thought she must be in love with this brilliant, dedicated, honorable, *passionate* man, and it cut her to the quick to keep admitting that all he needed of her was the answers she had some gift for uncovering.

She didn't think they had much more time to indulge his dark mood, and she wanted him to remember that Solter was no saint.

"Solter may have been the victim of a terrible life, Neil," she said at last, "but he became a monster no one could have stopped if he'd lived."

Neil gave her a glance to acknowledge the truth in what she said, then looked at the death grip he had on the steering wheel. He eased off, and let up the gas pedal until the old vehicle coasted to a stop.

"I think we need to go back now."

He stared out his window across the barren prairie. Nothing but weeds and cactus and a cloudless, late-afternoon Texas sky. There was nothing and no one around as far as the eye could see in any direction. "Go back for what, Andrea?"

His cutting stare hurt her feelings. He might be dedicated and sexy and brilliant but he had a long ways to go toward gracious. "There's still a great deal we don't know. Whether Leif knew Solter took Didi's life, if he really was blackmailing Solter—"

"C'mon, Andrea! He knew. Happelsmith said it—like any good ol' boy, he ran to money. He had to be blackmailing Solter all those years." Neil dragged a hand through his hair, and as she'd come to expect, paused at his neck to rub the tension away. "It didn't even matter if Solter cut him off, because he was a crooked pharmacist, and he knew Zolgen was a potential gold mine."

"I suppose it was no wonder that Solter despised drugs after what became of his mother," Andrea reflected. It really was surprising how accurately they had envisioned the real murder taking place. "Elbertson couldn't have cared less, except for the profit motive. He'd have followed Solter's tirades in the paper, known about the bad blood between you and Solter, and seen how he could kill two birds with one stone."

"Yeah. And you can bet your pretty little hide Elbertson is behind Peripeteia Enterprises."

Andrea shifted her legs so that her feet rested on the floor and she was sitting straight. "This is enough to take to the authorities, Neil."

He gave a long sigh. His tongue seemed locked to the pit of his mouth. Elbertson was probably sitting in the house that blackmail built, somewhere north of Amarillo, right now. Counting his money, laughing his ass off, profit-taking off Zolgen, maybe even sending money the other way now, subsidizing a vigilance committee back in Santa Fe.

The vigilantes might believe in their cause, might truly see themselves working toward making the world safe for upstanding, law-abiding citizens everywhere.

Elbertson, on the other hand, would have only one reason for keeping the vigilance committee alive—to keep the man he had framed for his brother's murder silent and at bay.

Or dead.

The vigilance committee had to be stopped. Solter's brother had to be stopped.

"Which authorities, Andrea?" he asked. He slouched in the seat and pinched the bridge of his nose. Closing his eyes, he rested his head against the back of the seat. "Who can we trust?"

Andrea rested her own head back. The problem was a serious one. To be effective, the vigilance committee needed only one individual in any law enforcement agency. What the agency knew, the individual knew, and the network of vigilantes thrived.

One mistaken presumption, one wrong move, would seal Neil's death warrant. The only person Andrea trusted beyond question was Miri Silverman. She made the suggestion to Neil.

"What makes you think she'll know anyone we can trust?"

"I don't know, Neil," Andrea admitted. "She has a lot of sources, a lot of friends. I know it doesn't feel like it from where we stand, but there have to be a few honest cops left in the country. Miri will find one."

Neil reached out and stroked Andrea's fingers. "You trust her." He trusted Andrea. She trusted Miri Silverman. What else could he do?

Andrea nodded. "With my life, Neil." With his life.

He straightened in his seat then and got out to stretch. Andrea followed suit. The sun had dipped below the horizon, and it would be dark soon. She went around the car to stand by Neil, to offer him a consoling touch.

One ankle crossed over the other, he leaned into the old car and put an arm around Andrea's shoulder. She rested her head on his shoulder. In spite of their desperate circumstances, she'd never in her life felt more taken care of than she did standing there cradled against him.

"It's time you went home, Boo." It killed him to tell her that, but it wouldn't do to show his feelings.

"Neil, we aren't . . . we haven't—"

"I know." He brought his chin low to rest on her head. "I know." Truth was, he didn't know exactly what she meant, but it didn't matter. He had his answers now—most of them, anyway. Answers enough to convince the prosecutors to drop the case against him. And that part done, there was no way he could justify keeping Andrea near to him, endangering her life even one more hour.

Squinting against the last warming rays of the sun, he steeled himself to overcome any resistance from her. "We'll find a pay phone and you can call Miri. It wouldn't be a bad idea to go stay with her."

"Neil, no." Her chin was unaccountably quivering, and she clamped her teeth shut for a moment. "I can't do anything from New York."

His arm tightened around her shoulders. "Maybe you'll be safe in New York." He refused to look at her, to set himself up for caving in to her stubborn pleas. "You're going home. Tonight. It might take days to set up a time and place I can live with, to sur—surrender." God help him, he could barely get the word out.

Her chin hadn't stopped its quivering, and now tears pricked at her eyes. "How will you—will I—find you again?"

"I'll call you every morning. When you're satisfied with whatever arrangements, I'll meet you. Anywhere you say."

"No." She began to shake her head. Her throat seemed swollen to twice its normal size. She pulled out of his arm and turned to confront him head-on. "I'll stay with you, and Miri can make the arrangements."

Neil bowed his head. She was so sweet, so loyal, so beautiful. What would it take to make her understand this was no child's game of hide-and-seek? That the price on his head only grew higher? That even she was no match for a bullet in the back?

"No."

"Neil, they won't do anything if I'm with you. They wouldn't dare!"

"You're wrong, Andrea." The stakes had already grown desperate for the vigilance committee. John Brice's appearance at Andrea's house proved that. "They'll stop at nothing."

"Then they won't stop with you," she snapped, willing him not to send her away. "I already know too much. I've already seen too much. They can't afford to let me—"

His hand snaked out and he grabbed her arm and pulled her to him. His lips went down on hers before she could utter another word of what they would do to her. The woman had an answer for every damned thing he could think of, and he was tired of thinking.

His arms closed around her and he crushed her to his body. She put her arms around his neck and shoved her fingers into his hair and pulled him deeper into his own fierce kiss. If he thought he was going to send her away, he had another thought coming. "I won't leave you."

"You will."

His hands seemed everywhere at once, stroking her back, her breast, trapping her jaw to brush at her lips, cupping her bottom. She moaned and let her head fall back, and his whiskers scraped her cheek and her jaw. His lips stroked her from the pulse point at her throat to the lobe of her ear. She wanted only nearer, and she bent her leg, then wrapped it around his, drawing herself still closer.

A gunshot blasted, and blasted again.

Stunned witless at the echoing blasts, Andrea sank against Neil. For an instant he went rigid, then he pulled her to the ground. He closed his arms around her, covering her body with his, protecting her head with his hands.

His head jerked up and he searched the horizon in every direction but saw no one. What had to be fractions of a second seemed like years before he registered the whooping cheers of boys he still couldn't see.

"Eeeeehaw! I got the little sucker!"

"Did not! Didn't you see that, dude.... Your shot on'y made 'im a lopear.... I'm the one that got him!"

Kids.

Relief sapped every cell of Neil's body. Weeds poked in his eye, and his elbow had whacked a rock when he went down, but all he could think about was the danger he'd put Andrea in. He dragged in one ragged breath, and lifted his weight off her. "Are you okay?"

"Fine." But her beautiful green eyes were round with ill-concealed panic, and it made him want to tear those rabbit-hunting kids limb from body. Most of all it convinced him that he was right. She had to get out, if not back to Santa Fe, then to New York and the one friend she trusted with her life.

He scrambled to his feet and pulled Andrea to hers. She saw the implacable look about his eyes, the steely determination that brooked no discussion.

Protecting her, he'd get himself killed. She had no choice but to leave him behind. She had to find someone smart and honest enough to listen to the truth, powerful enough to disband the vigilantes.

He helped her brush the dirt and weeds from her backside, then helped her into the car. He turned it around, its shocks protesting and the bottom scraping earth, then headed back toward the city lights.

NEIL CIRCLED THE BLOCK and came up on a northbound one-way street. The intersection had gas stations on the two far corners, and to their right, a convenience store. The place wasn't doing much business, and there were several parking spaces right in front. He debated parking in one of them, then discarded the idea in favor of the curbside.

Andrea got out and went to the pay phone near the entrance to place a collect long-distance call to Miriam.

The line was busy, still busy when the operator tried a second time. Andrea dug into her coin purse for a few quarters and dialed her own number in New Mexico to retrieve any messages. Her machine indicated there were three. She punched in the code to begin listening.

Miriam Silverman was the first. *"Andrea, listen. I've got some information on Peripeteia Enterprises. The account to which sales are credited is at the First Continental Bank of Amarillo.''* She recited an account number, then repeated it.

"The sales agreement purporting to sell the patent to Peripeteia Enterprises has Neil Caulfield's signature, but the date is wrong—unless Caulfield signed after he skipped bail. Is that possible? Anyway, the agreement transfers ownership to one Leif—that's L-e-i-f—Elbertson, E-l-b-e-r-t-s-o-n. Amarillo post-office box.

I hope this helps, Boo. Call me. And please, be very, very careful.... So long."

Leif Elbertson was Peripeteia Enterprises. The news didn't come as any surprise. They'd put it together hours ago. But the documents Miriam had seen proved Elbertson's connection, and possession of the Zolgen patent gave him an indisputable motive to frame Neil for the murder of Ben Solter.

All the right answers were shallow comfort. Neil had to first survive long enough to see justice done.

Andrea glanced back at him, slouching low behind the wheel of the car. She knew how jittery he was, sitting in the open for any extended period of time. She'd almost decided to hang up before the second message when she heard Mason Piers's distinctive baritone on the recording.

Piers!

"Vogel, listen to me, and listen well. I haven't got much time."

The strained quality in his voice made her straighten up and listen more closely. She glanced again at Neil, watched him checking his rearview mirror.

"You haven't got much time." He gave a phone number she recognized as his private line at home.

Automatically, her glance followed Neil's—behind the car. A squad car had pulled to the side, parking directly behind their LTD. Its rotating beacon lights and search lamp were off, the headlights and inside overhead lights on. The lone uniformed policeman looked to be consulting notes on a clipboard.

"They know where you are...." Andrea shivered violently. The vigilance committee, she thought. God help them, the vigilance committee knew, had them dead to rights on an Amarillo street corner.... *"Andrea—"*

She watched Neil straighten, his weight shifting, everything about him alert. The cop set aside his clipboard and tugged his cap on tight. Neil shifted out of park.

"—for God's sake—"

Terror mounting, she watched the cop close his door and withdraw the nightstick secured at his side. Neil did nothing, though she knew his gaze must be to the side mirror, watching the cop approach. Do something, for God's sake—something, Neil...

"—get somewhere safe—"

Safe?

She could do nothing. Couldn't move, or help or distract the cop. He drew very near. He held the nightstick at its base in his right hand, its business end in his left. He was a large man, tall and broad-shouldered, middle-aged but prepared for anything. He stooped and tapped Neil's window with the stick, demanding Neil get out.

"—and stay put!"

Stupidly, she stood there frozen, listening to Piers, listening to the disconnect, listening to the machine accessing yet another call. *"No way out."* She seemed thrust into the midst of some chilling, horrendous Hollywood set with nothing to do but watch the unfolding scene.

The cop readied his stick to bash in the window when Neil pulled the steering wheel with everything in him hard to the right and floored the gas pedal.

The tires spun and shrieked. The cop jumped clear, let the stick fly.

Chapter Twelve

The LTD lurched crazily into the convenience store lot, its rear tires bumping over the curb. Neil had the gas pedal to the floor when he jammed on the brakes. The car jolted to a screaming stop inches from Andrea.

The cop ran full-bore at Neil's side of the car. Cold and shuddering and scared out of her mind, Andrea dropped the receiver and jerked open the car door. The cop was pulling back hard on the nightstick.

She threw herself into the car and in the same instant the arc of the cop's nightstick ended in Neil's window, bashing glass in a thousand directions. Neil took a glancing blow to the left side of his head. He floored the gas pedal, and again the huge LTD lurched forward, throwing Andrea against the seat.

Oblivious to the glass and the roaring pain in his head, Neil swung out onto the opposite street, a southbound one-way. Andrea watched through the back window as the cop ran to his squad car, yanked open the door and flung himself in. The last she saw was a convenience-store customer diving into his own little VW seconds before the squad car peeled through the lot in pursuit.

Kneeling in the seat, watching out the back, she felt the glass littering the seat shred her lightweight linen slacks and slice into her knee. The siren screamed now, and the beacon lights flashed behind them. Neil whipped into an alley at the last possible second, and the cop car spun out to make the same turn.

The LTD emerged on a side street, its shocks pushed beyond endurance as it crossed to the alleyway on the other side. Neil turned at the next street into an old residential area, then doubled back behind a bar and grill.

He swerved into an overflowing metal garbage can, then drove by as garbage flew in every direction. The can fell spinning to its side, and when the cop caught up to it, it jammed between the squad car and an immovable Dumpster bin. Those few seconds cost him the chase.

Neil was operating on pure adrenaline. His scalp was bleeding, his eyes squinting. He drove through a zigzagging pattern of several blocks, searching every alley and side street for an inconspicuous place to abandon the car.

Andrea spotted one. "There," she pointed. "Neil, look."

Two runners of cement led from the old neighborhood street to a space deep in the darkness and shadows between two brick homes. He'd already driven beyond the drive. He backed the LTD in and up the short incline until it was hidden from street view, tucked tightly next to the back end of the larger house.

He switched off the old car, took the key out of the ignition and stuffed it deep into the seat crevice.

Then he felt the roaring pain in his head, and for a moment expected to pass out. But he'd been in this kind of trouble before and he knew he couldn't afford to let the darkness overtake him, to quit for even sixty seconds. He opened his car door and twisted his body to get out.

"Neil, wait! You can't—"

"What I *can't* do is wait, Andrea," he chided, his voice tight as a drawn bow. He forced himself to stand, to pull his weight out of that car. His head spun, and he damn near collapsed.

He clung to the white vinyl top of the LTD and let the dizziness pass. He didn't know when Andrea got out of the car. He didn't hear her door close, or see her come around the car, but there she was at his side.

Her medical, caretaking side took charge. She moved his left arm down from the top of the car so she could get closer to his head. A cloud cover blocked every star, even the moon, and the night seemed as dark as a cave. She ruffled his hair gently with her fingers to brush away the shards of glass.

She felt a swelling on the side of his head the size of a small child's fist, and the blood had clotted, matting his hair.

"Look at me, Neil. Please."

He endured her ministrations, wanting to flinch, to be left the hell alone. He shivered and brought his arm back up onto the roof of the car, then turned his head and rested his chin on his shoulder.

He opened his eyes, but she had to stand on tiptoe to come close to looking into them. She couldn't tell where his pupils left off against his midnight-dark irises, or even where the whites of his eyes began. But he blinked, and he was breathing at a more normal pace. His flagging energy seemed to recover by fractions. He might lose it all at any second, and she couldn't afford that yet, here.

"Neil, listen to me. Can you walk?"

Listen to her. He could spend a lifetime listening to her sultry Louisiana accent, but he didn't know if he could put one foot in front of the other. Still, he nodded. He would do anything he had to do. Anything, one more time.

He turned away from the car and draped an arm around her shoulders. Without her, he'd have crawled.

She had to abandon the beautiful little Christmas cactus, but she stuffed her things into Neil's day pack and shouldered the strap. Appearing to cling to Neil, in fact she supported him at every step.

They made it to the street. He called on every reserve, every survival instinct left in him. Forcing himself to stand taller, one square of sidewalk after another, he walked with her. He wanted to tell her how sorry he was for dragging her through his nightmare, but he saved his breath and his energy.

They walked for nearly an hour through the dark, mostly silent, neighborhoods. Dogs barked now and again, and every once in a while they heard people talking to each other in houses they passed. They covered what had to be a couple of miles, and none of the cars that drove by showed them the least attention.

At last Andrea spotted a lighted, old-fashioned neon bar sign, and they walked through the parking lot to the old brick building. At the recessed entrance, Neil took his arm from around her shoulders and opened the door. Casting him one more careful glance, she walked in ahead of him.

The barkeep, fortyish, scarecrow-lean and scarred from juvenile acne, looked up and waved. The minute he saw the clotted-over gash on Neil's head, his friendly smile vanished.

"Don't need no trouble in here now...."

Andrea looked up at Neil, clung to his biceps and smiled at the bartender. "He won't be any trouble, sir," she improvised, deliberately projecting female helplessness. "Some naughty, *ornery* little boy pitched a rock or somethin' through our car window."

Most of the clientele were on their feet, cheering a preseason football game. Mercifully, a booth came open at the back of the bar, and though it was by a window overlooking the parking lot, Neil could sit with his back to a wall. "Would you be so kind as to bring us a couple cups of steamin' hot coffee, please?"

The barkeep surrendered to her charm, and she clung to Neil, guiding him to the back booth. His head pounded like all billy hell, but he couldn't help admiring the way she'd handled the skeptical runt of a bartender.

Neil sank into the booth and let his head fall into his hands. Andrea flashed a smile for the coffee, handed the guy a five, then sipped gratefully at her cup. "Please. Keep the change. Oh, and do you suppose I could get a cloth with ice in it?"

The barkeep cast Neil a jaundiced eye. "This ain't an infirmary, lady."

"No, sir, it's not," she agreed. "Still, I'd really appreciate it." She blessed some lucky star, because he returned after a few moments despite his attitude and produced a thin chunk of ice wrapped in a hand towel.

She handed Neil the ice and sipped her coffee, keeping a close eye. His pupils weren't intolerably dilated or uneven, and though caffeine would never replace standard treatment requirements of head trauma, it would constrict the vessels in his head, lessening the chances of an intracranial hemorrhage.

"Neil, everything has changed now. I didn't get Miri—her line was busy, but—"

"Doesn't matter," he responded, his speech more hoarse, thicker than normal. "You're out of here, any way you can."

He had to get the big picture, here and now. Still she spoke softly, knowing their choices were scarcer by the moment.

"I've done things your way up to now because you knew better, Neil. Now *I* know better. I don't have a clue how you survived on your own when you were shot in the back, but I'm not leaving you alone with a head injury."

He scowled, the corners of his mouth turning down briefly, but even that effort hurt him, and he didn't argue.

She reached out to him, touching his hand. "When I didn't get Miri, I called my answering machine. She'd left a message—Elbertson is Peripeteia, just as we thought." He started to shake his head and flinched. She had to clamp her mouth shut to stave off a cry for the pain he was in. "Drink some coffee, Neil."

He sipped at the cup, holding his head still as he could. She needed to tell him the rest, but she thought it could wait until she'd spoken to Mason Piers. The walk had taken the edge off her anxiety, but returning his call was urgent.

"I'm going to try to find someplace to stay, Neil. I want you to sit here and keep that ice on your head. Okay?"

"Yeah." Fact was, he couldn't have moved if he wanted.

A pay phone that took only dimes hung on the back wall, twenty feet from their booth. Andrea got several dollars' worth of dimes from the barkeeper and placed the call. Piers answered on the first ring.

"Mason."

"Are you okay?"

Andrea breathed a short sigh of relief. He knew her voice. "For the moment."

"And your... friend?"

Despite his message on her answering machine, she didn't trust Piers as far as she could throw him. His call could be a trap easy as pie, and she wouldn't give him the time of day, much less any indication of Neil's state. "I have lots of friends, Mason."

"We don't have time for games, Vogel—"

"No. We don't. I trusted you this far, Mason, but I won't stay on this line indefinitely."

Piers sighed and swore. She could almost see him scrubbing the back of his thumb over his eyebrow. "What a bloody mess! At least tell me if you're someplace safe for the night."

"No."

"Or have anyplace to go?"

She stared at Neil coddling his head, giving her warning looks. "Maybe if I knew what I was up against—"

"A monster," he interrupted harshly. "An out of control, absolute-evil-incarnate monster!"

"Which you must have been party to, Mason. I've been to Solter's house."

She could hear his teeth clicking against his pipe, his lighter hissing, his breath as he drew hard on the stem. He knew she must be aware he was in too deep with the vigilance committee.

"The Bartlett baby," he offered by way of explanation. "Rod Bartlett's nanny did feed that baby those diuretics—"

"Oh, my God." Andrea gripped the pay-phone receiver and heard Miri's voice in her mind. *But the nanny did it, Boo.* Everything came crystal clear. Despite Andrea's verdict, Piers had overcalled her on the cause of death of little Melissa Bartlett. "Are you saying that Solter used your ruling to coerce you into the vigilance committee?"

"*Coerce* is a little…strong. He made it seem as though we all make mistakes, that the vigilance committee was there to…to correct the injustices of an inadequate judicial system."

Andrea felt a wave of nausea begin low in her body. "Did they murder the Bartlett's nanny?"

"I don't…I don't know. I don't think so. Solter used to preach at length on the role of fate in justice. He would say, 'She deserved to die, and so she drowned.'" He hesitated, dragged on his pipe and went on. "I wish…I have to believe you were right about Caulfield, too. I was wrong to bow to the pressure, Vogel. Horribly wrong. I know that now."

"What pressure, Mason?" she cried, shivering as though she'd never again be warm. "Solter was dead! You were free of what he knew—"

"Wise up, Vogel," he interrupted harshly. "If you've seen that operation, you know every filthy little secret was documented to the nth degree. Solter's cousin came forward and took charge of the committee, and what Solter knew, Elbertson knew."

"But he's a madman—"

"Do you think we don't know that? Do you think if we'd known at the time that he'd turn the Cause to this vendetta, to this . . . death squad, that we'd have gone along?"

He was rambling now, nervous, desperately anxious to justify what he'd done, what he'd become. Andrea glanced at Neil. Time pressed in on her like a vise, but she couldn't interrupt, couldn't stop the flow of Mason's desperate excuses.

The Cause. The vigilance committee had a name.

"We didn't see it coming, Vogel. At the time it seemed . . . well, it was fitting that Elbertson lead the manhunt for his cousin's murderer. He's a very compelling, charismatic sort, very strong-willed. He looks astonishingly like Ben looked. We were . . . seduced by that, by the man."

"Who else, Mason? Janine Tyler? John Brice?"

Before he could answer, the operator interrupted. "Another one-eighty, please, to continue." Andrea dropped twenty more dimes into the slot, and Piers picked up immediately.

"Tyler, Brice, Jay Frost, who clerked the Caulfield trial. There's an army out there, Vogel, dozens of cops sympathetic to the Cause and a half dozen active state patrolmen and FBI that I know of personally. Hell, Texas is crawling with them. . . .

"They know you're in Amarillo, they have license-plate numbers, descriptions—" He hesitated, and she heard him draw hard on the pipe again. "They have orders—specific orders to leave the kill to Elbertson."

"Oh!" Andrea clamped her lips shut, but not before Piers heard her small cry.

He murmured his miserable assent. She understood. "Everyone in town is scrambling to cover their asses," he intoned. "Solter's place has been dismantled—at least, the...the basement. Elbertson has gone stark raving mad with this vendetta, and they're all terrified he'll drag them down with him when he's caught."

Them? Could Piers possibly believe he wasn't every bit as culpable as the rest? If Elbertson's own feared him to that extent, what chance did she have of salvaging Neil's life, or her own?

"Mason, so help me—"

"Save it," he interrupted tersely. "There's nothing you could say that I haven't already thought. Listen, Vogel, and listen good. My wife, Cindy, has part interest in a secluded bed-and-breakfast outside Amarillo. Her sister runs the place. You must remember. If you can get there before Elbertson catches up with you, you'll be safe, at least for the night."

And then what? Andrea wondered. Neil wouldn't make it through another hour sitting in that booth, and her options were all gone.

Her fear for Neil, and her outrage at Elbertson and everyone connected with him, made her thoughts strung out, scattershot, insensible. She had no idea what bed-and-breakfast Piers thought she must remember. "Cindy's sister? Mason, why would I remember that? How—"

"Yes, you do!" he snapped impatiently. "You came to Cindy's mother's funeral. You met her sister. She's plain, unmarried. The two of them inherited the house, and she was deciding to turn it into—"

"Wait." She did remember. She remembered Cindy's maiden name, remembered thinking what a lovely name it would make for the B-and-B Cindy and her sister planned. Thorn-something or other. Thornbrook? Thornberry?

She reached for the grimy phone directory, a ragged string looped through a hole in the upper left corner. *Thornbloom.* She had only one question left for Piers, but she didn't bother asking. He might tell her the truth, he might not. Worse, he couldn't really know.

What were the chances that Elbertson had been a silent party to this whole conversation?

As she pondered this, the operator broke in again. Andrea disconnected, then immediately dialed the Thornbloom number. Vicki Thornbloom had clearly been expecting the call. She offered Andrea quick assurances of safety and a brief set of directions to her place, nearly twenty miles south and east. When Andrea recradled the receiver, Neil was already getting out of the booth and shouldering his day pack.

He wasn't happy with her, or the time she'd taken on the phone. She could see that. He swayed, perilously close to passing out from the simple exertion of getting out of the bar booth. Moments short of collapsing, he wrapped his arm over the pay phone. "Gotta get out of here."

She nodded and ducked under his arm, draping it around her shoulders to support him. He was white as paste, and though his pupils seemed stable, beads of sweat had broken out on his forehead and upper lip. "Neil, listen. I've talked to Piers, and I have a place—"

"You *what!*" In one desperate motion he straightened, turned, grabbed her jacket lapel and forced her back to the wall, her right side tight against the phone. "You little fool! You called Piers! He's one of them! How could you be so stupid?"

Tears sprang to her eyes. She stared up at him and took a shaky, uncertain breath. He hadn't hurt her. She didn't believe he would hurt her. He was chilled and in shock, and his actions were mostly beyond his control. All the same, he scared her.

"Don't make a scene, Neil. If you give that bartender any excuse—"

Neil swore under his own jagged breath. He still had a handful of her jacket in one hand, his other against the wall by her head. His reaction time had again slowed to sluggish, but he'd never seemed more dangerous, like a gut-shot coyote.

To control her own emotions as much as to know, she counted pulsebeats at his carotid, and his respirations every time his chest rose and fell. One of them had to stay in control, and it had to be her.

His eyes shot anger at her like darts at a target. "Why?" he bit out.

She cleared her throat, but never took her eyes from Neil's. She spoke in low tones impossible to hear beyond him, but clearly and slowly so that he would understand through the pain that must be clouding every sense.

"He left a message on my machine, warning me, Neil. Not to scare me, but to warn me. He confessed to his part in this and reminded me of a place we can go."

"Fine," he croaked, his jaw locked against the blackness that kept threatening his consciousness. "What in the sam *hell* makes you think you can trust—"

"Instinct," she snapped. "The same instincts that made you believe I'd help you, Neil. He's running scared—they're all running—" She broke off.

From the corner of her eye she saw the barkeep sidling toward them, gripping the handle of a scarred cutting board. She tried to breathe, but she couldn't. His eyes squinted as he gauged Neil's threatening stance over her, and she knew the instant his indecision and suspicion hardened to intent. In another moment he would blindside Neil with the wooden cutting board.

She had no time to warn Neil. She jerked his hand to her breast and threw herself at him. Wrapping her arms around his neck, she kissed him. She sensed Neil's confusion, but she had to make the barkeep *believe* there'd be no trouble in his place, that she'd been embroiled in nothing more than a lovers' spat, quickly begun, over now.

Neil's head swam. He sensed some vague threat. He didn't know where it was coming from. He knew Andrea was responding to it, warding off the danger, but he couldn't focus. Her lips touched his, he heard her moan, he even saw his own hand on her breast, but he'd never felt more disconnected. He was angry with her, wasn't he?

Somehow he understood that he must play along with her charade, and he kissed her, but God help him, he couldn't feel anything.

Nothing but the freight train roaring through his head.

"You two want to get the hell outta here? I don't need any o' this crap going on same as I don't need any damn troublemakers."

Andrea darted a glance at the bartender and backed down from her tiptoes, pulling a bit away from Neil. She didn't dare argue, and she didn't know how she'd get Neil to the Thornbloom. She nodded at the barkeep, begged for one more moment, then turned with Neil and walked across the badly scratched hardwood floor to the door.

The cold night air hit Neil full in the face. For a second he thought he'd throw up, but when the feeling passed his mind cleared a little.

They made the first turn, into the parking lot they'd crossed earlier. Neil felt as if he might get by without using Andrea for a crutch anymore, and he took his arm from around her shoulders.

He remembered suddenly what had triggered his anger, but the effort to stand there on his own two feet took everything he had. "Got a plan, Boo?"

Cabs were out, cops were out, thumbing a ride was out. "Get a car," she said evenly. She didn't move half a pace away in case he began to black out or his dizziness returned.

He glanced around the lot at the motley collection of vehicles. "One of these do, ma'am?"

She cast him a scathing look for his sarcasm and refused to respond to it. She caught sight of a young couple clinging to one another for support, laughing raucously and weaving about the half-empty lot, headed for an old Dodge. There was really no decision to make.

She turned on her heel and walked in the direction of the old Dodge herself, to intercept the couple. If there were a God in heaven, this couple would be too drunk or stoned to mind selling their car.

Sudden panic clawed in her stomach. She didn't know how to walk up to someone and ask to buy their car. She would make a fool of herself, they'd laugh at her.... But the couple, reeking of booze, was almost there. She had no time for idiotic fear. "I wondered if you'd sell me your car?"

Startled at her approach, the pair pulled up short and silent. Dressed in tattered jeans and sweatshirts, if either one of them had had a bath in the past week it didn't show. The girl's long blond hair fell in limp, greasy strands, and her boyfriend's was every bit as unkempt.

They stared at Andrea for several seconds and finally looked at each other as if they'd just landed the greatest sucker of all time. Then, typically paranoid, they regarded her as if she were setting them up.

The male of the pair found his tongue. "You some kind of undercover cop, lady?"

Bad idea. Neil was right. Her aptitude for intrigue was slim to nil. "No, I... No. I just need a car."

"Lonnie," the girl tugged at his arm, "maybe we should—"

"Well, it ain't worth the powder it'd take to blow it to hell. You find yourself some other set of wheels, okay, lady?"

The street lamps were dim and filthy. Cars drove by and, from the sounds of it, a brawl was breaking out across the street. The last thing they needed was to be anywhere near trouble. Andrea swallowed. "Look—"

Suddenly Neil appeared at her side with three hundred-dollar bills fanned closely between his fingers. He reached out and grabbed the guy by the front of his sweatshirt and stuck the bills under his nose. "Last offer, *Lonnie*. Take it or leave it, but do it now."

Wide-eyed with fear of Neil and the nasty-looking gash on his head, the kid dug some keys out of his front jeans pocket, but Potter County's finest chose that precise moment to drive slowly by them.

Chapter Thirteen

The adrenaline rush hit Neil the moment the sheriff's car came into sight. Experience told him this was no random drive-by, that the brawl beginning across the street had drawn the cruiser. He knew enough to stand there acting as if nothing was wrong. The kids didn't.

Lonnie threw the keys to the ground, snatched the bills from Neil's fingers and bolted, leaving the girl to catch up with him or not. She darted toward the alley, too, calling hysterically after him.

Andrea knelt to pick up the keys and watched the county cops pull to the other side of the street. Two of them vaulted out of their vehicle and disappeared into the middle of the roughneck crowd.

Relief flooded through her. Her hands shook, and she jammed the knuckles of her free hand against her lips to keep from crying. Crouched there, she doubted very much that she could stand.

Neil bent and took her by the elbow and drew her to her feet. He led her the few short steps to the ancient baby-blue Dodge Valiant, leaned with his back against the car, enfolded her in his arms and rested his splitting head atop hers. He knew how tired she was, how cold and spent and hopeless, and he hated to feel her shaking because it meant the dregs of her energy were wasting.

"Ah, God, Boo... I'm sorry."

No one should go through what she'd already suffered in the last twelve hours, and the worst of it was his own despicable behavior, shaking her, laying into her for being all kinds of a fool. Without her he'd have dropped out cold in the street somewhere, dead, one way or another, by morning.

Andrea pulled back and shook her head. "Please. No apologies." He'd lashed out at her, but he was badly injured himself. She spared a glance toward the brouhaha developing across the street, then looked up at him and touched his prickly whiskers. "Piers said the vigilance committee even has FBI, Neil. We have nowhere safe to go if—"

He brought a forefinger to her lips, hushing her. He knew all about their choices, their lack of choices. "Do you know where you're going?"

"Hopefully." Hot stinging tears pricked at her eyes again. She'd have given anything, anything at all, for this nightmare to be done. To stop his pain. "Do we get to follow my plan, just this once?"

He looked down into her sweet, heart-shaped face. Her eyes watered fiercely. He wanted to kiss her but if he bent his head that far the pain might finally get the better of him. He handed her the keys. "Yeah, Vogel. This once we'll follow your plan."

She tilted her face quickly down to hide the glimmer of tears from him and opened the driver's door. Neil closed it for her, not fooled at all. He flung the day pack into the back seat, then gingerly eased himself into the car.

The pain overcame him at last, and the blackness he'd fended off so long won out.

THE LITTLE VALIANT HAD a transmission unlike anything Andrea had ever seen. Push-button automatic. Marshaling every resource left in her, she gave Neil a quick appraisal.

Satisfied with the pace of his breathing, she switched on the car. The needle stuck stubbornly to the *E* on the gas gauge. The little car could be running on no more than fumes, and if she made it to a gas station before running out, it'd be the first piece of luck she'd had since leaving Glen Haven hours before.

God and all his angels must have been watching out for her, though, because when she pulled out onto the street the county deputies and several Amarillo cops were busy slinging one brawler after another into a paddy wagon. The car coughed and died, but not before she managed to get it beside a gas tank in what had to be the oldest surviving station in town.

An attendant meandered out, asked her what she wanted, how much, and did she need the oil checked.

She told him to fill the tank and leave the oil. Mercifully, she had a twenty left in her pocket. She paid the attendant, then forced herself to wait for the six-forty in change, giving the attendant no reason out of the ordinary to remember her. She drove away and headed south.

She avoided the interstate as Vicki Thornbloom had directed. For what seemed an hour, she watched the odometer roll over the miles to her turnoff. Her eyes stung. Oncoming headlights blurred and crossed. Neil was out of it, and she couldn't hold on much longer herself.

The country road wasn't well marked, but she recognized the rooster silhouette atop a mailbox in a row of a dozen others, just as Vicki had described.

The dark and quiet unnerved her. Neil's breathing seemed steady and deep, but he worried her, and the sound of her own voice was better than nothing, so she repeated aloud the brief directions Vicki had given. "Off the highway you'll come to the crest of a hill. At the bottom, turn left. Two more hills, then another left."

All kinds of trees and scrub brush now. She decided there must be a stream nearby to feed the wooded thicket.

Thornbloom came into view at last, a sort of Greek Revival architecture she recognized because of so many back home in New Orleans. Oddly, this one seemed meant for the odd Texas woods. Andrea pulled the car to the side of the house beside a late-model sedan and what appeared to be a well-cared-for fifties-vintage pickup truck. She turned off the Valiant's headlights and switched off the car.

Neil stirred, groaning, and she reached out to feel his forehead. He felt clammy now, despite the car heater she'd kept at full blast. Her anxiety rising, she got out of the car and ran to the front door of the house.

Clad in a long quilted robe, Vicki Thornbloom met her at the door with a concerned hug and a mug of hot coffee. Vicki was a large woman, standing six feet in her stockings, and despite her pretty, wide-set gray eyes, no one would mistake her for a great beauty. To Andrea she appeared an absolute angel of mercy and goodness.

"You made it."

Gratefully, Andrea accepted the mug and sipped at the coffee. "Yes. I . . . We made it." She saw that Vicki seemed aware Andrea wasn't alone, and she assumed Piers had made the situation clear to his sister-in-law. "Vicki, he's badly hurt, passed out cold in the car. I've got to get him inside . . . warm. Fed, if possible."

Shepherding Andrea through the entryway to the kitchen, Vicki murmured reassurances and plucked a set of keys from a hook by the back door. "There's a small guest house out back—better than upstairs for your purposes, I thought. Come see if this will do, then you can get him in and I'll warm up some biscuits and stew."

Fresh tears came to her eyes when Andrea saw the fire burning softly in the small guest quarters, and an antique four-poster bed nearby. There were candles lighted and strewn around the room. A cedar chest sat at the end of the bed, and pretty ivory lace curtains matching the thick quilt adorned a small multipaned window.

Vicki waited anxiously for Andrea's nod of approval.

"This will be perfect, Vicki. Are you sure you don't mind—"

"Mind? Honey, I'd have been heartbroken if Cindy and Mason hadn't thought to send you here. He's . . . Is he . . . Cindy thinks he could be in very deep trouble."

Andrea cleared her throat and backhanded the tear that had fallen despite her intentions. "I won't lie to you, Vicki. He could be."

The other woman clamped her lips shut and crammed her hands deeply into the pockets of her night robe. "Well, then, no tellin' but helping you folks out might make things go easier on him."

Andrea nodded. "I hope so, Vicki. I truly do. But I need to get—"

"'Course you do. Easier, maybe, to bring your friend through the side gate there." She pointed out the flagstone path to the gate, promised to bring out first-aid supplies and later a tray of hot food, then hurried off back to the house.

Andrea left the door ajar, then went to wake Neil. But just beyond the gate she found him huddled against the wall of the main house, cradling the day pack to his chest.

"Neil," she cried softly. "Are you . . . are you all right?"

He cleared his throat and squeezed his eyes shut. "Woke up a minute ago," he explained, grimacing. "Just followed the sound of your voices."

She took the pack and urged him in. "Come on. Let's go inside."

His skin felt cold and clammy to her touch, but he walked into the guest house without her help and sat on the hearth next to the fire. Vicki appeared at the door with a handful of old prescription vials—painkillers and such, a collection of first-aid supplies and a thermos filled with hot chicken broth. She gave Andrea a quick, encouraging pat on the back, then closed the door behind her as she left.

Andrea sorted through the pill bottles, selecting the most recent prescription for a reliable painkiller. She held the pills out to Neil with a cup of the broth. He took the pill, and she waited to make sure he got it down okay. Then she emptied the bowl of supplies and carried it, along with Neil's day pack, to the bathroom.

She spent a few moments washing. There were deep shadows under her eyes, and her hair needed brushing badly, but the hot washcloth did wonders to restore her.

Stripped out of her slacks, she sat on the side of the bathtub to pick stray pieces of glass from her left knee, then bathed the cuts. Shrugging out of her sweater and bra, she put on her nightshirt from the day pack. It left her legs bare, but the rooms were warm and her legs were nothing Neil hadn't seen plenty of already.

She filled the ceramic basin with hot, sudsy water and carried it out to the main room. Neil scooted over to the braided rug and let her have the hearth so she could have access to his head. The painkiller had already begun to ease the hammering. The rich scent of burning pine combined with the soft glow of the candle-lit room made him feel mellow.

And then there was Andrea, waiting on him, anticipating his needs, ready to tend his head wound, dressed in something he could have off her in two moves. He'd have to be blind or dead not to notice the slender lengths of her legs, or that she'd discarded her bra.

"Ready?" she asked.

He nodded, ready for more than her tending to him, and forced his eyes elsewhere. He flinched when she first applied the hot washcloth to his head. She bathed the dried blood from his hair and the scalp beneath, and when she had it clean enough to properly examine, she cried out softly.

"Oh, Neil. This is awful." *Awful* didn't describe the damage by half. The gash needed stitches, five at least.

Though a needle-and-thread kit were among her supplies, she didn't think he could tolerate the pain, and she had no anesthetic.

"It's fine. Just do the best you can. It'll heal." His head was spinning again, or the room was, and he thought maybe he'd been a little premature in thinking he was ready for more than her medical treatment. "Your knee looks pretty wicked. Don't forget to put something on that, too."

She tossed the soiled cloth back into the basin and reached for the Merthiolate and more gauze. "This is going to sting like crazy.... Hold on."

The antiseptic hit his raw nerve endings like a sledge-hammer, and he had to clamp his teeth shut to keep quiet. She held his head, and crooned and blew gently at the stinging, and crooned some more. When she stopped blowing, magically the burning eased off.

She picked two miniature butterfly bandages from the box and peeled the paper off the backs. Firelight glinted off the mahogany highlights of his hair where she parted it with a fingernail. She applied the tiny bandage, then another so that the edges of his head wound were pulled together.

"You're good at this. Gentle."

She laughed softly. "This wouldn't stand the scrutiny of an E.R. intern, but it'll have to do, I guess."

A quiet knock came at the door, and Andrea rose to answer it. Vicki Thornbloom delivered a tureen filled to the brim with steaming meat stew, and a tray with hot biscuits and butter and chokecherry jelly. She thought it was best if she never actually saw Neil, and she departed as soon as Andrea had the tray indoors.

Leaning against the hearth, his legs stretched out, Neil accepted the bowl of stew Andrea dished out, then buttered half a dozen biscuits. He'd consumed most of it before he felt half-alive again.

"Do you trust her?" he asked finally. "This relative of Piers?"

"Yes." She spread a biscuit with chokecherry jelly. He'd regained some color and seemed not to be in as much pain. But his question reminded her that he hadn't thought much at all of her judgment in calling Piers. "Do you think I shouldn't?"

"No." But it wasn't her question he answered so much as the underlying doubt. "Andrea, I'm sorry about what happened in the bar. The way I—"

"I know. But it isn't as if you didn't have cause. I should have told you before I called that Piers had left a message."

He felt he could listen now. "What did he say?"

Andrea touched the navy-colored cloth napkin to her lips and set aside her tray. "I told him that I'd been to Solter's house, so he knew what I must have seen. The vigilante setup. He called them the Cause."

Neil grimaced and rose to ladle another portion of stew into his bowl. "The Cause."

"Yes." She understood the contempt in his voice. They each sat quietly for several moments, while their spoons scraped steadily at their bowls of the rich beef stew.

At last Andrea set aside her china and silver. "Piers named names. Tyler, of course, and Brice. Jay Frost, who clerked at your trial, some state patrol. He warned me against the FBI, too. I assume that the minute an honest cop knows where we are, a well-placed Cause member knows also, state or federal."

Neil lost whatever appetite he had left. He'd have felt mellow in other circumstances, replete, able to lie back and appreciate her peaches-and-cream complexion in the firelight, her lovely green eyes. Her bare legs. But he knew their ploy to get out of Santa Fe unwatched must have failed. Someone had known exactly where they were headed and why, and he couldn't begin to imagine how he was going to get out of this one, or get her out.

The certainty wrecked the warm ambience. His head ached badly. "Go on."

Andrea sighed, weary to the bone of thinking this nightmare through to its inevitable conclusion. But if they had a chance at all, it would come of keeping one step ahead of Elbertson, and for that, they needed to examine every move.

"Okay. I would guess that all of them believe that vigilante rhetoric Brice was spouting, but Piers says Elbertson has gone over the edge. That every effort is focused on you—us. The order has gone out that we're to be tracked, but Elbertson wants the kill himself."

"The kill. Piers's word?"

"Yes."

Neil's oath came out on a whisper. "So Piers is scared. They're all scared. They've been feeding a monster who's feeding on them now."

Andrea nodded. "Exactly. Piers knows Elbertson—knows he was Solter's cousin."

Neil thought a moment about what else Piers knew, *why* else a man in his position as medical examiner would fall into a barrel teeming with bad apples. "Is Piers in this because he believes in it?"

Andrea swallowed. Old loyalty made her want to defend Piers. If Piers hadn't made the attempt to help, she'd never have come close to forgiving him his complicity. "No. He...made mistakes. I guess you could call them human mistakes."

If you were generous. Neil wasn't inclined to be anything of the sort. "Like what?"

"He's a doctor, Neil. Doctors close ranks. A friend of his, an orthopedic surgeon named Rod Bartlett, covered for his daughter's nanny, who fed Bartlett's baby a lethal dose of furosemide. Her father claimed the baby must have found the pills on the floor and ingested them herself. Mason believed Bartlett's story. He ruled the death accidental."

Neil shook his head and scraped at his beard with the backs of his fingers. It didn't even matter what had motivated the surgeon to protect the nanny. One doctor believes another, and he could see Piers buying into a friend's version of a terrible accident.

"So Piers's bad judgment is exposed," he speculated. "How? How did Solter come up with these things?"

Andrea shrugged. "We'll never know, except that he'd built a lifetime worth of contacts."

"But he was such a law-and-order freak. Why wouldn't he go after Bartlett?"

"Maybe he did. All he'd have to do was threaten Bartlett with one simple question in one column. 'What really happened to baby Melissa?' So Bartlett admits the nanny did it. Now Bartlett and Piers have to scramble to save their reputations."

"Or climb into bed with Solter and the Cause," Neil said. "Solter has Piers in his pocket for future reference, but then he's murdered. If we're right, and Elbertson murdered Solter, he has to intervene."

"A serious inquest could only hurt him—"

"So he uses Solter's leverage to force Piers to call off the investigation." Neil picked up his bowl again and began picking chunks of meat from the cooled stew. "How does Piers wind up blowing the whistle?"

"He hasn't. Not really. Warning me doesn't stop Elbertson."

"Do you think Piers even suspects it was Elbertson who killed Solter?"

Andrea got up and put her tray on the floor near the door. "I doubt it. But what if he does?"

"If he does, he took a big risk in warning you. Assuming Elbertson killed Solter and then took up where Solter left off with the vigilance committee, avenging Solter's death is the first order of business. What's to stop him from bumping Piers off for a traitor to the Cause?"

Andrea shuddered. If Neil was right, Mason Piers was in far more trouble than having to salvage his reputation. He could be next in line after Neil on Elbertson's hit list.

"I gathered that everyone Piers knows is busy covering their tracks. Elbertson wants vengeance, and he doesn't care who he takes down getting it. They're bailing out as fast as they can, Neil. Piers, too. Maybe calling me eased his conscience a little."

Neil just hoped Piers's gesture wasn't too little, too late. His throat thickened. His heart ached.

A piece of pine burned through and fell, sending a shower of sparks up behind him. He turned and reached for the poker to stir the coals, then tossed another log on the fire.

He felt like hell warmed over. The throb in his head was better but not absent, and his back ached—it would never quite be the same even under the best of conditions. And he needed a shower, for more reasons than one. "Mind if I take the bathroom first?"

"No. Please. Help yourself." She got up from her place atop the bed when he stood. "Neil, wait." She put herself between him and the bathroom long enough to take a pulse at his wrist.

His skin was heated, not feverish. She cupped his face in her hands, telling herself she had to evaluate his status. His eyes were bloodshot, and his pupils only slightly enlarged, but the intensity stunned her, and unwittingly, her fingers stroked his whiskers.

She wasn't naive or innocent in sex. She knew exactly how the birds and the bees did it. She knew about pheromones, hormones and endorphin chemistry.

But she knew nothing about the kind of desire she saw in his eyes, or why she felt so...aware of being the woman making him forget the gash in his head.

He never took his eyes from hers, but his hands went to her hips and he pulled her toward him. His thumbs found the points of her pelvis and circled them. His fingers splayed over her bottom, and he pulled her closer still until she felt the rigid measure of his arousal. All his strength and gentleness and honesty were condensed in that intimacy, and Andrea felt her senses overwhelmed.

His gaze drifted to her lips. He filled her world, and then he kissed the corners of her mouth, gently coaxing, urging. The rough, wet texture of his tongue touched the fullness of her bottom lip, seeking entrance. She heard her name whispered against her own lips before he took her mouth again.

A shiver passed through her. She was afraid—not of him, not of the kiss, but of how much she wanted him. Or how much it would hurt, surrendering to him, to the desire flaring between them, only to lose him when he no longer needed her.

Her moment's hesitation broke through the haze in his mind. It cost him, but Neil set her back, cocked his hands on his hips and stared at the floor. Of the two of them, he'd come to count on her to be the one to expect good things, lasting things. A tomorrow, and a tomorrow after that. When he spoke, his voice was hoarse, and pain had reclaimed his head. "I wouldn't hurt you, Andrea."

"No." Andrea closed her eyes. How ironic, to hear him use the word *hurt*. Did he think it didn't already hurt that he'd made her want more than he meant to offer? She swallowed, pursed her lips and tried to think how to be honest with him. "Not in the usual sense."

"How, then?"

"I'm a coward. I don't want to find out."

"You're a lot of things, but a coward isn't one of them." Lord, but his head hurt again, just to talk.

"You don't know me well enough to draw conclusions like that, Neil."

"You're wrong, Boo." But he didn't have the energy to list the ways.

She shook back her hair and ran her hand over the tangles that distressed her so. "Try not to get your hair wet, Neil. Your scalp wound won't tolerate it."

He caught her glance, then took her chin in his fingers to prevent her looking away again. "Are we going to pretend there's nothing happening between us?"

"It's asking too much, Neil, to expect—"

"The trick, sweet Andrea," he interrupted huskily, "is to know what you're asking for."

ASK, AND YE SHALL RECEIVE. Seek, and ye shall find.

Filled with the scorn wrought of a lifetime, Leif Elbertson stood inside his darkened house, staring out at the still darker shapes of his windmills in the night.

Ask? *A fool's errand,* he thought. All his life he had taken on the burdens of others. He had seen early in his misbegotten life that he possessed a potential so powerful, so expansive, so all-consuming that to waste it would have been criminal.

He reveled in power. At times he felt like a great mythic beast in the firmament, a constellation feeding on more than mere mortal beasts, growing stronger and larger and brighter, feeding on still more, ever-expanding into the heavens, dominating them until he should rise to challenge the sun itself for sheer stellar radiance. Such was the radiance and power he would train on the scum of the earth, enforcing natural law.

Only the fit survive.

But the good Dr. Vogel, pathetic former rising star of the still more pathetic medical examiner's office, threatened everything. His rage at her knew no bounds. What demon had possessed her? What unholy alliance had she made with a worm such as Neil Caulfield, the self-righteous prig?

He found her actions unimaginable. Traitorous. A vile echo of her boss, the weakling Mason Piers, who had not the conviction of a stone, or the will of a blade of grass.

Tyler. Frost. Piers. Cops too anxious to score. Surrounded by incompetence, by loyalties too thin to bear, by fearful sniveling fools, Elbertson was swamped with contempt.

John Brice. Now, there was a man of his word, a man who saw the Light, who knew what it meant to be loyal, to follow orders, to maintain standards, to hold fast in times of great adversity. John Brice. A true brother to the Cause. But even Brice, who had known Vogel and Caulfield would come snooping to Amarillo, who had managed to insert an APB into West Texas computers, who had put out the word that no one was to lay a hand on the pair of miscreants, even Brice had run up against a stone wall.

Brice had mistrusted Piers, whom he had watched, tailed, spied on and tapped. They knew that Piers had contacted Vogel. They knew he'd spilled his guts, revealing everything. *Everything.* They even knew that he'd offered her an impromptu safehouse. What they didn't know was *where*, but it was only a small matter of time.

Too bloody bad, but now Vogel would have to die with Caulfield.

Chapter Fourteen

When Andrea got out of the shower, Neil had fallen into a restless sleep.

She sat in her nightshirt for a while, staring into the flames, quietly searching for an answer to their plight. There seemed to be no safe retreat or advance, no way out, no possibilities left to them no matter how she rearranged the variables.

The realization left her feeling more vulnerable than she knew how to handle. Every other challenge in her life had lent itself to answers that led to reasonable actions. This time her answers proved more dangerous than knowing what questions to ask.

Before Neil had surfaced, she felt certain, Elbertson would have remained content to allow the threat of the vigilance committee to keep Neil underground. Now, though, they knew too much, and Elbertson could ill afford to let them live. A man who had murdered his own half brother wouldn't hesitate to kill again.

But of all the possibilities, of all the endings she could imagine, none affected Andrea more than the one that had Neil Caulfield bidding her goodbye. Her eyes watered, and her throat swelled. She sat there on the hooked rug in front of the hearth, her arms wrapped around her bare shins, and defied her tears.

The truth was, she couldn't stare into the fire long enough to vanquish that ending.

The fire died down in a spray of sparks as a small log burnt through. Andrea stoked the flames with more wood, a large, gnarled piece that would last awhile. She turned on a table lamp by the bedside, then stretched across the mattress to check on Neil.

His skin felt dry and warm to the touch. He apparently didn't appreciate her easing back his eyelids, but he didn't wake up, either. She knew his head must hurt very badly. At times he stirred and thrashed about and talked in his sleep.

His pupils were evenly dilated, though, and she began to worry a little less that he'd hemorrhaged into his head, or that the concussion would have any lasting effects.

She eased away to turn off the lamp, then curled up on top of the covers. The fire to her back, she watched the shadow play of firelight on Neil's head and shoulders and torso.

She would never tire of looking at him. Never. He wasn't a pretty man, or classically featured, but he was handsome and more ceaselessly male than any man she'd ever known.

The planes and angles of his forehead and cheeks and jaw were at once subtle and harsh. His hair grew sideways at the back of his neck. The sweep of muscle from his collarbone to the hard flat nipple buried in rich, almost black hair fascinated her.

Her fingers floated over his breast, no more than a feather touch skimming his chest hairs with her palm. Where he had stirred and thrashed, he became absolutely still. Where he had groaned, no sound escaped his throat.

She felt mesmerized by his silence, by the sensation that he was suspended in time and place, that he was hypnotized by her touch. She felt powerful and womanly in her ability to rouse him through no more than her barest touch.

With her eyes she had followed the path of her fingers hovering over him. Now she looked back at his face and found his eyes open, focused on her with such intensity that she lost the instinct to breathe.

He wanted her. He had a lump on his head the size of a child's fist, and a murderer after him, poised to kill. He had no reason to trust anyone, and yet he trusted her. More, he wanted her.

She began to pull back her hand, but she seemed invisibly bound, unable to move. He took her wrist and trapped her hand against the hard wall of his chest, and he never took his eyes off hers.

"Andrea." If his head hurt, he didn't know it anymore. The aches in him now were confined to the ones she stirred with her touch. "Don't . . . stop." His voice was thick with sleep, but his heart raced. He brought her hand where she could feel the rapid beating, then covered her chest with his hand, to feel the pulsing of her heart.

His hand was sure, gentle, and his fingers stroked her neck. "You know what you're asking, this time?"

She could only nod mutely, caught between the sensations he caused and the cautioning question he posed. But this time, she knew.

She saw that he was sad. But she didn't ask why. She knew. Life had taken everything dear to him and taught him how foolish it was to believe in whatever was lasting and good in return. Before Solter's murder, he'd fought back. He'd almost forgotten the bad parts.

Almost.

She wanted to make him forget the bad parts again, if only for a little while. Nothing more. She touched his whiskered jaw, then bent, slowly, to bring her mouth to his. She rubbed her cheek to his, then kissed him. He let her, trying to be still, to stay passive.

"Are you all right?" she asked him.

"Yes." *Don't do this,* he warned himself. He thought he understood her motives. She was scared, and she needed to be held. She'd seen him badly injured, and she needed to hold him. He just didn't think she understood—or had ever accepted—that going fugitive with him wasn't some noble refrain of ''you and me against the world.''

But her mouth was so sweet, and her kisses so warm and soft. Ah, God, but he wanted her.

''Andrea,'' he whispered, some part of him still needing to warn her. He guessed that in the end he must expect that somehow he would be cleared of Solter's murder, somehow vindicated, or he'd never have come back at all.

What he didn't believe was that there was a chance things would ever work out right for him and Andrea. He was attracted to her as to no woman he'd ever known, but his life was a wreck, and the last thing he wanted was to use her for some cheap sexual liaison. ''I don't want to hurt you.''

''You won't,'' she promised him. He no longer needed her. She knew that. Every moment he spent looking out for her safety was a moment he wasn't concentrating on his own. She understood that.

It was his hopelessness that hurt her heart.

She trailed her fingers again over his torso, molding her hand to the masculine shapes and contours of his chest. She felt the slight trembling in his body and in her own. She had never wanted a one-night stand, but before Elbertson's brand of evil justice caught up with them again, she would give him something to believe in.

He shivered with the pleasure of her touch. Mirroring her, he drew his hand down her chest. His fingers spanned both her breasts. He touched her in small circles, his palm to her nipples. A fire began to spread beneath her skin.

''Oh, Neil . . .''

She started to unbutton her shirt, but he took her hand away. ''Let me.'' He pushed himself up and discarded his briefs and bunched pillows behind his back, then took her hand and guided her astride his thighs. He looked into her eyes and held her hand with one of his, stroking her knuckles with his thumb, and undid buttons with the other.

Twelve buttons before he was done. She watched his fingers. Her breathing grew shallow as a child's. Twelve buttons. She felt wild with the need to be touched. Twelve.

He parted the shirt then, beginning at her collar. His fingers guided the fabric back from her collarbone, past her breast, dragging it over her nipple, pulling it past the fullness of her breast. Then he was done, and she saw the wildness in him, and she smiled, thrilled at the moan of desire he gave.

"You're so beautiful." He raised his knees, and she slid into him, and the friction of the hair on his legs against hers made her breath catch in her throat.

He let go of her hand and touched her heated, throbbing core and traced a nipple with his lips, then the other nipple with his tongue. He brought her to the edge again and again. Then he eased her panties aside, and when he entered her she looked into his eyes and her surprise filled him.

He moved, thrusting into her, wanting all she had to give to him. "It's so good with you," he murmured. "So damn good."

She clung to him, to his shoulders, thinking how special this was. How extraordinary, she kept thinking, her wanting, her need for this, with him. She fitted herself against him as if it were their thousandth time, instead of their first. She loved the smell of him, the sounds of their bodies together, the look of him, the feel of him.

"Neil," she whispered. "Neil."

"Andrea."

Even then, he worried. Don't be sorry, sweet Andrea, he thought. Please, God, don't be sorry. He cupped her face with his hands, and kissed her deeply. *What if we had forever? What if I loved you?*

But he didn't say it, only tried to make her feel forever instead. There was such a need in him—that he might love her, that this might be his only time with her.

He leaned forward and enfolded her in his arms, crushed her to him and rocked her, back and forth, back and forth, and he never once noticed the aching in his head.

When they peaked, when he brought her to pleasures higher and more exquisite than she'd ever imagined, then she truly was sorry, for these few hours could never have been enough.

SHE WOKE AT DAWN, huddled in his arms beneath blankets and the thick, downy comforter, her hand resting lightly on his bare hip. She didn't think he was asleep.

She covered his hand, which cupped her breast, with her own. How could the night have passed so quickly?

"Neil?"

"Mmm. Don't move." His head ached like crazy, but it was nothing compared to the need in him to hold her.

He endured her sleepy, insistent orientation questions one more time. His head hurt, yes. It wasn't unbearable, no. He knew who he was, he knew where he was, he knew how he had gotten there. She didn't ask, but he also knew how he had come to hold her through the night like this. How he felt.

He wanted to mention that, but he didn't. Who was he kidding? *I love you, sweet Boo.... By the way, do you want to pull another gangster-style getaway today?*

He didn't want to think about that now, or about what an ass he'd been to put her in the path of the vigilance committee.

"Do you need more painkillers, Neil?"

He drew her closer. Her body felt soft and warm against him. "I'll let you know."

What he needed was a way to get her out of Leif Elbertson's cross hairs.

IN THE END IT WAS Clerk of the County Court Jay Frost who came through.

Leif Elbertson stood poised on the deck of his fortress, aiming idly at a hapless doe antelope through the cross hairs of the scope on his Smith & Wesson rifle when the map came through on his fax machine.

A map. How gloriously concise. *X* marked the spot. Up one county road, down another. Thornbloom was the name. The maiden moniker of Cindy, wife to the whining traitor, the medical examiner himself, Mason Piers.

How he hated whiners!

Piers. Another instance of the immutable laws of the universe at work—there was a sucker, a *fool,* born every second of every minute. The world could tolerate just so many fools before it collapsed under the collective weight. Every great civilization in the history of mankind had crumpled in the wake of the fools it so vaingloriously suffered.

Well, *this* civilization would not topple, he vowed. He had only to look around him for the proof. Black against white, man against woman, rich against poor, fundamental good against the ever-more-pervasive evil. There was a terrible backlash coming in this society, and he, *Elbertson,* stood at the pinnacle.

It was his duty, his highest moral obligation, to rid this society of its pretenders, the ones who gave lip service to the righteous while they whored around in every imaginable arena—sex to politics to banking to housing. There were many, many pretenders more important than Neil Caulfield, but few were so sly and none so urgent to dispatch.

Dispatch.

Such an elegant, sanitary term for a final solution. Neil Caulfield and his Louisiana doxy pretender bitch must be *dispatched.*

The very survival of the Cause itself depended upon it. Stellar strategist that he was, he trusted no one but himself with the task.

WHEN ANDREA WOKE AGAIN it was nearly three o'clock in the afternoon and Neil was out of bed, in the shower. The shuttered window let in almost no light, but the fire had been prodded back to life with a little care and a few pieces of hardwood kindling.

Languorous, she stretched, and scooted into the still-warm impression left by Neil's body. The warmth and scent of him lingering on the bed linens evoked stirring, vivid memories in her body, and she ached. His mouth, his tongue, his fingers, his sex—every liberty was an intimacy she had given him.

She listened to him turn off the shower, and to the silence that followed. He wasn't one to sing in the shower, she'd never heard him whistle, and other than to murmur her name, he'd barely made a sound making love to her.

Was he so outwardly solemn by nature, or had his months on the run made him so deadly quiet? She had never been boisterous, but she hummed to herself and sang with the songs she liked on the radio. She regarded such sounds as human and life-affirming and joyous.

It only drove home to her the differences between them.

The sight of him emerging from the bathroom dressed only in his jeans stiffened her resolve. He needed her, and would need her long after these days and hours were a memory. She would be there.

She sat up in the bed, drawing the sheet up with her to cover herself, and leaned against the slatted headboard. "How are you?"

"A shower helps." He followed her shape beneath the comforter with his eyes, and his gaze lingered on her full breasts. He swallowed. "You . . . help."

He took the towel from around his naked shoulders and rubbed gently at his head. "I'll live, I think. What about you?"

She smiled. She could see the lump on his head from here, but it didn't seem to affect him, or take anything away from him. And it was a start, that they wouldn't pretend nothing special had happened between them last night. "Me, too."

He sat on the stone hearth. "We have to get out of here, Andrea."

She wondered if that were true. If he intended to send her home. "And go where?"

He let the towel fall back around his shoulders and drew a deep breath. "Nothing has really changed. The best thing is still for us to separate. You—"

"No."

He'd expected a protest, but not her flat refusal. "No?"

"No. I've changed my mind. I don't think we should separate. The Cause is disintegrating, Neil. All we have to do is help it out—wait it out. The whole operation is bound to fall apart soon—"

"None of that matters." Elbertson was still out there. Could she believe for one minute that he didn't intend to succeed, with or without his vigilance committee?

"Of course, it matters! We could go to Judge Medina and expose the vigilance committee—or the news media, for that matter. We could have Miri hire legal counsel to splatter a protest of the Zolgen deal with Brightmark all over the papers, and file suit to recover your patent. Mason will help us, Neil. I know he will. He—"

"Is probably dead right now," Neil interrupted harshly. "Dead, Andrea. He betrayed the Cause. He betrayed Elbertson. Do you think he has a snowball's chance in hell after that?"

He watched the color drain from her sweet, heart-shaped face, and felt like a brute. It wasn't in her to think of such things, to even conceive that a man she so clearly trusted and liked despite his grave mistakes could die for doing the right thing. Goose bumps broke out on her arms, and her beautiful bowed lips compressed to a bleak, thin line.

Things still had the potential for disaster. Neil could have cited her chapter and verse; more essentially good people were already circling the drain. But he couldn't stand to see her so crushed, and he relented.

"You're right, Andrea. All of those things need to happen."

She broke off her stricken gaze and gave a quick shake of her head. He got up from the hearth, jerked off the towel and left it lying where it dropped. He sat on the side of the bed and took her into his arms. He didn't know what it was like to have enough faith in humanity to be shaken, but he knew he didn't like what it had done to her.

Her arms went around his neck, and the sheet fell away to her waist. She pressed herself tightly to his body. Her forehead rested against his shoulder, and her softly rounded bare breasts flattened against him. She was so small.

Parting from her would be the hardest thing he'd ever done, and the things that needed to be said hurt him. He stroked her silky, raven-black hair and breathed in the scent of it. "If you go back, you'll be safe. The vigilance committee won't lay a finger on you—or Elbertson, for that matter—if you make them believe I'm coming back for you."

Make them believe... Her arms tightened around him for an instant, then fell away. She had first to make herself believe. She leaned back. Her breasts were uncovered. He couldn't help looking, and she knew that.

"Don't do this, Boo."

"Will you be back for me, Caulfield?" Maybe she wanted him to look. Maybe she wanted him to take her again, to make love to her again. Or maybe she wanted him to fill himself with the need of her, so that he would come back for her, because otherwise, she simply didn't believe him.

Neil swallowed, and the air fled from his lungs. He couldn't take his eyes off her. Her nipples were dark, honey-hued and swollen, and he so ached to kiss her, to taste her, his own flesh filled and hardened unbearably.

She saw then what it took for him not to touch her. She felt awash in sudden, selfish shame. It crippled him to want her; she'd never in her life done anything so wanton and shabby, and she drew the sheet upward to cover herself.

"Neil, I'm . . . I'm sorry."

His fist uncurled. He touched his fingertips to her lips to silence her, then touched her through the linen barrier. "Not me." He grinned shortly, and when the smile faded he looked into her eyes and thumbed her tender, aching areolae through the fabric until she gave a soft cry. "Speaking for myself, sweet Boo, I've never had—" he cupped her "—so much . . . reason for coming back."

She nodded solemnly. "Then I'll go home, and make them believe."

SHE SHOWERED AND DRESSED in clean jeans and an ancient Tulane University sweatshirt. She'd promised Neil to do as he asked . . . go home, play the part of the waiting woman, and in the meanwhile, do everything she could think of to destroy the vigilance committee that was Solter's legacy and his brother's most powerful weapon.

She opened the bathroom door and asked Neil to bring her hairpins. She'd agreed, but she hadn't promised to like it. She dashed a tear from her cheek, then pulled her wet hair into a knot at the top of her head. Neil leaned in the doorway watching her, and held out the pins.

"I'll never speak to you again if you get yourself killed."

A corner of his lips curved up in a tender smirk. "Never is a very long time, Vogel."

"Well, I mean it."

"Of course you do. Your prissy little bun's off center, you know."

"It is not." But she twisted this way and that, trying to see in the mirror. "Is it?"

"Never mind." He reached out and scooped a handful of her sweatshirt and pulled her close to him. He held her for at least the tenth time since he'd sworn it was the last, and she clung to him. He needed some diversion badly. "D'you think we could get something to eat?"

"I'm sure." She straightened and left his arms, sensing he wouldn't touch her again. She searched through the day pack for keys to the Valiant. "Do you feel all right to drive?"

He nodded, and took the keys when she found them.

"Okay, then. I'll go see Vicki about some food, and I'll meet you at the car?"

Again Neil nodded, then watched her dart up the path to the main house. He shouldered his pack and took one last look around the room, at the English ivy draped over the window and the pine cones in a basket on the mantel. He'd never been one for nostalgia, but he wouldn't ever forget this gracious little bungalow where he'd made love to Andrea Vogel.

Andrea got into the Valiant, divvied out roast beef sandwiches Vicki had already prepared, then kept a watch on the bungalow in the side-view mirror. By dusk they were nearly to the cattle guard in the road and she could no longer see the old Greek Revival-style dwelling.

They went another quarter mile when a single rifle shot exploded into the car's right front tire.

Neil swore and jerked the wheel hard to the left, but the battered little car spun off the country road and crashed head-on into the culvert.

Chapter Fifteen

The car pitched into the solid earth of the barrow pit wall, and Andrea was thrown forward. Instinctively she threw her hands out in front of her to save herself from the terrible impact, but she became trapped on her knees on the floor of the car.

The eerie silence was broken by two more shots slamming into the old car, one at Neil's door, the second at the decades-old windshield. The glass was brittle, shattering in every direction. Dozens of tiny shards were driven into Andrea's cheek and she screamed.

Neil couldn't believe his vile luck—nor could he stomach the blood on Andrea's cheek. He shoved her still lower with his right hand and jerked at his door handle with the other. It was jammed tight by the wrenching crash and the earth as the car listed to the left side.

He swore again and threw himself upward, across Andrea's side of the bench seat, trying for her door. Another shot tore into metal toward the rear of the car, and he expected the bullet to set off an explosion in the gas tank. He braced for the blast, then lunged at the door again when it failed to happen.

It took him two more superhuman efforts to reach the door and force it open against the pull of gravity, anchoring himself with his foot against the steering wheel. "Get up, Andrea. For God's sake, get out!"

She struggled upward, fueled by fear and adrenaline pouring through her body, but the effort to pull herself free proved too great, and Neil all but threw her out.

She fell awkwardly to the ground, and in another instant fell again as Neil leaped from the car and covered her body with his.

"It's got to be Elbertson." Instincts fired in him at a frenzied pitch. Both right wheels of the Valiant were off the ground and spinning slowly, and he knew the smashed-up car, turned half on its side, blocked the firing line of the rifle shots.

There was one chance in ten that they'd get away from the car before the shooter managed to make it blow, and one chance in a hundred of escaping the bullets if they escaped the explosion.

Neil gauged the distance to the other side of the barrow pit and the deep cut of a dry creek bed, then dragged Andrea with him, lunging and stumbling over the side. Another shot bit into the dirt, then ricocheted inches from their heads, a fraction of a second after their fall.

Shaking uncontrollably, Andrea hiccuped and swiped at her cheek. Her hand came away bloody, and she hiccuped again, fighting off the panic and revulsion the sight of her own blood caused her. Again she hiccuped. "Neil—"

He shook her shoulders and made her look at him. "Andrea, stop it now and listen to me! Can you do that? Can you listen to me?"

She clapped a hand to her mouth to silence the frantic little cries accompanying every breath, and nodded.

Neil's heart twisted in his chest over her gesture, but he had no time to waste thinking what this woman meant to him. He jerked up the leg of his Levi's and pulled out his .32 automatic pistol.

"I want you to stay here, *right* here, and count to a hundred. I'm going to make a run for it, to decoy the bastard in the other direction." He saw the protest rising in her eyes, and gave a warning shake of his head. "It's our only chance, Boo."

"Neil, you can't possibly—"

"Make it two hundred—that'll give me something over three minutes—then run as fast as you can, back to Vicki's. I'll try to circle around and take her old pickup, but you'll have to be gone by then, do you understand? Both of you, or he'll kill all three of us. Get on a bus for Albuquerque and make sure Vicki stays clear of here for tonight, at least."

Still helplessly shaking, plagued by her hiccups, she had no trouble understanding his intentions or his plan, but for the first time in her life, she knew what it meant to feel hopeless. Between them, Neil was the expert survivor, and she would do what he told her no matter what.

"Where shall I go?"

"Solter's place," he said without hesitation. "If they've dismantled their operations, it's the last place they'll look. Give me forty-eight hours—"

A barrage of shots rang out in quick succession, and in nearly the same instant the bullets spewed up the earth, tearing into the eroded, age-old riverbank above them. Neil covered her again with his body as clumps of dirt rained down on them.

In the aftermath they heard triumphant, crazed laughter, and Neil knew that Elbertson was firing not because he had them clearly in his sights, but for the sheer terror value.

Neil sat up and grimaced, pointed his gun overhead and back, and fired. Elbertson's tactics gave him away, and for the first time, Neil took heart. A professional, practiced, *clever* assassin would just do the job and walk away.

Andrea didn't understand why he'd responded that way, wasting a bullet. "Neil?"

He smiled, a bittersweet kind of smile, and rested his head back against the embankment. "He's playing with me. He's a fool, and it won't hurt him to think I'm running scared."

She gave a small cry and reached out to touch his face. "Aren't you ... scared?"

He took her hand and kissed her fingers. "Yeah. But I'll make it back to you, Andrea. I promise."

He threw himself over the opposite edge of the dry creek embankment and lit out in a crouching run with only the brush for cover. It occurred to him at the last possible second that Elbertson might go for Andrea instead, and Neil figured he had to take that option away from Elbertson.

He made a moving target of himself, scrambling on a parallel course with the creek bed. Elbertson fell for the ploy and fired at Neil, and the earth spit dust at his heels where the first bullet hit.

"You're a dead man, Caulfield. A dead man!" Elbertson shouted, taunting. "You've never been anything more than a buffoon, a cretin in a league of bleeding hearts, and now, boy, you never will!"

Forty. Forty-one. Counting, drawing ragged, torn, ineffectual breaths, Andrea shuddered violently. She lost sight of Neil, and the odd, jeering diatribe chilled her to the bone. But she knew Neil must be still on his feet.

No one would bother mocking a dead man.

Still racked with hiccups, Andrea shivered hard. The night air was chilly, the sun was nearly down. She clasped her bloodied hands together and forced herself to count. *Eighty. Eighty-one. Eighty-two.* She made it to ninety-seven before another rifle shot echoed back, and a count of one hundred and thirty before another small barrage came.

At two hundred she was on her feet and running. Neil had accomplished what he'd set out to do, decoying Elbertson away from her and Vicki Thornbloom, and now she had to do her part. A stitch caught at her side, but she kept a killing pace until she topped the rise and could see Thornbloom. The sight of Vicki, bundled in a heavy white sweater and pacing her galley worriedly, gave Andrea the impetus to keep going. Another hundred yards.

Just another hundred. The sun set. The darkness came on quickly, but she headed for the porch light.

One more muted shot rang through the chilly night air. Andrea crumpled to the ground fifteen feet short of Vicki Thornbloom's front door.

"My Lord, child!" she cried, dashing to Andrea, bending over her. "Are you all right? What happened to your cheek? I could have sworn I heard rifle shots! What's going on?"

Her hiccups were gone now, but Andrea was on her knees in the dust for several seconds before she could catch her breath enough to answer. "Vicki, there's no time—"

"Of course there's time, child," Vicki interrupted, cupping Andrea's grimy, bloodied face with her warm hands. "Of course there is. We need to get you inside where it's warm and safe, and clean up your cheek. My *heaven,* your cheek looks just awful!"

"Vicki, listen to me!" Andrea took hold of her hands and shook her. "Those *were* rifle shots, and they are no accident. There's a man out there who means to kill us all, and we have to leave here!"

Vicki straightened. Mason had told her how serious the situation was. She had lived a lonely, self-sufficient life, and even this news didn't set her back much. She planted both hands on her knee and pushed herself to her feet, then assisted Andrea up. "Where's your young man?"

NEIL WENT DOWN with the last shot Andrea heard. The bullet tore a hole the size of a grapefruit in his jeans and carved a deep, jagged furrow over muscle and ligaments in the calf just below his right knee.

But the bullet didn't lodge, and the streaking fiery trail of pain only made him move faster. He rolled behind a clump of mesquite, then off a canyonlike wall, a fall of three or four feet.

The fall jolted his leg and sent pain screaming through him. He stamped his foot and gnashed his teeth, but the nausea racked him. He sniffed, dragging his left sleeve across his sweaty brow, and took those few precious seconds to plan another hundred yards.

The Thornbloom woman lived within spitting distance of the northwest end of the Palo Duro Canyon park. Anywhere else in and around the plains surrounding Amarillo, and he'd have been down in the first five minutes. Down for good.

Between the dark and the rugged landscape on the edge of the canyon lands, he had a chance. His head was killing him and now his leg was ripped up and bleeding like all hell, but Elbertson had tired of the game and the jeering. Neil figured he had an hour's worth of consciousness left in him, and a quarter of an hour back to Thornbloom's pickup.

He'd kept relentlessly to the cracked, dry creek bed. Outside the brush and scarce vegetation, it provided some decent cover. Even when it hadn't, he'd stayed close, establishing a pattern, giving Elbertson every reason to believe he wouldn't risk another course.

Neil listened for a clue to Elbertson's position, but he heard nothing to give away the presence of another human being in the dark Texas night. The pain from hip to ankle was almost overwhelming now, and he knew he couldn't come out of another minute's inactivity.

He crammed his .32 automatic into the waistband of his jeans and hauled himself back over the dry, wind-eroded bank. He scrambled through brush and weeds, moving forward on his forearms and knees, willing himself beyond feeling the pain, focusing every scrap of his attention on his yard-by-yard progress.

He counted off what ought to be twenty yards, then rolled over and lay on his back, listening for pursuit. He let another half minute pass, then picked up a clod of dirt, rose for an instant on his knees and hurled the clod southward with everything in him. It fell downstream of the creek bed. He heard a rustling noise in the brush maybe thirty yards to the north.

With any shred of luck at all, Elbertson would pass him by. He was clearly a decent marksman, but he hadn't come prepared to track his quarry. It had been a crucial mistake to give Neil half a chance, and he thought Elbertson must be cursing himself by now.

Live and learn, sucker. Ignoring the roar of pain in his head and his leg, belly-crawling, Neil strained to listen for Elbertson. When he saw the solid dark outline of Thornbloom's roof, he didn't give a damn anymore where Elbertson was.

He'd made Andrea a promise he intended to keep. He got to his feet and ran through the thickets and brush and into Thornbloom's pickup.

Reaching beneath the steering column and dashboard for the wires to bypass the ignition, he ran his nose right into the keys. The humor of the situation struck him before he slumped sideways and passed out cold.

VICKI HUSTLED ANDREA INTO her car, then went inside for her keys. Andrea got in and let her head rest against the seat back. Her hiccups were back and her abdomen ached. She couldn't think what she should do next, but Vicki seemed to be handling it all. In a little while, she promised herself, she'd go to work on a plan.

Vicki drove like a madwoman, and when she saw the smashed-up little Valiant in the ditch, her lips compressed into a thin, angry line. She sped past the car, and minutes later headed north on Canyon Drive, finally exiting for the access road near town. Several blocks off, she pulled up in front of an old tract house with a nearly unreadable sign in Spanish hanging from its porch.

"Estella Marquez," Vicki told her. "An old friend. She sells tamales and green chili, and she'll let you use her bathroom."

Vicki purchased a carton of green chili and flour tortillas and then spoke quietly with her friend. Andrea found the tiny bathroom. The porcelain had been chipped or worn away in the sink, and the mirror had given way to large rusty patches, but the bathroom was clean and the hot water was exquisite. Andrea rinsed away the worst of the grime and blood from her hands and face. Her cheek did look awful.

She knew plastic surgeons who would take her to surgery in an instant to deal with the glass shards in her cheek. As a child of three or four she'd fallen on wooden steps and come up with the palms of her hands covered in splinters. Her mother had refused to let her colleagues anywhere near Andrea's hands.

In a few days, the skin had sloughed off the layer of childish skin infested with splinters. God willing, her cheek would do the same.

But her bloodied cheek was the least of her concerns.

Something had gone terribly wrong. She'd known from the second she fell at Vicki's feet and heard that last shot. Neil had been hit. She didn't know how badly he was hurt, or if he were dead.

He wasn't dead. He couldn't be. But what about the next time, or the time after that? Elbertson had to be stopped; she had to find a way.

She accepted a woolen poncho and an old felt-fur hat from Vicki's trunk. Vicki helped her put on the blanketlike coat and settled the hat on her head. Andrea forced herself to eat half the carton of green chili and a couple of the small flour tortillas while Vicki drove to the Trailways station on Tyler Street.

Vicki had already left the key to her pickup in the ignition for Neil, and a couple of hundred-dollar bills. She pulled her sedan to a stop at the curb to leave Andrea off and handed her another hundred in twenties.

"Vicki, this is too much—"

She gave a quick shake of her head. "Your ticket home will eat up most of it. What else is an old broad like me to do with her money, anyway?"

Andrea smiled briefly and reached out to squeeze Vicki's hand. "A bus ticket is one thing, Vicki. Your truck is another. I don't know what will become of it—"

"Doesn't matter," Vicki declared flatly. "Doesn't mean a hill of beans." She fell silent for several long moments. "I was a bit of a hellion, Andrea. One nasty scrape after another. Mason Piers was there for me every time—and saving my behind was never cheap, I can tell you. He never could abide a friend's troubles."

Hot tears stung at Andrea's eyes for Mason Piers. He hadn't been able to abide her troubles, either, and now he might well be dead. "Vicki...I...Mason—"

"I know." Her eyes trained on a derelict heading into the bus station, Vicki pursed her lips and gave a short, sharp sigh. "I've been trying to reach my sister all day long."

Andrea guessed Vicki had long ago thought about what might happen to Mason—which didn't prepare her for losing her sister. "I'll try, too," she promised. She didn't think the vigilance committee, or even Elbertson, would go so far as to kill Cindy, but reassuring Vicki now seemed a hollow, pointless gesture.

"I'll be staying at the Hyatt for a few days." Vicki planted her hands on the steering wheel and stared straight ahead. "I'd appreciate it very much if you can get the message to my sister."

Andrea murmured her assent, then slipped quietly out of Vicki Thornbloom's car and watched her drive away. Andrea's own complicated emotions were riding too high, especially her feelings for Neil Caulfield and her fears for him. She could understand Vicki's need to hide her emotions.

She made her way into the terminal, purchased her ticket from a disinterested clerk, then found a seat in the waiting room, where there were few other people nearby. She drew her legs up in front of her body on the seat, settled the poncho around herself like a tent and let her head rest on her knees.

It was only eight o'clock, and she had well over an hour to wait.

Huddled in her seat, Andrea felt her wrist for her mother's gold bangle. It wasn't there. She remembered now that she hadn't worn it since before the hike to Solter's place. She knew that the bracelet was only a symbol of strength, but she really needed such tokens right now.

She felt scared and bereft. Though defiance was Andrea's ingrained answer to adversity, just as it had been for her mother, she had no special gift for intrigue. But she wouldn't die. She had to prove to Neil Caulfield that she could survive, and she would.

She thought the wizened old man taking tickets gave a double-take when he saw her, and that the driver couldn't stop looking at her. But no matter how curious they seemed, no one made a move in her direction.

She thought she knew why. Long after she boarded the nine-thirty Trailways bus headed west out of Amarillo, she was still thinking of Mason Piers's last words to her. Elbertson wanted her dead, and the fact that no one came near her only proved he wanted to kill her himself.

THE POLICE AT THE OTHER end of her five-hour bus ride were anxious. Andrea K. Vogel, the former deputy medical examiner, was wanted, but not *Wanted*. That kind of crap went on all the time. What made this unusual was the jurisdiction problem—that, and the fact that the assistant district attorney out of Santa Fe, Janine Tyler, insisted on driving Vogel from the bus station in Albuquerque back to Santa Fe herself. With a police escort, of course.

There were so many violations of procedure here, not one of the cops wanted to touch the scenario with a ten-foot pole. The safest thing was to let the assistant district attorney have her way, drive an escort the sixty miles and forget the whole thing.

The bus arrived at 1:30 a.m., taking into account the return to mountain standard time. Andrea had slept sporadically, her sleep haunted by visions of that billy club shattering the car window, glancing off Neil's head.

Fatigue claimed her. She felt disoriented and vague, and she wondered whether she would wake in time to catch the first morning bus back to Santa Fe if she fell asleep in the Albuquerque station.

Janine Tyler was the last person on earth she'd have expected, but the moment she got off the bus Andrea caught sight of Tyler with a cadre of uniformed officers. Defiance rose in her, and she forgot how tired she was.

"Janine. How kind of you to arrange a ride home for me. The layover was going to be a killer."

Tyler pursed her lips, deliberately choosing to ignore the sarcasm. "You look like hell, Andrea."

"Maybe that's because I've been through hell in the last forty-eight hours." She took off Vicki's hat and, with her fingers, combed her hair, which was thick with blood and tangles. She'd intended to clean up a bit in the bathroom on the bus, but had never quite summoned the energy. "What do you want, Janine?"

Tyler took her by the arm and began walking toward the exit of the bus depot. "We have to talk. Now. It can't wait."

Andrea kept putting one foot in front of the other, but she had no intention of talking. "I have nothing to say to you in any capacity, Janine. Arrest me if you like, but I still won't have anything to say that you'd want to hear."

"Then you can listen." They'd arrived at Tyler's car, the police following at a close range, and Janine unlocked the passenger door, then opened it. "Get in."

"I don't think so."

Tyler swallowed and stepped back, letting go of Andrea's arm. "Andrea... please."

"Janine... please," Andrea mocked. "Do you really expect me to trust you? I'll ride with the nice policemen."

Tyler all but stamped her foot. At nearly two o'clock in the morning, under the unflattering lights of the bus terminal parking lot, the assistant district attorney didn't look her best, either. There was something almost desperate in her hushed insistence. "Andrea, there's a great deal more at stake here than you know!"

"What, pray tell?" Neil's life was at stake, but Andrea only gave an impassive stare and challenged the assistant district attorney again. "Or is it that you're afraid of what I *do* know?"

Tyler hadn't thrived in the D.A.'s office on faint-hearted instincts, and Andrea knew that. There was no point in trying to back Tyler into a corner, or in tipping her own hand to disclose everything she and Neil had discovered.

But there was no way, either, knowing Janine Tyler's ties to the Cause, that Andrea would ride with her. "Don't force the issue, Janine, or I'll simply become so violent that one of the cops will have to ride along with us, anyway."

She turned on her heel and walked straight to the policemen waiting on the assistant district attorney, opened a squad-car door and got in.

Tyler held a terse conference with the officers, apparently conceding to Andrea's demand. She heard Tyler tell the officers to meet her at the offices back in Santa Fe. Tyler's anger and embarrassment were obvious from her gestures and tone, and Andrea gave a silent hurrah.

The ploy bought her an hour to think and something of a psychological edge, but once in Santa Fe, neither small advantage relieved the stark reality that she was to be held at Tyler's whim to the full extent of time allowed by the law.

The two of them faced off again in a spare, windowless interrogation room one floor away from Tyler's office. Andrea knew some of Neil's worst nightmares were set in rooms exactly like this. *Please, God, Neil. Make it back.*

The assistant district attorney sat across a six-by-eight table from her. Her eyes were as bloodshot as Andrea's, and her voice seemed meager. Tired. Even conciliatory. "Do you know how much trouble you're in, Andrea?"

"I have a fair idea." Andrea gestured toward her bruised and bloodied cheek as if the injury alone proved how dangerous her situation was. "Do you?"

"These things happen when you resist arrest—"

"That's not how this happened, Janine."

Tyler grimaced. "None of that matters now, Andrea," she snapped. "The fact of the matter is, you have stolen files belonging to the county, harbored a fugitive, aided and abetted Caulfield's escape time and again. I could lock you up now and throw away the key for twenty years, and any jury in the land would make it stick."

"But you won't, will you? Because it's Caulfield you need to apprehend, and if I land in jail, you'll never see him again."

Tyler got up from the straight-back chair in anger. "Are you threatening me now, as well?"

Exhaustion took its toll on her reactions, and Andrea flinched. "No. I'm not threatening you—or telling you anything you don't already know. If anything happens to me, Neil Caulfield will disappear forever."

Tyler sat down again and took a deep breath. "Look, Andrea. Let's make this easy on both of us. Tell me where Neil Caulfield is, and I'll drop all charges we might make against you."

"Dead—or dodging bullets." If Elbertson had succeeded in killing Neil, wouldn't Tyler already know? "Can I go now?"

"Andrea—" Tyler closed her eyes momentarily and gave a sigh "—please. I know it's late, I know you're tired and hurt, I know—"

"Hurt, Janine?" Andrea cried. "You don't live in the real world at all, do you?" Tyler might be a prosecuting attorney, but all she regularly saw of violence was summed up in police photos. She was stuck in some safe, abstract little world where people didn't bleed and die, they were . . . *hurt*. "Tell me this, Janine. Was the Solter murder prosecution assigned to you or did you ask for it?"

Tyler sat stonily, refusing to react. "I hardly think that matters at all."

"No more than the truth," Andrea said. "In the end, all that matters is what the jury can be made to believe, isn't that right? No matter who suffers, or who pays? No matter what the truth?"

"I had motive, opportunity and method dead to rights," she answered wearily. "I believed that Neil Caulfield committed that murder, I prosecuted, and I would have won a conviction."

"No doubt garnering the highest praise of law-and-order patriots the world over."

Tyler's chin rose defensively. "Yes."

Andrea cast her a pitying glance. "You'd have won the same attention prosecuting the *right* man, Janine."

Chapter Sixteen

The night was dark as sin, the landscape hellish, and Elbertson stumbled. His heart squeezed tightly in his chest, and for a moment, he couldn't breathe.

He despised such subtle reminders of his mortality. Had he survived so long, come so far, overcome such adversity only to fade ignominiously away? To let Caulfield wreck the makings of a true and just society?

No. Nothing worth achieving ever came simple. Injustice had plagued him from the moment of his birth, but he was stronger for it. More powerful. Forceful enough to restore order where there was none, to bring light where darkness reigned, to achieve what human beings had dreamed of but never achieved.

True and lasting justice.

He was a rising star in the firmament of the heavens; it was the first and most telling revelation he'd ever experienced, that as a boy of eight, lying in his meager bed, staring out the window in the tar paper walls of his bedroom, he was bound for greatness. Such elegant reversals, such peripeteias, made one truly appreciate life.

He dusted off the knees of his pants and continued on in the pitch black. Of a certainty, he'd jeopardized his own grand scheme by toying with Caulfield. The scum had escaped, somehow eluded the instrument of his own death, one more time.

But, Elbertson decided, trudging along, no longer making the effort to proceed unheard and unseen, it would have made for an inelegant conclusion to this episode to have been given a maladroit adversary to vanquish.

Besides, he might now relish a little longer the thrill of victory, for it was of an equal certainty that Caulfield would not survive long. His chemical invention was an insult to the survival of the most lowly, and his actions were an affront to the natural laws of the universe.

The profits of the fiendishly ill-conceived work, Zolgen, had been funneled from the dummy corporation to the efforts of the Cause. Yet another in a long line of the aesthetically pleasing reversals he had engineered.

Peripeteia Enterprises.

At last he reached his four-wheel-drive vehicle. He was mightily tempted to torch the Thornbloom property, to punish the succorer of his enemy, but he saw no finesse in it. Days ago, his anger had made him promise retribution, but he had risen above such petty, destructive inclinations, intent now upon the restoration of order.

Caulfield must die, of course, as must Vogel, though not before he confronted them. Not before they understood and appreciated the most beloved of his peripeteias....

JANINE TYLER'S HANDS were tied. They had been from the start. Andrea suspected that she still had hopes her career could be salvaged, but that wouldn't happen if word got out that she'd engaged in vigilante politics.

Andrea said nothing of the vigilantes in the six hours Tyler kept her, or of Elbertson, or her conviction that it was Elbertson who had killed his brother. Janine was still almost certainly a pipeline to Elbertson himself, and Andrea wouldn't arm the assistant district attorney with their suspicions, thus giving Elbertson the advantage of knowing everything they knew.

The only saving grace of this night, Andrea thought, was that Tyler didn't truly know Neil.

Andrea had told the assistant district attorney that she would never apprehend Neil if Andrea were in jail. He'd disappear again, and her case would hang in legal limbo— as damaging politically and to her career as if she'd failed to secure the conviction.

If Tyler knew the kind of man Neil was, she'd know that he would never sacrifice Andrea's freedom for his own. He'd proven, more times than she cared to remember, that he'd choose her safety over his every time.

But Tyler didn't know that, and so she made yet another error in judgment. She let Andrea go free.

Andrea called a cab from a telephone outside the D.A.'s reception area, and turned to go. Tyler walked out with her and stood waiting. The air was brisk despite the glaring early morning sunlight.

There were dark shadows beneath Tyler's hazel eyes, and her honey-blond hair, ordinarily so sharply styled, hung lifelessly. Andrea thought she looked as if she'd spent more sleepless nights than this one, and wondered how a woman with such intelligence and drive had gone so far astray.

"Off the record, Andrea," Tyler said, "do you know where Caulfield is?"

"No. But you must know that I wouldn't tell you if I did."

Tyler rubbed her upper arms with her hands, as if to get warm. "I wish none of this had ever happened, Andrea. I think...we were...we might have been friends."

Andrea swallowed, feeling suddenly as sorry for Janine Tyler as Neil had felt for Ben Solter when he'd learned that Solter had taken his own mother's ruined life. She couldn't condone the assistant district attorney's lack of judgment, but she could understand her ambition, her desire to have

Solter's approval. "You were doing what you thought was right."

Tyler shook her head. "Not lately."

The cab drove up and honked, but Andrea didn't move. "What does that mean—*not lately?*"

Tyler bit her lip and hugged her arms to her body. She stared across the street at a newspaper vending machine. "When I was a little girl in Kansas, my father ran a game-bird hunting club for rich men. He supplied them with trained bird dogs and shotguns and ammunition. They'd pick out the pheasants they wanted to shoot from a chicken-wire pen, and they'd always pick the pretty ones. The crossbreeds with feathers so beautiful it made your eyes hurt."

Biting her lip, she broke off. Andrea said nothing, and at last she went on. "My daddy would catch the birds and stuff them into a grain bag. Afterward, he'd take them out into the fields and let them go. All day long I would hear the hunters' shots, and I'd cry. But he'd say, 'Business is business, baby, and them birds're business.'"

She shaded her eyes with her hand then and looked straight at Andrea. Her chin puckered, staving off the tears in her voice. "Mason Piers is already dead, Andrea. If I were doing what I thought was right, I'd have had you locked up in Albuquerque where you would be safe."

NEIL REGAINED consciousness in the half hour before dawn. Cold and stiff, he was slow to rise off the pickup bench, slower still to orient himself. He laced his fingers behind his head. He sucked air in through his nose, gritted his teeth and forced himself to bend his wounded leg at the knee.

The pain nearly caused him to black out again.

Shivering violently, he took hold of the steering wheel. He fought to stay conscious, to think. The Thornbloom woman's car was gone. Only this pickup remained. He searched the darkness around him for the slightest hint of another presence, then the rearview mirror. He rolled down the window and listened, hearing nothing, only the silence of the predawn night.

He straightened, bringing his body into place, then pushed in the clutch pedal and turned the key in the truck ignition. It whined and turned over and whined again without success. He gritted his teeth and plunged the gas pedal to the floor despite the pain roaring up his right leg. At last the engine came alive.

He shifted into neutral and let off both pedals, then sat there blowing warm air into his cupped hands, waiting for the heater to produce enough warmth to help him come alive himself.

He thought Andrea must have escaped. That the Thornbloom woman had stayed away. But neither conclusion eased his mind much. Elbertson would go after Andrea now, and she was smart, able to figure out the most complicated problems, but she didn't have the survival skills of a ten-year-old street kid.

He didn't think Elbertson would toy with either of them again. He had to get to Andrea, to protect her at all costs. Elbertson would know this truck, which meant every cop in five counties would be out for him, loaded for bear. He figured he had about one chance in a hundred of getting out of state in this truck.

Warmer now, he spotted the hundred-dollar bills on the dash and his day pack on the floor. More grateful to the Thornbloom woman with every passing moment, he started to pocket the bills when he felt the .32 digging into the small of his back. He stuffed the bills into his shirt pocket, then reached behind and pulled the automatic from his waistband.

The torn, jagged edges of his jeans scraped over his wound, and after the pain subsided, he knew by the feel of warm blood that he'd torn the wound open.

He swore and bounced his hand hard off the steering wheel. He jerked open the door, then reached for the day pack and pulled out his sweatpants. He eased out of the cab and stood leaning against the truck for a moment.

He kicked off his athletic shoes, then gritted as he stripped the torn, blood-crusted jeans from his body. He rooted around in the day pack for Andrea's nightshirt, wrapped the whole thing tightly around his bleeding calf wound and tucked the end beneath the bulk.

By the time he drew on the sweatpants, his head throbbed mercilessly, and by the time he'd driven the miles of dirt road beyond the smashed-up Valiant to the highway, he knew he didn't know where he was, whether I-40 lay to the north or the south. He'd been sleeping when Andrea made the drive the night before.

He sat there at the intersection, the truck rumbling, the heater fan churning, for what seemed hours. He couldn't remember ever feeling such indecision, such uncertainty, but he knew his wounds had a lot to do with it.

That, and the overwhelming necessity to get back to Andrea before Elbertson found her. He couldn't afford the luxury of wasted time, a wrong choice.

He drew a deep breath and turned north. Within a few miles he spotted a sign announcing the exit ramp to I-40, and he knew by the grace of providence he'd made the right choice. He took the westbound interstate and pulled off at the truck stop where he and Andrea had eaten dinner two nights before. There were no less than three Texas Department of Safety patrol cars parked in the lot.

He drove the truck over a curb at the back of the property and ditched it behind the building, then headed into the men's room.

Outfitted to accommodate truckers, there were lockers, latrines, showers and sinks to wash up by. A clock hanging on the wall told Neil it was five-fifty in the morning.

Three men stood scattered at various sinks, shaving. Neil walked in, forcing himself not to limp. He dropped the day pack on the floor beside him, stuck his head under the sink tap, lathered with soap from a wall well, washed up and listened to the idle talk among the others. Two of the truckers were heading west in the next hour.

Neil pulled a wad of towels out of the dispenser and rubbed his arms and face dry, waiting for a lull in the conversation. "One of you guys interested in a paying passenger?"

"Which way you headed, buddy?"

"West. Santa Fe."

"I'm headed west, then on up to Denver," the one farthest from Neil said. He was balding and small, but the kind of small that masked scrappy, iron strength. "What kinda bucks you talkin' here?"

"Fifty."

"Make it a hundred, and we've got ourselves a deal, pardner."

Neil hesitated only long enough not to seem desperate. He nodded. "A hundred, then. When are you taking off?"

"Now soon enough for you?"

Neil shouldered his filthy day pack and headed out the door behind his ride. "Which rig?"

He rode in silence, pretending sleep, listening to the scratchy exchanges of the truckers on the CB radio. The sixteen-wheeler had covered a hundred miles before word started passing between the truckers.

The cops were looking hard for an armed and dangerous man, thought to be seeking asylum or a means of escape from the Amarillo vicinity. Neil remained still, his legs drawn up so that the wound wouldn't stiffen, his eyes closed, listening to some disembodied voice scratch its way through a fair description of him.

If it weren't for bad luck, he thought, he wouldn't have any freaking luck at all. God. He was so tired. The last thing he wanted was to make this guy sorry he'd ever taken on a passenger.

Neil opened his eyes and watched realization dawn on the trucker, and knew he had no choice, not with Andrea's life hanging in the balance.

He reached down and slid the .32 automatic from the holster on the inside of his left leg. He held it in his right hand, braced with the left and rested both at the wrist on his knees, aiming straight at the driver.

"Your lucky day," he said. "Get me to Santa Fe, keep it at an even sixty-five, and I won't have to use this."

ANDREA FELT AS IF the breath had been ripped out of her. She forced herself to turn, to leave Tyler standing there, to walk away and get into the cab. She gave the cabbie brief instructions to her home. And then she began to shake.

Mason Piers was dead.

Andrea had no illusions left, not one. Elbertson had ordered her bagged and released, just like the pretty pheasants. Janine understood that it was her own life on the line if she defied him.

Heaven help them all. All the rising stars, burning out, falling over their own ambitions and petty faults. Her throat ached. Nausea roiled in her. She didn't know what had become of Neil, though she thought Tyler wouldn't still be asking where he was if Elbertson had managed to kill him.

The cab dropped her at her home fifteen minutes later. She punched in the garage-door-opener code, then closed it behind her. Doodle was frantically happy to see her, and though by the dog's behavior she doubted that anyone had come into her house, the old retriever was nearly deaf now, and Andrea checked out the whole house. Satisfied that she was alone, Andrea fed Doodle, shut her in the garage and gave her an enormous bone-shaped dog biscuit.

She tried Piers's home phone number over and over again, but there was no answer. By the time she took a shower, doctored her cheek with an antibiotic ointment and dressed in warm, comfortable sweats, Cindy Piers called Andrea.

"Andrea," she greeted her tonelessly. "Mason is dead."

"I heard, Cindy. I'm so terribly sorry. But I'm worried about you now. Where are you?"

"Andrea, they tried to make it look like a suicide," she said, ignoring the question in her grief, "but Mason would never do that. Never!"

"I know, Cindy. I know. Where are you now?"

"At the hospital." She sniffed and let out a strained little sob. "They had to bring Mason here to declare him dead.... Do you... do you know what's become of my sister?"

"Yes, and I think she's probably safe—but Cindy, I... My phone line may be tapped."

"Did she go to a friend's?"

"No." Andrea struggled to come up with a hint so Cindy would understand that Vicki had gone to the Hyatt in Amarillo. "She didn't leave town, but if she were traveling, do you know where she would stay?"

"Yes, the... Yes. If I called her there from here at the hospital, would it hurt anyone?"

Andrea thought there probably was a way, even in a hospital with hundreds of outgoing lines, for such a call to be traced or tapped. Elbertson might seek revenge on Vicki Thornbloom for hiding them away, but she doubted very much that Mason Piers's widow would be worth Elbertson's attention now.

Heartbroken, she listened for a few moments more to the teary ramblings of Mason's widow, then urged her to go somewhere where she could feel safe.

She hung up then, as certain as she could be that Cindy would look after her own safety. Weepy-eyed and emotionally strung out herself, she would rather have called Doodle inside and upstairs and clung to her old pet and cried herself to sleep waiting for Elbertson to come after her. But she'd promised to meet Neil at Solter's place, and she would be there come all the hellfire and damnation promised in the years of her childhood religious upbringing.

ON IMPULSE, SHE STUFFED her illicit copy of the medical examiner's file on Solter's murder in her backpack along with a few frozen breakfast burritos and, at the last moment, a pair of wire cutters. She headed out her back pasture by ten-thirty. She thought about taking Doodle along this time, but the poor old thing might only get into terrible straits being so deaf.

She jogged until her side ached from a lack of oxygen, then ran harder. Sooner or later she'd get a second wind. Nothing could make her slow down. Andrea avoided a rocky slope though it took her twenty or more yards out of her way, then continued on.

Solter had been a powerful writer, Andrea thought, paid in the hundreds of thousands for his opinions. He must also have been a genius at pushing all the right buttons, at touching the responsive chord of people all around him.

He'd appealed to Janine Tyler's career aspirations, praising her law-and-order position publicly, pandering to her ego.

He'd played up Mason Piers's feeling of remorse over his ruling in the murder of the Bartlett baby, persuading Piers that such miscarriages of justice could be overcome by the Cause.

She didn't know what had motivated John Brice. It was possible that Brice had had a vigilante mentality to begin with, and Solter's Cause provided the appropriate outlet. But it was Solter who had been all things to all people, the standard-bearer of the Cause.

Andrea came to the summit of the final hill and began picking her way down as fast as she could. The surprise was that Elbertson had walked right in and picked up the standard as if he owned it, and that Janine Tyler and Mason Piers and John Brice and countless others had followed along like good little sheep instead of the responsible, intelligent people they were. Why?

Why?

She was haunted by her memory of Mason's anguished explanations: *We didn't see it coming, Vogel.... It seemed fitting.... He was a very compelling, strong-willed sort....*

She couldn't accept it. Nothing justified their behavior. It didn't matter if Elbertson knew everything in the files Solter had compiled over the years. He wouldn't have had Solter's forum to use the information. And yet they *had* obeyed Elbertson.

There was a reason. There was always a reason, and she was more determined than ever to find it. She felt on the verge of discovery, and she dreaded it. She would begin at the start, tear apart every supposition they had made, every fact they'd accepted for the truth, and somewhere, she would find the reason.

She searched for signs of life. Running scared themselves, none of the vigilance committee would show up here, but the thought hadn't escape her that Elbertson might. Elbertson *would* show up, sooner or later.

She saw nothing to make her suspicious. Avoiding the trip wires, which seemed to loom enormously now that she was aware of them, she went to the back of the house and opened the housing on the fuse box. She remembered vaguely which fuses Neil had pulled, but she had no hope of duplicating his expertise. She threw the main breaker, knowing all power to the house would be cut off right along with the alarm system.

What she could not have known was that throwing the main breaker would have the exact same electrical consequences in the alarm system as breaking a window. A contact point was broken, and somewhere in a monitoring facility in Santa Fe, the alarm system installed on Ben Solter's property shrilled a warning.

Chapter Seventeen

Andrea took a .357 caliber automatic pistol from the gun case in Solter's study and loaded it. She'd never fired a weapon outside a test site in a lab, but she had no doubt that she could and would use it if she were threatened.

She closed the gun cabinet and made her way upstairs, and began with the "Separated at Birth" mock-up of the brothers, which she peeled from the inside of what had been Ben Solter's medicine cabinet. She put the pistol on the floor at her feet, then sat on the edge of the tub for long moments, staring at the photos and at Elbertson's scrawled taunts.

The photos were as poor and grainy as she remembered—one, the newspaper file photo of Solter, the other a snapshot taken in a prison yard, presumably of Elbertson. She played a what-if game with herself.

What if it were Solter and not Elbertson in the prison yard snapshot? Or neither of them? What if Solter had written his columns from jail? What if Solter had gone certifiably insane after murdering his mother and Elbertson had taken over his brother's life, each of them living as the same person in some kind of shared, twisted psychosis? Each possibility seemed more far-fetched than the last.

She got up from the side of the tub, retrieved the weapon from the floor and wandered downstairs with the mock-up in hand. Intending to study her own file of the Medical Examiner's investigation, she sat down at Solter's desk, set the mock-up and the .357 carefully to one side, then withdrew from her backpack the papers she'd crammed in earlier.

The room was musty smelling, and the silence around her complete. She read for over an hour, poring over every fact, every conclusion. At the end, she knew no more than she had already known. She felt restless, as if she were wasting her time. She could reexamine every scrap of evidence, but nothing in that file would resolve her uneasiness.

Why, in the aftermath of Solter's demise, *why* had the key members of the vigilance committee so readily accepted Elbertson? Mason Piers was unlikely to have taken over, but why not Janine Tyler? Why not John Brice?

He was so compelling . . . so like Ben. . . .

How like Ben? she wondered, realizing then that she had never seen a decent picture of Elbertson, that she didn't really know what he looked like. The snapshot in the prison yard was poor, from a distance of several feet and taken by something like an old Brownie camera rather than a 35mm.

If she were to characterize the man in the prison yard photo in one or two words, they could be *arrogant* or *cocky,* even . . . *condescending.* She would never have thought, offhand, that Elbertson was compelling, or able to inspire the support his brother had so effortlessly won.

What was it about Solter that had made him so appealing, so popular, so easy to follow? She took the photographs from the M.E.'s file, and the measurements of Solter's cranium that had caught Neil's interest.

She stared at them, as if they could tell her what kind of magic Solter had made. She began manipulating her numbers, calculating odd ratios, playing with the figures. Caught up in possibilities she couldn't even have described, Andrea slid the mock-up closer.

She opened Solter's desk drawer and took out a twelve-inch ruler. She turned the ruler to its metric side and applied it to the newspaper photo of Solter.

She became quickly frustrated with the poor quality of the blurred photograph. Urgent niggling doubts crossed her mind. She was wasting her time. A dead body was a dead body, and Solter was dead.

Still, she couldn't help thinking where she'd seen better photographs. She ran back up the stairs to Solter's bedroom, and there on the wall was the photo gallery she remembered, catching for all time the success and popularity of Ben Solter.

There were several sharp, excellent photos of him on the wall, and she took two of them—one was a side view, the other, face-front. *Norma lateralis, norma frontalis.*

It would be nice, she thought, if cranial measurement could predict criminal behavior, or a man's power to inspire and lead, but they couldn't. Adolf Hitler had been a short, unattractive, common little man, and no one could have predicted that, beady eyes or no, he would incite an entire nation of people to evil.

Solter was different. He'd been an attractive, distinguished-looking man, and he'd had an aura about him, even on film, that captivated people.

She fooled around with the nasal index and a couple of critical craniofacial angles. All photographic measurements were tricky at best. Some were impossible, but calculating backward she arrived at a factor that took into account the smaller relative size of Solter's face and head in the photograph, and each of her comparison calculations matched within acceptable ranges of error.

But when she compared the interorbital distances to the biorbitals—measures between the eyes and then from the outer edge of one eye to the other—the resulting ratio was off.

Andrea frowned. Maybe she'd made a math error. She dug into the desk drawer for a calculator and began again. She remembered telling Neil that Solter's eyes were set closely together, but in the photo the eyes appeared to be set apart at a more normal distance. She made the measurements again, then calculated the results three more times. She wasn't wrong.

Her fingers began to shake.

She picked another obvious, simple measure, the distance in centimeters from the point at the back of the jaw to the center of the chin, gonion to menton. Then another, from the bony protuberance at the eyebrow level to the back of the head, the glabella to the maximal occipital point.

She began to hear and feel her own pulse in her ears. She factored in her corrections for the photographs, and still those measurements failed to match.

"Oh, my God." The body she had autopsied was not Ben Solter's.

It took Neil a solid hour to drag himself to the rise above Solter's place. It would take him another half hour to skirt the house and approach from the back. He fought with himself every step of the way, forcing one step after another.

He saw the broken window in the back door from a hundred paces, and from half a dozen paces that the fuse box had been tampered with. When he limped close enough to swing open the door and saw the main breaker thrown, he sank to the ground, helplessly laughing. All this time, all this way.

Cutting the power at the source was so...Andrea. She had probably cooked their goose.

His gut ached from laughing so hard. He was so damned tired and he hurt so bad that he couldn't stop.

Collapsed on the ground, his legs stretched out and his back leaning against the wall, he didn't know if he was laughing or crying. Either way, his nose was running and the closest thing he had to a tissue was his shirtsleeve.

He made the supreme effort to raise his shoulder and turn his head, and then he saw Andrea fly out the back door into a perfect firing-range stance, leveling a .357 at him with both hands extended straight out from her shoulders. He began to choke on his laughter again.

"Dammit, Neil!" she cried, letting her arms fall back. "I could have shot you!" Tears flooded her eyes, and her heart pounded. Relieved that he was alive, utterly angry at him for scaring her, she'd have throttled him in an instant if she could just have seen clearly. "What is so damn funny?"

Neil sobered up then. He'd never before heard her swear. He saw how badly shaken up she was and he knew she wanted an answer. And that he loved her. "The fuse box, Boo."

Her chin went up, and she just stood there. "What about it?"

He sat where he was because he didn't think he could get up. "I'm no expert, but tripping the main circuit ought to trigger the alarm exactly like breaking in."

"Oh." Her eyes closed, and she let out a choppy, frustrated breath. "Neil, I... Maybe we should get out of here."

He planted his left foot close to his body, then eased himself up against the wall. "How long have you been here?"

She cleared her throat, and he could see that her chin was quivering. She was too preoccupied with her mistake to notice that he couldn't stand on two feet, let alone walk. Another minute of the pain and he wouldn't care if someone amputated his leg.

"You mean, how long has it been since I switched off the breaker?"

"Yeah."

"An hour, maybe a little longer... Neil, I have to show you something—"

He swore. He couldn't keep the grimace of pain off his face another second. "Come here. Quick."

She saw the pain he'd been struggling to control, and she darted to his side. "It's your leg, isn't it? Your right leg?"

He ground out some sort of agreement, then clamped his mouth shut while she helped him inside.

"If I triggered the alarm, why hasn't there been some response?"

"If we're lucky, security was monitored by the vigilance committee, and—" God help him, he was almost there. Almost. "—no one will come."

"And if we're not lucky?"

"Then they're so scared of us that they're calling out the militia." He managed a quick grin.

"That's not even funny," she scolded, but it so relieved her to see that he had a joke left in him that she smiled as well.

"To Solter's study, okay?" he directed.

He sank onto the sofa in the study, oriented so that he could watch to his left outside the immense picture window without making himself a target. She wanted to see his leg, but he grabbed her hands.

"It'll wait, Andrea. Honest to God, it will." His eyes didn't stay still two seconds, looking at her, keeping watch outside. "What did you have to tell me?"

Kneeling on the carpeted floor by the sofa, she saw clearly the implacable look in his dark eyes and knew he wouldn't let her deal with his wound. Knowing him, she knew how serious the wound must be that he had to hide it from her.

He had just breached her personal version of the Mason-Dixon line, and if he didn't know it, so much the better. She would show him what she'd discovered, and then she'd call an ambulance.

"I don't believe . . . Neil, Solter isn't dead."

He jerked his head toward her and stared disbelievingly. "Better start at the beginning."

She got up long enough to retrieve the photos and her calculations, then returned to his side. She held up the better photograph of Solter in one hand and her own craniofacial illustrations in the other. "This man—" she indicated the photo, then the illustration "—is not this man."

Neil glanced outside again, then from the photo to her work. "How... Are you sure?"

She nodded. "As sure as I can be. It would take exhuming the body to prove it, but the body I autopsied wasn't Ben Solter."

Strapped with the constant pain, nervous as hell to be lying there propped up like a rag doll, Neil fought to clear his thinking. "Was it Elbertson?"

"It must have been, Neil. There's no other explanation. But see for yourself." She showed him all the calculations she had made in comparing Solter's photo to her measurements at the autopsy.

"Most of these measurements are so close that there's virtually no difference. But these three—the length of the jaw and the different spacing of the eyes—are too different for any margin of error."

Neil closed his eyes and let his head fall back to the thick arm cushions behind him. "Then what you're saying is that if Elbertson is the stiff, Solter is alive."

"Yes." She hesitated for a moment, thinking he needed a moment to digest her theory. She could see that he was in pain and, for a time, couldn't remember when he hadn't been. She should probably have called the ambulance then, but he rallied a bit.

His lips turned up in a tired smile. "Tyler will have to drop the charges against me then, won't she?"

She felt tears prickling at her eyelids. He never quite believed the good news, no matter what it was, but she'd never seen him when he couldn't find something to tease about.

"There's still a dead body to account for, Caulfield. Tyler won't let go of that."

"No. I guess not." He stared out at the forested land-scape and thought a moment. He was glad, really, to be distracted from the unremitting pain. "How did you discover this? What made you do these comparisons?"

"Nothing made sense, Neil, after a while. Things like why Tyler and Piers and the rest would let Elbertson walk in and take charge of the vigilance committee. I asked Mason. I remember asking him why he didn't bail out of the Cause the minute Solter died."

"Why didn't he?"

"Because we couldn't."

Andrea jerked around at the sound of another voice; Neil flinched and had hold of his gun in an instant, for all the good it did him. Janine Tyler stood in the doorway to the study, hostage and at gunpoint, rigid with fear.

"Janine! What—"

And there was Ben Solter behind her, a short-barrel shotgun trained on Janine's head. Behind Andrea, trapped reclining on the sofa, Neil swore. He didn't dare move while Tyler stood under Solter's gun, but his tension multiplied a thousand times.

"Ah, Dr. Vogel of the unholy alliances." His deep sar-casm was so at odds with the congenial tone of his voice that Andrea was left speechless for a moment.

"Let her go," Neil said, concealing his own weapon. "Let both women go, Solter. This is between you and me. It always was."

Solter ignored Neil, though his kindly expression re-mained. Somewhere, in some way, his pleasantries man-aged to purport absolute control. This was the man who had convened a powerful vigilance committee, no matter what name he called himself.

"Andrea—may I call you Andrea?—it is indeed a very great pleasure to meet such an astute woman.... But I see we should explain our presence."

He smiled as if he were surely a welcome sight to them, then guided Tyler by the gun at her head into his study. He put down a thick briefcase next to his desk, but the gun barrel never wavered so much as an inch from the base of Janine's skull.

His voice was as cordial as his humor; he chilled Andrea to the bone. "Tell them, my dear."

Janine's face expressed her loathing for Solter. She looked at Andrea. The gun at her head was a powerful motivator for doing as she was told. "The vigilance committee installed an escape route, a tunnel that leads from a hidden door downstairs to a trapdoor a hundred yards out."

Neil swore, interrupting her, but she continued while Solter sat relaxed and at ease behind her. "There were still things I wanted to get out of here, Andrea." She glanced quickly at Neil, at the gun he held. "I went to the trapdoor for my own protection. Solter was there."

Except that he held a gun at her head, his treatment of Tyler was gentlemanlike and exemplary. He gave the smallest bow, then indicated Janine should take a seat in one of the matched brocade wing chairs across from the sofa.

He took the other chair, and the gun was no longer pointed at Janine's head, but squarely at her chest from a range of no more than four feet.

"Perhaps you would be so good as to put down your gun," he suggested, at last looking at Neil. He waited until Neil had complied by tossing his pistol onto the floor several feet away. "Dr. Vogel, you were about to explain why my merry little band of vigilantes felt compelled to continue on. Please."

Solter's pretense of a chat between friends sickened her. "You murdered your brother."

He smiled. "Yes. Among friends, I must admit that I did."

Solter made her skin crawl. She felt Neil's rage at his powerlessness in the situation. Janine Tyler's life hung in the balance, and neither of them doubted that he would sit there in his cream-colored brocade chair and pull the trigger, sullying the matching chair with Janine Tyler's blood.

"Things must have been very confused among the vigilance committee," Andrea said. "Everyone thought you were dead—no one knew what to do or what would happen next. Then you came along in the persona of your brother, apparently very strong-willed and charismatic and determined to find your own murderer.

"We thought Elbertson had pulled it off, Ben," Andrea continued softly, watching him, despising him. "But you're the one who pulled it off, aren't you? The switch, the—"

"Yes. The switch." There was a look of supreme satisfaction about him. "The ultimate peripeteia."

Neil and Andrea exchanged glances. Miri Silverman had suggested they look up the word, and they both had to wonder if they'd have caught on sooner had they taken her advice.

"Elbertson would have killed you, wouldn't he?" Neil asked softly, in a voice so low he knew Solter could only take it to be taunting. Neil couldn't stand risking Janine Tyler's life, but unless something changed radically, they'd all be dead within an hour. Solter meant to kill them all. "He was a selfish, greedy, blackmailing bastard, but did he suspect what a menace you had become?"

"He couldn't have cared less what I had become," Solter argued, but in a tone appropriate for some happy little gathering. "He intended to kill me with an injection of the Zolgen sample I had appropriated from Caulfield's lab, you see, and I couldn't let that happen."

"So you decided to use his plan," Andrea said.

"He had only one decent plan in his life. I owed it to him to use it," Solter insisted. "He volunteered—at gunpoint, I must admit—to don my clothes and jewelry. So you see how it was that you discovered a suit coat of his in my closet.... He had a choice—the injection of a fatal dose of Zolgen, or a bullet through the head. He took his chances. With the mildest persuasion actually, he injected himself.''

''It was simple for you, wasn't it?'' Neil asked, not bothering to mask his scorn.

''In the grand scheme of things,'' Solter said affably, ''I am, and always have been, a far more significant player than my departed brother.''

Neil glanced at Tyler, who sat disbelieving. ''You didn't know Solter well enough to recognize him when he showed up on the doorstep claiming to be his own cousin?''

Solter laughed, still the gracious host to a gathering among friends.

Janine's chin rose defiantly, and she stared at Solter. ''He was different.''

Solter smirked, but then he paused, took on another posture in his chair, another expression, his entire demeanor transformed into the west Texas good-ol'-boy cliché his brother had been.

Andrea and Neil exchanged glances, stunned by the simple, convincing portrayal. It was as if Solter were an accomplished actor, a human chameleon adapting to another environment altogether.

As if he were his brother.

''You give me too much credit by half, girlie,'' he taunted Janine, his voice and words subtly altered to suit his brother's persona. ''You must remember,'' he said, staring at her, fondling his trigger, ''I was dealin' with dolts too caught up in their own pathetic little dramas to pay proper attention.''

''You disgust me,'' Janine hissed, her face contorted with rage. ''You spout law and order and then murder your own brother! You're lower than a snake and I will see you in hell.''

Solter only smiled. ''Properly so, for a cluster of fallen stars, don't you think? But don't count on it, Janine. I have fought the good fight for far too long to suffer such a fate.''

Feeling betrayed beyond belief, Janine uttered a low, fierce growl of fury, prepared to spring at Solter, aiming to tear him apart. Andrea flung herself across the room, out of his line of fire, and in the same instant, Neil lunged off the sofa in the direction of his discarded gun. At some point during the desperate struggle the sound of police sirens began to wail in the distance.

Janine hurled herself at Solter. He altered the position of his gun and slammed the butt into Janine's head. She slumped into his body.

Pinned to the chair, howling in rage, he tried to get up, but the weight of Janine's body foiled him. Andrea gained her feet, jerked up the briefcase he'd brought in and hurled it at Solter with all her might.

He deflected the case with his forearm and arose like a phoenix out of the chair. Janine's body fell to the floor. Roaring vile epithets at Andrea, he turned and brought the shotgun to bear on her.

The second expanded in her. She heard the sirens approaching and understood that the police were at last responding to the alarm she had triggered. Her mistake, her ineptness at intrigue had at last paid off, but too late. They would be too late.

She stared at Solter, stared at the shotgun that would blow her apart, then searched the room for Neil, for one last look at Neil. She loved him, but she would die. Tears erupted and she cried out Neil's name and then choked.

She would die. She heard the shot. She waited for the sensation of her body being torn apart.

Then the instant shrank back to real time and it was Solter's body crumpling to the floor, not hers. She cried out and her tears blinded her, but in another second Neil was there, taking her into his arms.

Her body trembled violently. Neil closed his arms around her. "Breathe, Andrea. It's okay. It's going to be okay.

Come on, breathe with me.'' He drew a deep breath, urging her to follow him, then another and another.

When the police came through the door, Neil was still holding her. Janine Tyler had come to. The officers started firing questions. One of them took Neil's gun. Grimacing with pain, Janine took charge. Solter's body was photographed and then removed. Finally Janine looked at Neil, uncertainly at her own hands, then back.

''Too little, too late, Mr. Caulfield,'' she murmured, struggling with tears. ''But I'll see that all charges are dropped and your records expunged.'' She glanced back to check on the police officers still in her charge, then turned to Andrea. ''Is there…is there anything I can do for you?''

Andrea looked up at Neil. ''Yes. Call an ambulance.''

Chapter Eighteen

"I'll accept your apology anytime, sir. It seems I am entirely suited to intrigue."

Lying in his hospital bed, Neil looked up from the newspaper he was reading. Andrea stood in the doorway of his room wearing a fuzzy soft pink sweater dress, and except for her skinned knee and scraped cheek, she looked fine. She came into the room, followed by a bouquet of balloons. She put down her small pink leather shoulder bag and sat in the easy chair beside him.

Postoperative pain pills had him feeling mellow. She made him feel the pull of tears and powerful emotion in his throat.

Nothing about her was suited to intrigue but her undying faith, and that was what he craved. What he loved most.

"Too bad," he murmured, taking her outstretched hand. "I'm fresh out of apologies." No one would be testing her fitness for intrigue again. Not if he had anything to say about it. He let go of her hand and held up the paper. "This says the bigwigs have voted unanimously to offer you the office of interim medical examiner."

"They have," she answered softly, revealing her bittersweet pride in the offer. "Think I'll take it, too."

He smiled at her, and for the first time since she had known him, his smile filled his features. "That's good, Andrea. You deserve the job."

She nodded, staring at her fingers turning her mother's gold bangle on her wrist so she wouldn't blatantly covet the feel of his gorgeous, manly chest. It wasn't the *job* she was thinking of now at all. "And what do you deserve after all of this, Neil?"

He took a deep breath and set aside the newspaper. He could have named on the fingers of one hand the creature comforts he'd craved for so long while he'd lived his fugitive existence. He had all those things again now.

But there were other things. To have his mother back, and his kid sister. To regain his place in the scientific community. But he knew now that he'd trade them all for Andrea Vogel's permanent attentions. And when he looked at her again, it wasn't a smile in his eyes, but the naked sizzling need of her.

She recognized the ache. It mirrored her own. She'd learned enough in life, always being the smart one, to know Neil Caulfield might never expect that things would come out right. But that was Neil, and she respected him, just as she knew he valued her differences and strengths. She was willing to offer him possibilities forever after, if he would only accept them.

If only he would tell her.

"Miri wanted you to know she's got some high-powered Manhattan attorneys working on recovering your Zolgen rights." Andrea paused. Neil said nothing, only nodded, closed his eyes and leaned back into the pillows. Could she be so wrong about what was between them, when she had such a reputation for being right? For her faith? "So," she said. "We all live happily ever after."

"Do we?" He gazed at Andrea, at her widow's peak and her pretty green eyes and her precious bow-shaped lips. He swallowed. Commitments weren't his forte. If he'd learned anything in his life, it was that nothing good ever lasted.

Nothing this good, anyway. But he was tempted to try. Sorely tempted, because he liked the man he was when he was with her. He stretched out a hand to her again. She came to sit on the bed next to him, and held his hand.

God. What a lump there was in his throat. "I'm grateful to her, Andrea, but what I really want is nothing Miri Silverman can recover."

Her fingers curled unwittingly tighter around his. "What is it, Neil, that you truly want?"

His eyes passed over her—her eyes to her neck to her breasts beneath the pink dress, back to her eyes. "Truth is, Andrea, I'm in need of a particular rising star."

Had her heart stopped, midbeat? "Real stars are forever," she warned.

"I'm counting on it."

Her eyes went all watery again. He had learned to count on something. On her. "Good thing, Caulfield. I'm in need of a particular heaven."

**Relive the romance...
Harlequin and Silhouette
are proud to present**

by Request

A program of collections of three complete novels by the most
requested authors with the most requested themes. Be sure to
look for one volume each month with three complete novels by
top name authors.

In June: **NINE MONTHS** Penny Jordan
                               Stella Cameron
                               Janice Kaiser

**Three women pregnant and alone. But a lot can
happen in nine months!**

In July: **DADDY'S
          HOME**   Kristin James
                      Naomi Horton
                      Mary Lynn Baxter

**Daddy's Home... and his presence is long
overdue!**

In August: **FORGOTTEN
           PAST**   Barbara Kaye
                     Pamela Browning
                     Nancy Martin

**Do you dare to create a future if you've forgotten
the past?**

Available at your favorite retail outlet.

HARLEQUIN®
I N T R I G U E®

Hop into a pink Cadillac with the King of Rock 'n' Roll for the hottest—most mysterious—August of 1993 ever!

#237
HEARTBREAK HOTEL
by Cassie Miles
August 1993

All Susan Quentin wanted was a quiet birthday, but she got lots more: sexy greetings over the radio, deejay Johnny Swift himself—and a dead Elvis impersonator outside her door. Armed with only sunglasses and a pink Cadillac, could they find the disguised "King" killer amid a convention of impersonators at the Heartbreak Hotel?

Don't be cruel! Come along for the ride of your life when Johnny tries to convince Susan to love him tender!

ELVIS

THREE UNFORGETTABLE HEROINES
THREE AWARD-WINNING AUTHORS

Untamed

MAVERICK HEARTS

A unique collection of historical short stories that
capture the spirit of America's last frontier.

HEATHER GRAHAM POZZESSERE—over 10 million copies
of her books in print worldwide
Lonesome Rider—The story of an Eastern widow and the
renegade half-breed who becomes her protector.

PATRICIA POTTER—an author whose books are consistently
Waldenbooks bestsellers
Against the Wind—Two people, battered by heartache, prove
that love can heal all.

JOAN JOHNSTON—award-winning Western historical author
with 17 books to her credit
One Simple Wish—A woman with a past discovers that
dreams really do come true.

Join us for an exciting journey West with
UNTAMED
Available in July, wherever Harlequin books are sold.

MAV93